THE LUST GAMBIT

THE LUST GAMBIT

STEVEN G. JACKSON

King Family Press

THE
LUST GAMBIT
STEVEN G. JACKSON

King Family Press
Shanghai
San Francisco

Book Cover and Interior Design by Steven G. Jackson
Edited by Mary Altbaum
Author Photo by Ryan Christopher Jackson
First Edition
Printed in the United States of America

ISBN: 978-1-7355528-7-3 (Trade Paperback)
ISBN: 978-1-7355528-5-9 (Ebook)

Library of Congress Control Number: 2023914379

This is dedicated to my Dad. Of all my novels, this was his favorite.

CHAPTER 1

Valentine's Day, San Juan Capistrano, CA

Nick Hardy pondered the department-store application.

Have you ever had an alcohol, drug, or gambling conviction or problem?

He glanced down at his tight, yellowish T-shirt, which read "Tequila is my favorite color," and laughed, which caught the attention of the hefty woman seated near him.

"Sorry," Hardy said. "I guess I didn't think my wardrobe through this morning. Do you think I get credit for hitting two out of three on the vice question? Or do I need to pick up some weed and nail the trifecta?"

"They said no talking," the woman whispered. "I really need this job."

Hardy admired her Panama hat. "Speaking of weed, that's a nice lid."

She cracked a smile. "Shhh."

Hardy put his finger to his lips. "Right. Sorry." He returned to the form and debated how honest he should be in answering the question, then looked back at the woman. "Pretty sucky way to spend the afternoon, huh? Applying for a job you know you'll hate?"

Silence.

"I run a martial arts studio. I'm only here because my regular referrals from the local battered women's clinic are drying up."

She made eye contact for the first time. "You help women?"

Hardy pulled out a business card. "In case you know someone. I help women lose weight, too." He put up his hands. "Not that you need it."

She hesitated. "Gyms make me self-conscious. Too many people."

"My client's insist on discretion. All sessions are just me and them. Name's Nick."

"I'm Flora." She considered the card. "I suppose it couldn't hurt to look. I do need to turn this application in first."

While she turned in her application he tore his up and tossed it in the trash.

I wouldn't last a week.

He hopped into his Mustang, grateful he still owned one prized possession. Flora followed him to his studio in the Historic District of San Juan Capistrano.

As Hardy and Flora entered his first-floor studio, Hardy's yellow lab jumped him. Hardy hugged Bear and gave him a treat.

"Good boy, Bear. This is Flora. She's okay."

Bear came up and sniffed her hand. "How old?"

"Close to double digits. A rescue. Okay with women, nervous around men."

They stepped across the wrestling mats covering most of the concrete floor. Hardy pointed to a couch with a sheet and blanket next to an open suitcase holding a pile of clothes. "Take a load off."

"Movie fan?" Flora asked, noting the dozens of posters lining the walls. "Ryan Gosling, George Clooney, and Brad Pitt. I guess you know your clientele."

Hardy stared at the posters, reminiscing. "These are all films I had a part in. I worked as a stunt man for ten years."

She pointed to a series of photographs of Hardy working in action scenes. "Is this you?"

"Yeah. They don't like to let those out in the open, but I dated the photographer, so I ended up with some."

"That's so cool."

Hardy trudged to his desk and pulled a bottle of tequila and two short glasses out of a drawer. Bear squatted on his bed and licked his lips twice while watching the tequila. "Then I turned thirty, and the work dried up. They like their action figures young. Drink?"

"It's the middle of the afternoon."

Hardy reversed course and sat down on the desk.

Flora examined the couch and stayed on her feet. "So you make a living just helping women? Seems like a limited market. Those studios for kids seem to be packed all the time."

Hardy glanced at the eviction notice on his desk and shuffled some papers to cover it up. "I'm not really a 'kid' kind of guy."

She eyed him. "You're a Hollywood kind of guy?"

Hardy's face glazed over. "It's not as glamorous as it sounds. I did have offers to work private security for some stars, but I turned them down."

"Why?"

"I'd be protecting a lifestyle I don't care for. Your demons eventually get you."

"You have demons, do you?"

Hardy fought back the memory of his final intervention for his mother. "Don't we all?"

"I suppose we do." She eyed the couch. "You don't live here, do you?"

"It's temporary." Hardy considered the recent bad streak at the poker tables, and made a fist. "My luck's due to turn. But don't worry about me. Bear and I do fine." He leaned in. "So, is this private enough?"

Flora hesitated, her eyes flinching. "I'm sorry. This isn't for me." She gave him a sad look and escaped, easing the door closed on her way out.

Bear rose and plopped his head in Hardy's lap.

Before he could revisit the tequila, his cell phone rang. "Hardy."

"Hey, cowpoke," Bret Flint said in his Texan accent. "I told you quitting the force and getting this PI gig with Alice Polk would score some serious side benefits."

Hardy admired Flint's selective memory. "I recall you getting asked to leave the police, due to tampering with evidence. To protect me."

"We both know it was an accident. You didn't deserve to go through a murder investigation."

"Thank God you landed on your feet. Again."

"Pard, I keep telling you, all Texans are lucky, 'cause we were born Texans. And, today, you get to be lucky, too. I scored us an invite to the most exclusive Valentine's shindig in town. A pool party at Alice's estate. She's expecting a whopper. I'm in charge of security and Alice says you can help. She's even paying us. Get over here fast as you can. It'll be a blast."

Hardy straightened up. *Paying us? I guess my poker game can wait.*

Hardy rubbed Bear behind his ears and glided to the suitcase, digging out a wrinkled pair of gray slacks.

This should be a breeze. Nothing bad ever happens in Laguna Beach.

CHAPTER 2

Laguna Beach, CA

Hector "Matadamas" Mendoza gripped the burner phone tighter. "I can kill Sara right here. Right now."

"No," came the reply. "It's personal for Rivera. He wants to off her himself. Your job is to grab Sara and her son at the party. Before seven."

The ocean breeze tugged at Mendoza, dressed in black, next to his teenage son. His reflective sunglasses couldn't keep his eyes from wincing from the sun's midday assault. He scratched at the scar on his cheek. "Her home would be safer."

"If she's taken at home, the investigation on who gave her up might blow back on me."

"Why by seven?"

"The American's switched tunnel surveillance, and we haven't paid the new guards off yet. So the tunnel under the border is out. The US border guard on our payroll gets off at ten. You must make the deadline. Understand?"

"Sí. We'll get in position and let you know when we have them."

"Only call if something goes wrong. Drive them straight to Rivera's mansion in Ensenada. Remember. Get to the border by ten."

Mendoza hung up. He could see the hilltop estate of Alice Polk across the canyon. He smiled at his son. "Today, you break into the family business. You will learn to love your job, as I do."

CHAPTER 3

Alice Polk's Estate, Laguna Beach

Hardy arrived unfashionably on time and found Flint on the patio, standing next to their host. Alice held a half-filled Bordeaux glass, talking up a chap with gray hair and eyebrows like Santa Claus. She looked fifty-something in a cocktail dress designed for another era. Hardy sneaked in behind Flint and his ever-present tan, waiting for a convenient moment to startle him.

"Seriously, Rod," Alice said in the voice of a female Louis Armstrong. "The Lust Gambit hasn't been pulled off in ages. The target has to be a genuine megalomaniac."

Hardy leaned in closer, intrigued by the contradiction of Alice's voice and her demure appearance.

"You didn't ask for a recent stock con," the gent said with a British accent and a hint of mischief. "Or an easy one. You asked me for my favorite. One I'd pulled off, back in the day, when we had to resort to such things. And that's the Lust Gambit."

Alice stiffened. "Perhaps we shouldn't discuss our past. Tell me, would technology make it easier today, or harder?"

"Harder," Rod said. "Too many automated checks. Too easy to trace your moves."

"I'm not so sure." Alice cocked her head. "Computers also allow instantaneous transactions. If you do it right, you can move money around and still hide your trail." She peered up at Flint. "Mr. Flint, what do you think?"

"I agree with you, boss."

"Because I'm right, or because I write you those big checks?"

"Well, I admit to being a huge fan of those big checks. I have my eye on a piece of a business jet."

Hardy looked to the sky and shook his head, then grabbed Flint from behind and put him in a headlock. Flint jerked, but couldn't break free.

"Seriously," Hardy said. "A business jet? What, the Goodyear Blimp wasn't available?"

Hardy released Flint. Alice stared at Hardy in what he hoped was amusement, but might have been amazement.

Flint shook his uniform back into place. "Alice, this is the security help I told you about. Nick Hardy, meet Alice Polk. The stockbroker to the stars."

"Appreciate the gig," Hardy said.

"Let's hope you're irrelevant." She turned to Flint. "I have a new assignment for you. I need you to find a long-lost colleague. I . . . ," she paused, then grinned mischievously, ". . . tutored her in Spain. She won't make it easy for you. She guards her privacy fiercely."

"Not to worry," Flint said. "I can find anybody."

Alice shook her head. "If only you had real money, Mr. Flint. The Lust Gambit would work splendidly on you."

Flint didn't shy away. "As I've told you many a time, Ms. Polk, I'm from Texas. Being boastful comes as naturally as a dust storm in the panhandle."

Alice grunted. "Try not to break your arm, patting yourself on the back."

Hardy decided to bail Flint out and pointed out toward the blue Pacific, which sparkled as the early evening sun hovered over Santa Catalina Island. "How do you get any work done around here? I'd spend all day staring at the ocean."

She eyed him curiously. "Another chamber of commerce sunset in paradise, I suppose. Which will mean more tearing down and rebuilding on this hillside. More new neighbors." She shuddered. "It's nothing to be pleased with."

Flint brushed back his disorderly blonde hair. "You need this colleague for a stock deal?"

Alice's head shimmied. "No. I'm more interested in rekindling our *personal* relationship."

"I'll get on it right after the party," Flint assured her. He motioned toward the pool bar and Hardy followed him. "Pard, check out that blonde by the diving board. Who-eee. Reminds me of that girl in Cancun."

Hardy scanned the grounds. The pool was surrounded by hard bodies and cocktails. Women outnumbered men by two to one. "Where are all the guys? There's hardly any here."

Flint laughed. "Just like Alice likes it."

"You mean?"

"Oh, yeah. But most here tonight are straight. You couldn't ask for better odds."

"That blonde can't be older than twenty," Hardy said.

"That's only ten years' difference."

"For me. Fifteen for you."

"Fifty bucks says she won't care," Flint said. He pointed out a brunette with olive skin in a white cocktail dress that clung to her slim figure. "See the Latina babe? That's Sara Cruz. She works for Alice. She's off limits to me, but I told Sara about you. Come on, I'll introduce you."

"I'm not here to find a date." Hardy glanced at the crowd. "Too rich for my taste."

"Hey, it's time you got back in the saddle."

Hardy gave Sara a closer look. She wore a gold pendant, hovering just over the curve of her breasts, and her two-inch heels looked like they'd cost more than his best suit, back when he had a suit. "I have to admit, she's hot. Anything I should know?"

"She wears a ring, but I don't buy it. She never mentions anyone except her son."

"A son? No thanks. I just want to get paid. Women are a complication I don't need."

Flint put his arm around Hardy's shoulders. "It's been three years, pard. Just go talk with her. Have a cocktail. Be friendly. You're a stud, remember?"

Hardy thought back to being left at the altar. "Even studs can choose to take a break."

"Just one more thing," Flint said. "Alice is sweet on her."

Hardy stared incredulously at Flint. "Sara's gay?"

Flint laughed. "I wouldn't jerk you around like that. But it's fun to watch Alice get rebuffed for once in her life. Sara needs the gig, so she tolerates the mild innuendos."

"Won't it piss Alice off if she sees me with her? Might be blowback on you."

"Don't sweat it," Flint said. "I'm going to find Alice her hidden lady. She'll be happy."

"Mr. Flint," Alice called. Hardy and Flint looked back at her. She peered longingly at Sara, then back at Flint. "Do you plan to do any work tonight?"

Alice strode back toward her mansion. Like a well-trained golden retriever, Flint followed after her, his hair flapping in the breeze like a wagging tail.

CHAPTER 4

Mendoza noted the scene below him from behind a parched bush on the hill above the Polk estate, his teenage son crouched next to him. Guests mingled in Laguna Beach cocktail attire, which ran the gamut from upscale bathing suits to smart casual.

He did tell me to call if something went wrong. He exhaled and hit the final digit on his phone, sweat pouring down his face.

Rivera will kill me if I fail. And my boy.

The voice on the other end answered in a hushed voice. "I told you not to call me."

"She's here," Mendoza said. "But no sign of the boy."

"I just found out he's home with a sitter."

"Should we take her and then go get the kid? It's almost seven."

"Take her now. I'll worry about the kid."

"*Bien.*" Mendoza hung up and motioned beyond the house, toward his car parked on the street. "It's time. Go get changed."

"Sí, Papa."

"You know why you must go in first?"

"She will recognize you, and might run before we can get her."

"*Correcto.* They'll never see you coming. I'll be outside waiting. And listening. Once you have her, I'll come in and we'll be away before they get help."

CHAPTER 5

"Nobody moves, or I shoot!"

Hardy jerked his head toward the voice, his instinct to defend fully activated.

A young man stood on the diving board with a mammoth squirt gun. He flashed it around the party. "I mean it. Everybody freeze."

Hardy relaxed as a football came flying from the balcony and knocked the goof into the pool. Everybody laughed. Hardy followed the ball's flight and saw Flint making a Heisman pose.

"Reminds me of the time I threw six touchdown passes in high school," Flint called out to his captive audience. "Texas state champs."

The crowd roared. Couples started splashing each other, first with their feet, then with their arms as dozens ended up in the pool, voluntarily and otherwise. Someone turned the music up, and the guests raised their voices to be heard.

Hardy turned to look for Sara and found her within arm's length. She was staring up at Flint. "Leave it to Bret," she said.

He stared at her, his determination to stay unattached feeling some resistance. She was even prettier up close. Her softly curled brown hair with reddish highlights glimmered in the sun. Hardy caught the subtle orchid scent of a perfume he recognized from romantic walks in Hawaii. He decided to trust Flint's instincts about her marital status. Ring, or no ring, he smiled, the sort of smile he reserved for photo shoots.

"Yeah," Hardy said, a little louder than necessary to compete with the music. "He's something."

She shivered. "It makes me cold just watching those guys in the pool."

Hardy watched the sun nearing the island. "Yeah. It hit eighty today, but it'll get cool in a hurry once the sun goes down." He glanced at her dress. "You have a jacket or something?"

"Inside. So, how do you know Bret?"

Hardy offered his hand, but she didn't take it. "I'm Nick Hardy. I think Bret told you about me."

Her body relaxed. "Ah, so you're the infamous Nick," she said with a smile. "Bret did say you were coming to help him with security. I hear you two go way back." She shook his hand, her firm grip belying her delicate frame.

"Yes, we met at a beach party when he was a cop here in Laguna, and it was the start of a beautiful friendship. I didn't even have to let him win at roulette. Or kill any Nazis."

She cocked her head, confused.

"*Casablanca*," he said. "That's the last line of the film."

"Never saw it."

"What? Oh, Sara, you need to fix that. Greatest movie ever."

"When it comes to the greatest ever, I'm a *Gone with the Wind* kind of girl."

Hardy smiled. "A solid choice, but wrong. I'll take it as a personal challenge to convert you."

"Just what I need. Someone else trying to convert me." She smiled as she said it, as if she was sharing a joke with herself.

"Like Alice?" Hardy said.

She stopped smiling. "Bret told you, huh?"

"Just a little. I promise my conversion won't be such a big deal."

Sara laughed out loud. "You're funny. What do you do? A PI like Bret?"

"I run a martial arts studio. I work closely with a local women's clinic."

"Seriously? That's so cool. What got you into that?"

"It's a boring story. How about you? What do you do?"

"Alice is teaching me to be a stockbroker."

"Now *that* sounds exciting."

"It's okay. I start here at five every morning, so that part sucks. But there are worse places to work. Still, there are many other things I'd rather be doing."

"Like what?"

"Astronaut. Race-car driver. Anything fast."

Hardy looked down on her, unable to contain his grin. "Now *that's* cool. Uber-cool. What's stopping you? Family obligations?"

Sara blanched. "What do you know about my family?"

"Nothing. I see the ring, that's all. But, just between the two of us, Bret thinks it's a prop."

Sara took a deep breath. "He should mind his own business."

"So, you *are* married?"

"Is that important?"

"Well … ."

"Just what do you think is happening here?"

"I don't know. Just getting to know you."

"Nick, I'm sure you're a terrific guy, but I'm not looking for new friends." She turned away. "It was nice to meet you. Enjoy the party." She hustled across the patio toward the house, leaving Hardy standing alone. He set his drink down and chased after her.

"Sara. Hold up."

He caught up with her as she reached the patio under the balcony. The music pounded off the walls and ceiling under there, and Hardy winced. He took Sara's arm and she spun to face him.

"Nick, I need to go."

"What'd I do? We were just talking. Harmless, right?"

"You didn't do anything," she said, stress lines etched on her forehead.

Hardy glared at the stereo, the blasting still getting on his nerves. "Hey," he yelled at the guy manning it. "Turn that down, will you?"

The guy lowered the volume just a touch.

"Really, you're great," Sara said. "I know you're working, but it's an easy gig. I'm sure there are women here hoping to hook up. I'm just not one of them."

His instinct was to follow her. *She's interested in me. I can tell. I haven't been interested in anyone since everything went to hell. But there's something about her.*

He chased after her. Before he could catch her she backed out of the doorway into the patio. Her face was ashen, her body stiff.

"Sara?"

She moved her eyes toward him without turning her face, which stayed riveted straight ahead. "I've got to get out of here."

Hardy stepped up to see what she was staring at.

The hallway was vacant except for a Latino youth in a white delivery outfit, carrying a long floral box. He was scanning the inside for someone to deliver the flowers to.

Sara grabbed Hardy's arm in a viselike grip to turn him back and then slid sideways, getting out of the deliveryman's sight line.

"Sara? What's wrong?"

"Nick, I need your help. If I call for Bret that delivery boy will hear me. You're my best chance."

"At what?"

"Escape. That delivery boy was sent here for me. His father's an assassin who works for my cousin."

Hardy tensed and gave her a perplexed expression. "An assassin? Your cousin? You're not serious."

"We can discuss my dysfunctional family another time. Right now, I need to get out of here."

"He's just a kid." The delivery boy advanced toward the patio. "Looks like he's delivering flowers."

Sara grabbed his hand and pulled him toward the corner of the house. "I'm telling you, he's here to kill me. Are you going to help me, or not?"

"He's not going to hurt you while I'm here. I'll check it out. Stay out of sight."

Before Sara could protest, Hardy stepped into the doorway and came face-to-face with the delivery boy. He scanned him for weapons and didn't see any bulges. The kid appeared to be about eighteen, and harmless. Even so, he kept up his guard. "Can I help you?"

The boy looked up at Hardy, his eyes narrow slits. "I have a delivery for Sara Cruz," he said in a thick accent, his voice menacing.

Hardy considered the size and shape of the box. *Could you fit a rifle in there?*

"I'll see that she gets it," Hardy said, cutting the kid off when he tried to pass him.

"My instructions are to deliver it personally."

"I need to see what's inside."

The boy stood his ground. "That's none of your business."

"I'm security, and I'm to check all incoming packages."

The Latino set the box on a nearby table. "Knock yourself out."

Hardy undid the ribbon on the box and opened the top, finding a dozen long-stem roses.

"Okay," Hardy said. "She's not here right now. I'll see that she gets them."

The boy paused and glanced at his watch. Hardy pointed back at the front door. "I'll see you out."

Hardy waited for the boy to budge, but he held firm. Hardy reached into his pocket and pulled out a twenty-dollar bill. "Here you go."

The Latino smiled and pocketed the bill. When his hand emerged from his pocket, it held a pistol, aimed at Hardy's heart.

CHAPTER 6

"Kid, you don't want to do this." Hardy stared at his assailant, calculating how to disarm him.

"I'm not a kid."

"Leave him alone," came Sara's voice from behind Hardy. "You came here for me."

Hardy glanced back and found Sara standing in the doorway, her arms up.

"Sara," he said, "go back outside. *I got this.*"

The teen stepped aside so he had a clear shot at Sara. "Come with me," he said. "Nobody has to get hurt. We're just going for a drive."

Hardy tensed, ready to strike, when Flint's voice boomed from above. "Hey!"

The boy looked up at Flint, which provided Hardy all the distraction he needed. He leapt forward, grabbing the gun and flinging it to the side, where it skid across the marble floor, landing on the fireplace hearth. Hardy pinned the boy's hands behind his back.

"I've got him," Hardy said. "Get the gun."

Flint retrieved the gun and put the safety on. He waved the gun in the boy's face. "What gives, bucko? Why do you want Sara?"

The boy smiled. "It's a family matter. And we will have her."

Hardy heard a gravel throat-clearing and saw Alice standing at the top of the stairs. Her glare caused him to swallow.

"Not tonight, kid." Flint dialed 9-1-1 in his free hand. "The only thing you'll have is a long stay in the pokey."

"We'll see."

Hardy didn't like the confidence in the kid's voice. He looked back at Sara, who had dropped to her knees. *She's terrified. Whatever this threat is, they wouldn't have sent a boy to do it.* "He's not alone."

"Police are on their way," Flint said, scanning the room.

Hardy reached over and lifted Sara to her feet. "What does his father look like?"

"Like him. Bigger. Big scar on his cheek."

"We've got to get her out of here," Hardy said to Flint.

Alice was walking down the stairs, concern apparent on her face. "Mr. Hardy, you take Sara. I need Mr. Flint to stay with me. There's a path on the side of the house. It's hidden from the backyard by bushes, and from the outside by a high wall. There's a gate. You can get out east of the house, out of sight. Use the side door in the next room."

Flint concurred. "No worries, pard. We'll be fine."

"Okay." Hardy took Sara's hand. "Let's go." He led Sara into the next room, which was opulently decorated but otherwise vacant, and out the side door.

They emerged in a narrow gravel walkway, hidden as Alice had described. Hardy checked right toward the bushes, noticing the sun disappearing behind Catalina, then pointed left toward the gate. "There."

Behind them, they heard the delivery boy yell, "Side yard!" before being muffled.

Sara bolted, Hardy in tow, to the gate that led to the front of the property. Sara shoved on it, but a padlock barred their passage.

CHAPTER 7

Footsteps rattled on the gravel behind them, approaching the penetrable barrier the bushes provided, louder with each step.

Hardy didn't hesitate. "We'll have to climb over. I'll give you a boost."

"I'm wearing a cocktail dress."

Hardy tried not to laugh. "And you look damn fine in it. I'll try not to look."

"You do that." Sara put her foot in his interlinked hands and he boosted her up to the top, where she swung herself over and disappeared on the other side. He peeked.

"You okay?" he asked.

"Fine. Hurry!"

Without waiting to look back, he climbed onto the gate. As he reached the top he glanced back and saw a figure barging through the bushes at the far side of the walkway. He made eye contact with a scarred Latino, dressed in black, and they glared at each other until the Latino drew a gun.

Hardy fell to the other side and they ran the two dozen steps to his Mustang, scrambled in, and sped toward town.

"Your cousin sent that guy?"

"I've already said too much. Just drive."

Sara dug through her purse and produced an iPhone, her nerves causing her to fumble it twice before she got enough control to dial. "Shit. Is anybody following us?"

Hardy glanced in the rearview mirror. "No."

She disconnected the call and tried another number. "I need to pick up my son. Can you take me?"

"Sure."

"Go south on PCH. To Dana Point."

Hardy turned left onto the Pacific Coast Highway and floored it.

She glared at her cell phone. "No one is picking up." She turned to Hardy. "What if they've already taken him?"

Hardy could feel his blood pressure rising. "How old?"

"Six. Why isn't the sitter picking up? Not answering at home or on her cell."

"You think it's connected to the guy with the scar?"

"Hard not to think that."

Hardy saw the despair on her face. "We should call Flint. He has police contacts."

"No cops."

She dialed again. She sat up straighter as somebody picked up on the other end. "Deputy Garcia, I think I've been made. At a party at Alice's. I'm being driven home by a man I met at the party. Nick Hardy . . . Five, ten minutes . . . No, I have to go home. Esteban is there and nobody's answering any of the lines." She paused to listen, then responded in a louder voice. "Your security rules are the least of my concerns right now."

She hung up and glanced in the side mirror again. Hardy checked his own mirror and didn't see anyone.

"Jesus, Sara, what's going on? Who's the deputy? A police officer?"

"Please just get me home." Still the loud voice.

"Flint can tell us what's going on back at Alice's. Maybe they caught the guy."

Sara gave Hardy an uncertain expression, then sagged into her seat. "Okay, on one condition. Just find out what's going on. I don't want Bret confronting the assassin."

Hardy handed Sara his cell phone. "Can you dial it for me? It's in the favorites list."

She took it and dialed Bret, putting it on speaker.

"Pard, I was just about to ring you. You clear?"

"Yeah. We're driving to her place. You're on speaker. A guy tried to follow us out the side. Figures to be the dad. Any sign of him?"

"I'm told some guy skedaddled through the back and out the side. Must have been him. But I didn't see him."

"What about the boy?" Hardy asked as Sara dialed her sitter again, to no avail.

"The police have him tied up. You should take Sara to the station. It'll be safe there."

Hardy queried Sara, who shook her head. "She called a cop. I think he's meeting us at her place. Her son was there. The sitter's still not answering."

"Holy Jesus," Flint said. "Okay, what can I do?"

"Will Alice let you leave?" Hardy asked.

"Yeah. She's asking everyone to leave. Said something about us being real party killers. You know what this reminds me of?"

"Not now, Bret."

After a moment of silence, Flint said. "Right. I'll let you know of any happenings at the station. Call me when you can."

The phone line went dead.

"Where to?" Hardy asked.

"Turn left on Niguel Road. Then first left. I live in the apartments."

"That's funny. I jog down here all the time. How come I never see you?"

She tried her cell again, without success. "I don't go out much."

"Maybe they walked down to the beach," Hardy suggested. "The reception down there can be a little flaky."

"Maybe. It'll be dark soon. They'd have to come home, right?"

Hardy glanced at her wedding ring. He decided to give her a chance to come clean about being single. "Shouldn't we call your husband?"

She stared out at the sea. "He's out of town."

He was about to say something when she sat upright and pointed into the park on their left, where a young boy ran along the crest of the hill in the last snippet of daylight. A man ran after him.

"There's Esteban," Sara exclaimed. "That guy's chasing him."

CHAPTER 8

"Hang on," Hardy said as he swerved his car into the parking lot.

Sara didn't wait for the car to come to a full stop, jumping out and flinging her heels to the side.

The stranger caught up to the screaming boy and picked him up off the ground, throwing him over his shoulder.

Hardy jumped out and tried his best to catch up with Sara, who flew across the grass. The guy disappeared over a knoll. As Hardy came over it he saw the young boy running at the bottom of the hill near a street lamp. The stranger was chasing him again.

"Esteban, come here!" Sara screamed. "Quick!"

The boy stopped, saw his approaching mother, squealed, and ran toward her.

The man stopped chasing the boy when he saw them, but he didn't run away either. Hardy stepped between him and the boy in case he changed his mind.

Esteban reached his mother just as they heard a voice call out from below. "Sara?" A Hispanic woman approached carrying beach toys. "What's going on?"

"Teresa, where were you?" Sara asked, gathering her son in her arms.

"We've been playing on the beach." She pointed at the stranger. "This is my brother. Visiting from Mexico."

Teresa said something to her brother in Spanish, which Hardy didn't understand. She came up to Sara and shook her head. "You are always so stressed. No good."

"You're right." She reached into a pocket in her dress and handed Teresa a pile of cash. "This should be about two weeks pay. I'm moving."

"When?"

"Immediately. Sorry for the lack of notice."

Teresa took the money, scowled, and left with her brother. "Loco," she muttered.

"Jesus, Sara," Hardy said. "That was kind of abrupt. What the hell is going on?"

She eyed him with uncertainty. "I don't want to talk about it. I just want to take Esteban home and wait for Deputy Garcia."

"I'll take you."

"No. You've done enough."

"If your cousin knows where you work, how do you know he doesn't know where you live?"

"Because if he did, he'd have taken us there, quietly, instead of at a crowded party."

Hardy couldn't argue with her logic. "Okay. How long before Garcia gets here?"

"He's forty minutes away."

"Okay. I'll take you home and wait with you."

Sara tried to glare at him, but he could tell her heart wasn't in it. "I told you, I can take care of myself."

"I believe that. But it's not open to debate. I'm not leaving you until I know you're safe."

She stood silently, then smiled. "Okay. I'm just around the corner. You can park in my space, since my car is still at Alice's. But first, I'd like you to meet my son. Esteban, this is Mr. Hardy."

Hardy knelt down to match his height. "Hello, Esteban. How was the beach?"

Esteban tried to hide in his mother's arms, but managed a smile. His olive complexion matched Sara's.

Hardy looked up at Sara. "He's wonderful."

"He's my world. What's left of it, anyway."

CHAPTER 9

Rivera Compound, Ensenada, Mexico

Manuel Rivera took the phone from his right-hand man, Alberto Delgado, and pointed his index finger at his guest, the mayor of Ensenada.

"You see that?" Rivera said, moving his finger toward the ocean from a balcony at his Baja estate. "Do you know what that is?"

The mayor squirmed. "No, sir."

Rivera squeezed his fist. "It's power. I'm like the surf. Unrelenting. Uncontrollable. I am what powers the economy. Do you understand?"

"Sí."

Rivera leaned back in his chair and sipped his iced tea. "Good. Let me be clear. Your city administrators and police need to do a better job of supporting me. Fully. Unconditionally. Do I need to remind you what happened to the last mayor?"

The mayor sweated profusely. "I did not mean to disrespect you, Manuel. Some of my men have complained about helping you."

Rivera continued to ignore the caller on the line. "Then get some better men. Or I'll find someone who can."

He motioned for the mayor to depart, leaving him alone with Delgado.

"Who is so important that you interrupt me?"

"Matadamas."

Rivera took the call. "Do you have her?"

Mendoza's voice sputtered. "I, I am on her trail. She left the party before I could take her."

"My contact led you right to her. How did you lose her?"

"She might have recognized my son before I could take her."

Rivera narrowed his eyes. "Tell me you have her in your sights."

Another pause. "I'm trying to intercept her."

Rivera made a fist. "You're *trying*?"

"I know where she's going. I'll have her soon."

"Do not fail me. This is personal."

Mendoza hesitated. "I understand. I will retrieve her. She's certainly gone for her boy, which will put her squarely in our hands."

"I hope you are correct. For your sake."

"May I ask a favor?"

"You fail me, and then have the cojones to ask for a favor?"

"Laguna Beach PD captured my boy. I could have rescued him, but I did as you asked and went for the girl instead. I'm a few minutes away from her home. But I left my boy in the hands of the police. Can you get him back?"

Rivera mulled that over in silence.

"He wants to work for you, Manuel. That should count for something."

"I will take care of it. But if you don't deliver the girl, saving him will be pointless. Understood?"

CHAPTER 10

Alice Polk's Estate

Flint turned the Latino teen over to his old partner from the police department, who handcuffed the boy and shoved him into the back of his squad car. A second officer was speaking with Alice on the front steps as guests grudgingly departed.

"No sign of the kid's daddy?" Flint asked.

Flint's ex-partner, Billy "Mongo" Buchanan, didn't make eye contact. At five-foot-two, one hundred thirty skinny pounds, he seemed to swim in his uniform. "Nothing. We don't really know what to look for, since nobody saw him, or saw his car. *If* he was even here."

"He was here, Mongo."

"So you say. Now, if you'll excuse me, I have real police work to do. And honest men to work with."

Mongo walked away, leaving Flint to stew. He pulled out his phone and dialed Hardy.

Hardy answered on the first ring. "Hey, Bret. We found Sara's son."

"That's fine as cream gravy. Listen, there's no sign of the kid's daddy. He might be headed your way."

"Sara says nobody there knows where she lives. Not even Alice. She thinks it's safe."

Flint watched the teen sitting in the squad car. "They found her here. You know what I can't figure out? Why the daddy didn't fight for his boy."

30

"Unless he's hot on our trail and intends to finish the job first. I think I'll take Sara to my studio. That should be secure."

"I'll hang here and see if we get anything out of the kid."

"Will they let you talk to him? They're still pissed."

Flint glanced at Mongo. "That they are. Mongo is here."

"Shit. Don't give him any excuse to arrest you. He's looking for payback."

"Yeah. Gotta go."

He hung up and approached the squad car. Mongo stepped between him and the suspect. "Where you going?"

"I'm trying to get a lead on the daddy. Maybe the kid will spill something."

Mongo refused to budge. "Not on my watch. You're a civilian. The pros here will do the investigating."

Flint sighed and stepped into the house to check on Alice.

CHAPTER 11

Near Sara's Apartment, Dana Point

Hardy took Sara by the arm. "He's coming. We've got to go."

Sara set her son on the ground. "Who's coming? Garcia?"

"The guy your cousin sent. Flint thinks he knows where you live."

Sara's eyes grew wide. She knelt down, holding her son in her arms. "How is that possible?"

"People aren't that hard to find these days."

"I'm supposed to be."

"We can go to my place. He doesn't know who I am, or where I live. We can wait for your deputy there."

"What about my stuff?" Sara asked, her voice shaky. "Esteban's toys. Clothes."

"Too risky. We need to get you both to safety. Then we'll figure the rest out."

Esteban plopped onto the grass. "I want my toys."

Sara leaned down. "We must go now, sweetie."

"No!"

Her eyes starting to leak. "Do we have time?"

Hardy felt bad for both of them, but shook his head. "Your pursuers could get here any second."

Esteban reacted by shrieking at full volume.

Hardy perused the top of the hill, half expecting a brigade of bad guys to come charging over. "We don't need this kind of attention right now."

Sara dropped to her knees, facing Esteban. "Esteban," she said firmly, "you must stop. I will buy you new toys. Right now, we need to go with Mr. Hardy."

Esteban stopped yelling and swallowed. "Why, Momma? Why does this keep happening?"

Sara hugged him, tears falling down her cheeks. "I'm sorry, baby. It's going to be okay. Let's go up the hill. I bet if we ask nicely, Mr. Hardy will go to a drive-thru and we can get your favorite cheeseburger."

"I want tacos," Esteban said.

Hardy grinned. "Tacos it is. But only if we leave now."

They hurried up the hill to his car. After getting Esteban seated, they started to get in when a loud screech froze them. A large sedan came barreling around the corner from PCH, then ran a red light, and raced into Sara's apartment complex.

Hardy climbed in to drive, and Sara got in the back with her son.

"That's him, isn't it?" she asked.

"Afraid so. Let your Deputy Garcia know where we're heading." Hardy jotted the address down. "Don't worry." He pointed at the car entering Sara's apartment complex. "This guy doesn't know where we're going."

The sky turned darker.

CHAPTER 12

Alice Polk's Estate

Flint found Alice at the walk-in bar off her family room, pouring another glass of red wine.

"You okay?"

She glared at him. "Seriously? What about this could be described as anything remotely close to okay?" She gulped down some wine. "Any word on Sara?"

"She's with Nick. He'll take good care of her."

"Why would anyone come after her?"

"Beats me," Flint said, shrugging. "We don't really know much about her."

"You did her reference checks."

"Yeah. All came back clean. Flawless, actually."

Alice set her glass down and leveled her eyes at Flint's. "Nobody is flawless, Mr. Flint. Perhaps we were charmed into overlooking that."

A gunshot rang out in the driveway.

Flint recognized the sound of a sawed-off shotgun. *Not the police.*

Another shotgun shot, followed by pistol fire. Then a crescendo, making it impossible for Flint to differentiate.

Flint's first move was to step in front of Alice. "Get down!" She ducked behind the bar. "Stay here."

"You don't have a gun," Alice said. "Don't be a hero. Just lock the front door and come back here."

More shots. All shotgun now.

34

Flint grabbed a fireplace poker. He waved the sharp end in front of him as he charged the open front door. "They're not interested in us. They want the kid."

"And just what do you plan to do with that imbecilic poker?"

"I haven't a clue." He ducked behind the entry wall and peeked outside.

All four police officers were down on the concrete, blood surrounding their bodies. A low-riding Chevy raced away from the scene. The teenager was gone.

"Mongo!" He stepped out onto the tile entry outside. "Oh, Jesus, Mongo, don't die on me."

He crossed the courtyard and kneeled next to Mongo. He checked for a pulse, but knew from the wound in his forehead it was futile.

"Alice," Flint screamed, "call 9-1-1! Tell them *officers down*. I'm in pursuit."

He didn't wait for a reply. He raced to his Porsche. He dialed Hardy as he sped down the hill toward the Coast Highway.

Hardy answered. "Hey. You're on speaker. We're almost at my place. All good, so far."

"It's FUBAR over here," Flint said.

"What happened?"

"A gang attacked and took the boy. The police officers are all dead. Must have been at least four gunmen to get the jump on them."

"Shit," Hardy murmured. "Mongo?"

Flint slammed his hands into the steering wheel. "He's gone."

Hardy paused. "Oh, no. Sorry, man."

Sara interrupted. "Are you okay?"

"Yeah. I was in the house with Alice when they attacked. I'm hot on their heels now." Flint paused. "When I catch them, I'm going to rip their fucking hearts out."

Flint slammed on the breaks as the car in front of him stopped for a yellow light. "Dumbshit." He blasted his horn, then swerved around the cautious driver and ran the light. "Not you, Nick. I need to know where you hang your hat, Sara. I can catch up to them there."

After a short pause, and some mumbling between Hardy and Sara, she came back on the line. "Villas at Monarch Beach, on the corner of Mariner and Niguel."

"Thanks."

"I'd ask you not to tell anyone," she continued softly, "but I guess my place is burned anyway. Who's Mongo?"

Flint sighed. "My old partner at the police department. He and I had a falling out over a case." He shook his head. "Now I'll never get to fix it."

"You have backup?" Hardy asked.

"No," Flint said. He glanced at the fireplace poker on the passenger seat. "I could use some."

"Aren't you armed?" Sara asked.

"I don't usually carry."

"But you're a private eye," Sara said.

"You've been watching too much TV," Flint said. "My work for Alice is about checking out CEOs and the inside scoop on companies."

"I'll call it in," Hardy said, "and send someone to Sara's place. Do the killers know you're following them?"

Flint scoured the road in front of him, looking for the Chevy. "I don't see how. But I haven't caught up with them yet."

"Where are you now?" Hardy asked.

"Coming down PCH. Turning on Niguel."

"I still don't get how they know where I live," Sara said.

"Somebody figured it out," Flint said. "Listen, what do I do if they split up after their rendezvous?"

"Focus on the father and son," Hardy said.

"Sara," Flint said, "you ready to tell me why these guys are so hot and heavy to find you?"

"Not yet," Sara said. "But I owe you."

"I'll start a list," Flint grunted.

He edged his Porsche up near the entrance to the apartment complex and cut his lights. He could barely make out the lowrider parked next to a Cadillac in the advancing fog. The smell of the sea rode in with the wind. "Hey, I caught up with them. They're hitched up in front of Sara's apartment complex. There's the teenager. He's getting into a Caddy. Must be the daddy's ride. The Chevy is pulling out."

"Do you think they spotted you?" Hardy asked.

"Not a chance," Flint said as he ducked while the Chevy sped past him. "The Chevy just left. I got the license number."

The Cadillac roared to life and eased toward him.

"The Caddy's moving. Must have already checked Sara's place and found it empty."

Flint glanced in his rearview mirror after the Cadillac passed by and saw an AK-47 poke out of the driver's side. Flint ducked as bullets whizzed past him, shattering his back and front windows. The next shots took out his rear tires.

"Bret!" Sara yelled over the phone. "What happened?"

Flint stayed huddled in his seat until the barrage of bullets stopped. He chanced to look in his side mirror and watched the Cadillac peel away. "Jesus Christ! The guy blew out my window and tires."

"You're not hit?" Hardy asked.

"I'm okay. But they're gone. You know what this reminds me of?"

"What?"

"Nothing! He fucking shot at me. How did he know I was here for him? This is nuts."

Sara interrupted with a panicked voice. "Bret, this may seem even crazier, but you can't tell the police about me."

"Are you overdrawn at the mental bank?" Flint asked, raising his voice. "They killed four of my friends. And tried to kill me."

"I have a US marshal on his way. Deputy Marshal Garcia. He can take it from here."

Flint hesitated. "A US marshal? He's after this man?"

"He will be now," Sara said. "Can you just leave it to him? He won't want the police involved."

Flint opened the Porsche's driver's door and stepped out, surveying the damage. "You better have a damn good reason why. I'll have this towed over to Nick's. Y'all owe me some answers."

"I'll tell you what I can," Sara said.

CHAPTER 13

Hardy's Studio

After a quick meal and a bedtime story, Esteban fell asleep holding his new best friend, Bear, on Hardy's sofa bed. Hardy poured Sara and himself a few shots of tequila, and they sat on a floor mat near his desk. He kept the studio fluorescents off. A thin line of light snuck past the blinds from the lit-up parking lot.

Sara stared at her drink. Hardy tapped her shoe with his. "You're safe here."

Sara met his gaze. "Yeah. What could go wrong?"

Hardy recognized the sarcasm. "Your deputy will be here soon."

"Right." She sat up. "Can we change the subject?"

"Sure."

"So, is Nick short for something?"

"Nicholas. My mother used to call me that when I was in big trouble." He smiled. "She called me that a lot."

"Seems fitting that I call you that then. I've been nothing but trouble for you."

Hardy smiled. "Hey, what self-respecting guy doesn't enjoy the whole damsel-in-distress deal?"

When Sara didn't smile, he lowered his voice. "Look, I don't mean to make light of your situation. I know it's dangerous and sucks every which way. You want to tell me what's going on, or wait for Bret?"

Sara stared into her Tequila. "I'm not supposed to talk about it." She fiddled with her wedding ring, then noticed Hardy staring at it. "You were right. I just wear the ring to ward off Romeos. I've had enough."

"What can I do to help?"

"You don't even know me."

Hardy paused, his mind going back to a memory he'd hoped he'd buried forever. The moment his life had turned to shit. His sister. *Dead, because I didn't bother to save her.* "I can see you need help."

"You've done so much already. Deputy Garcia will come get me soon and I'll be out of your hair. Can I ask you something?"

Hardy bobbed his head. "Sure."

"You seem to be taking this all in stride. Why aren't you freaking out, getting caught up in something so dangerous?"

Hardy put thoughts of his sister back in the dark space he kept them. "I was going to ask you the same thing."

Sara blinked away some moisture forming around her eyes. "Sadly, this has become the norm for me."

"Guys chasing you, trying to kill you?"

"Sort of. The threat's always there."

"You said Garcia's a US marshal? This all sounds like WITSEC to me."

She stared at Hardy and sat back against the wall. "Screw it. I'm leaving the program anyway, so you may as well know what you've gotten yourself into." She waited, then continued. "Yes, I'm in the Federal Witness Security Program. I'm Garcia's witness."

"Why do you need protecting?"

"I saw a murder in Texas. Committed by my ex-fiancé, Victor Ortega."

Hardy's heart pounded, her summary hitting too close to home for comfort. "Your fiancé?"

"Ex. A childhood sweetheart thing. Over long ago."

"He's the one after you?"

"No. Victor wouldn't have the nerve. But he works for my cousin, Manuel Rivera. Manuel sent the assassin."

Hardy swallowed as he tried to process that. "Your cousin is trying to kill you?"

"He doesn't want me to testify against Victor. Considers Victor family."

"And *you're* not?"

"I rejected the family business. As a teen I worked for him. They trained me to be a computer hacker. When I realized the business he was in and why he had me hacking, I bailed. So, no, I'm kinda disowned."

"I feel like I've heard the name Manuel Rivera somewhere."

"He runs the largest drug cartel in Mexico. He's been in the news."

"Jesus, Sara." Hardy ran his fingers across the top of his head. "How long have you been in WITSEC?"

"Over a year," she said with considerable bitterness. "I still don't know if we did the right thing. I hate WITSEC so much." She paused. "Sorry for whining."

"You're not whining. It's a tough deal."

"Manuel continues to search for me—and my brother, Juan, too. Juan was at the murder scene, though he didn't see Victor pull the trigger like I did. My husband was also there."

Hardy sat up straighter, surprised more by a feeling of disappointment than the actual surprise. "Husband? I thought it was just for show."

Sara tilted her head. "Where do you think Esteban came from? Manuel had my husband killed after the murder in Texas."

Hardy felt relief, then shame. He could see the energy draining out of her. "Is your brother here?"

"He's in WITSEC somewhere. They decided it best to split us up. Playing the odds one of us gets to trial alive."

Hardy gazed into her eyes. "I'm sure the marshals know what they're doing. You'll both get there just fine."

"Garcia's boss, US Marshal Presley, he seems concerned."

"Any idea how Rivera's guy found you tonight?"

Sara gazed at the angelic Esteban. "No. Now I'll have to move again, and start over. That part is the toughest, uprooting Esteban like that."

After a moment, she reset her smile and returned her attention to Hardy. "You're taking this awfully calmly. What's your story?"

"I stay pretty even-keeled. Part of being a stunt man, where all hell is breaking out around you, everybody's yelling instructions, lots of time-sensitive pressure. If you blow one of those scenes it costs a fortune to redo it. Bret refers to me as 'ice man' because he thinks I never show any emotion."

"Never?"

Hardy thought back to his past. "Almost never."

"What about your personal life?"

"Well, you already know what I do. I used to do stunt work. I live here for now."

Sara snapped her fingers. "C'mon. Give me the good stuff."

Hardy laughed. "The good stuff, huh? I wish I had some. I'm single, and have been since my fiancée bailed on me."

"That sucks. Why'd she do that?"

Hardy involuntarily made double fists. A sharp pain drilled upstream as the nerves in his arm lit up. He took several deep breaths and tried to calm himself, only partially succeeding. "Things went downhill after I killed her father."

He put his palms up. "I guess neither of us has much luck when it comes to exes."

Before Sara could react, headlights flashed through the window as they heard a car pull into the parking lot outside. Bear jumped up and barked, but stayed on the bed. Esteban rolled over, but stayed asleep. Hardy, relieved for the interruption, got up and peeked through the blinds. "It's Bret."

"He wasn't followed, was he?"

Hardy glanced down Camino Capistrano and observed the normal flow of traffic. "Looks good." He watched Flint get out of the cab of the tow truck and pay the driver.

As the tow-truck driver got out to unhook Flint's Porsche, a sedan screeched into the parking lot. A large, Hispanic man in jeans and a blazer jumped out and pointed a gun at Flint.

"Freeze," the man yelled.

Hardy jerked back from the window, shielding Sara. "Stay down. They found you."

CHAPTER 14

Bear barked furiously at the alarm in Hardy's voice. Hardy signaled to Bear to be quiet, and he immediately complied.

Sara folded into Hardy. "Is there a back way out?"

"Emergency exit by the bathroom. Grab Esteban."

Hardy watched a short Caucasian man dressed in a suit get out of the driver's side, his gun ready. No sign of the man with the scar.

"Wait," Hardy said. "You recognize them?"

She peeked through the blinds and let out a sigh. "The big guy's my handler, Deputy Garcia. The other is his boss, Marshal Presley. They're the good guys."

Sara opened the door and called out to the marshals. "He's with me. Get in here."

Garcia relaxed and lowered his weapon. Presley flashed a badge at the tow-truck driver and told him to carry on. They followed Flint into the studio without asking permission and shut the door behind them, both visibly relieved to see Sara. Garcia glanced through the blinds, then motioned for Sara to join him on the other side of the room.

Presley stayed with Hardy and Flint while Bear checked him out for cool smells. Presley topped out around five-six, but Hardy could see he was all muscle, and all business. His black hair clung to his head in a sweaty mess. Pockmarks from an earlier ambush of serious acne littered his face. "I understand we have you two to thank for getting her out of there tonight."

"She tells me you're the local US marshal in charge of protecting her in WITSEC," Hardy said.

"Seriously?" Flint said.

Presley jerked in Sara's direction. "She said what?"

"She also said she wants to drop out," Hardy said.

Presley paused, then yelled at Sara. "Sara. What the hell?"

Sara glanced away from Garcia, midsentence. "I told him the truth," she said defiantly. "He risked his life for me. He deserved to know why."

Presley stared her down until Sara went back to her conversation with Garcia. Presley looked back at Hardy and Flint. "She's a wonderful person, but she can also be a handful. As stubborn as she is smart."

Hardy laughed. "I've only known her a few hours, and I see all of that." *And more*, he thought.

"Listen," Presley said, "I need to know you'll keep all this to yourselves. The identity of our inspectors is just as sensitive as the identity of our witnesses. We take precautions beyond what the FBI, the CIA, and the NSA do, combined." He glared at Sara. "I need you to forget about all of this."

"No problem," Hardy said. "What happens now?"

"We'll have her relocated, and the fact that you met her won't be an issue, since you won't know where she is." Hardy could see from Presley's expression that he cared deeply for Sara and her safety. "If you want, I can post stakeouts at your homes tonight."

"I can take care of myself," Flint said. "So can Nick. And we've got the Bear on our side. Personally, I hope they show up. They killed my friends."

"I heard," Presley said. "I'm sorry."

"I'll find them."

"I hope you do," Presley turned to Hardy. "We need to get her out of here." He switched gears and yelled over to Garcia. "Deputy, let's move."

Garcia left Sara and marched to Presley. His massive arms bulged in his jacket. A scar ran across his forehead below his brown hair. Bear growled as Garcia approached, but stopped when Hardy signaled to him.

"She swears he's Rivera's guy," Garcia said, "but the description doesn't match anyone from Rivera's team."

Sara joined them. "Nicholas, I don't know how to thank you. You too, Bret. I think I better go with them. I have a lot to figure out."

"You're staying in WITSEC?" Hardy asked.

"For now."

Hardy turned to the marshals. "Can you give Sara and me a minute?"

He took Sara by the arm and led her to the other side of the room.

Presley checked his watch. "You have twenty seconds."

Once out of easy earshot, Hardy turned to face Sara. "Are you okay?"

"I'm okay. I'll be in a new city with a new identity tomorrow. It sucks, but it's my life."

He surprised himself, and her, by pulling her toward him. He was pleased she didn't resist. "You sure about going with them?"

"Leaving the program is a big decision. Sometimes, I'm too impulsive. Truth is, I'm scared. I try to act like I'm taking all this in stride, for Esteban's sake, and nobody likes a whiner, but Manuel is a bad man. And he'll never stop."

"Will I hear from you again?"

She eased her head back and forth. "Afraid not. I wish we'd had a chance to get to know each other. I would have liked that."

"Me, too."

She gently pushed herself away. "My getting out of your life is best. I'm a bad person to be connected with. Everyone who does gets hurt. Or dead."

He shook his head. "Bad things happen to good people sometimes. That says nothing about who you are."

"Thanks. That's very kind."

Hardy fished out an old business card that had his cell phone number on it and offered it to her. "If you ever need anything, call my cell. Any time, day or night."

She laughed. "That's sweet of you, but I can take care of myself. Serious kickboxing. With Manuel and Victor in my life, I prepared myself."

"Really?"

"Really." She sighed. "They won't let me keep your card. I need to cut off all links to my past and present." She reached out for his hand. "I wish I could stay in touch."

Presley stepped over to them. "Sara, it's time. Thanks for your help, Mr. Hardy. And your discretion. You're sure you don't want a guard here?"

"We're good."

Sara picked up the sleeping Esteban, and Presley wrapped one arm around her, leading her away. Hardy didn't care much for the way he held Sara as they left. He didn't know why, but he felt like she'd be safer with him.

And you'd be happier having her around. He shook that confusing thought off and watched them drive away.

Flint idled up next to Hardy. "You know what this reminds me of?"

"What?"

Flint put his arm around his friend. "Not a damn thing."

CHAPTER 15

Hardy watched Sara vanish. He felt empty. "Do you think she'll be okay?"

"They know what they're doing. She's in good hands."

"I hope you're right. Something doesn't feel right. We still don't know how they found her in the first place. Who's to say they won't track her to her next place?" He turned to Flint. "Or here?"

"I hope those bastards do try to find us," Flint said. "I have some payback to give out. Just in case, I'll go to my place to get us some firepower. Lock the door and keep the lights off. I'll be back in less than an hour." He took Hardy's car keys and left without waiting for a reply.

Hardy lay down on his bed and closed his eyes, Bear joining him, exhaustion trying to overpower him. But he stayed awake, listening for suspicious sounds outside, and recalling a scene from three years before.

*****

Hardy stood in the guest bedroom of his future parents-in-law along the coast in Laguna Beach, his fiancée, Mona, at his side. The lifestyle of the rich and famous never ceased to amaze him. The size of this guest room easily surpassed his apartment, and the silver and gold decorations were probably worth more than his savings.

He winced at the tone of Mona's father, Richard, yelling at Mona's mother, Nancy, in their bedroom down the hall.

"Is it too much to ask," Richard screamed, "for a little respect. I told you this is important to me."

Mona's frown told Hardy she'd heard this act before.

"Do I need to go in there?"

"Oh, no. That will just make it worse. They'll work it out. They always do."

"He never lays a hand on her, right?"

"No. Never."

Hardy didn't hear much conviction in her voice.

A crash down the hall startled both of them. Hardy reached for the doorknob.

Mona's hand tried to stop him. "Please, Nick."

"Somebody could be hurt," Hardy said as he forced open the door. He raced to the parent's bedroom and knocked. When no one answered he let himself in.

Richard stood over Nancy, who had a gash on her forehead. A large rug was crumbled up in one corner on the hardwood floor, as if someone had slipped on it.

"Are you okay, dear?" Richard leaned down, extending his hand.

Mona came in and passed Hardy, joining Richard in helping Nancy back to her feet.

"Damn rug," Nancy said, not looking anyone in the eye. "I swear, we need to replace this. That's twice I've slipped on it."

Hardy watched Richard force a hug with Nancy, who seemed to allow it out of a sense of responsibility. Mona went to the bathroom and came back with a wet washcloth, applying it to Nancy's head.

Hardy stepped in closer. He saw a bruise on the other side of Nancy's face, away from the gash.

"What happened?" he asked Richard.

He turned to Hardy. "Isn't that obvious? She slipped and fell. She's always been clumsy."

"That might explain the gash. It doesn't explain the bruise on the other side of her face."

Richard straightened. "What are you, CSI? Mind your own business."

Hardy ground his teeth. He leaned down next to Mona, addressing Nancy. "Did you slip on your own? Or were you helped?"

"I just fell." Nancy said. Her face lost it's pink coloring.

She's terrified. For herself? Or me?

Hardy felt powerful hands grab his shirt collar and pull him up. He was spun around and pinned against the bedroom wall.

"What the fuck do you think you're doing?" Richard asked.

Hardy took a moment to plan his next move. It turned out to be a moment he didn't have.

Richard sent a booming punch into Hardy's gut. Hardy doubled over, and Richard released his grip, which was all the leeway Hardy needed.

He counterpunched to Richard's throat, not enough to break his windpipe, but enough to slow him down. Richard staggered back as Mona screamed for Hardy to stop. As Richard reached for Hardy's throat, he stepped on the turned-up corner of the rug. Richard lost his balance and fell, smashing his head against the bed's hardwood footboard.

*****

Hardy heard his car pull up outside. He sat up, his back moist and sticking to his shirt, as Flint came back in. Bear gave him a cursory glance and went back to sleep.

Flint carried two handguns and a shotgun. "All quiet here?"

Hardy stood and stretched. "All good."

"How you holding up?"

"Okay."

Flint waited for Hardy to continue. When Hardy didn't, he charged ahead. "She really affected you, didn't she?"

"What do you mean?"

"Sara. When you speak of her your face turns hotter than a preacher's knee."

"I just hope she's okay."

"Pard, I think it's more than that."

"It's not like I'm ever going to see her again."

Flint leaned forward. "It's a good thing to care about someone again. Maybe she's the kick start you needed to get back in the game."

"I'll get back in the game when the game is worth playing. It's not like you're leading the league in finding Mrs. Flint."

Flint ignored him. "I stay away from relationships because I want to. You do it because you were hurt."

"I wasn't the only one. I also screwed up your career."

"Forget about what happened to me. I did okay."

Hardy lowered his voice. "I messed up both our lives. How do I just forget about that?" He paused. "Can we talk about something else?"

Bear stood and came over to his master. Hardy rubbed Bear's head while he licked Hardy's hand. "It's okay, Bear. Daddy's fine." Bear cocked his head and continued licking.

Flint waited, then tread into even deeper waters. "Have you cut back on the poker? And the drinking?"

"Jesus, what's with the third degree?"

Flint didn't back down. "You've been pissing away your money ever since Mona bailed on you. You turned down security work in Hollywood that would have paid the bills. You're living here. You went through your savings, didn't you?"

Hardy thought about telling Flint that Mona may have been the trigger, but wasn't the original sin, but kept quiet about his sister. He dismissed Flint with a stiff wave of his free hand. "Just worry about yourself, will you?"

"I'll stop worrying about you when you grow a pair and stop sulking like a cat at the dog pound."

"Hey. You have no right . . ."

Flint tensed up and leaned sideways to see around Hardy.

"What's up?" Hardy asked, temporarily abandoning the verbal assault he was planning.

"I think a man just passed by outside."

Bear barked a warning shot toward the door. Hardy grabbed him by the collar. "Stay, boy."

Flint stood up and walked to blinds, one of the pistols pointed ahead. He eased the door open and peeked both ways. "No one here. Maybe I imagined it."

"Should we check the perimeter?"

"Nah. Probably nothing."

Flint closed and latched the door, then took a post at the blinds. "I'll stand watch for a while. You get some shut-eye. I'll wake you in a few."

Hardy knew Flint's powers of observation were reliable. If he said someone was there, someone was. And Bear didn't bark for the fun of it.

He didn't sleep much.

CHAPTER 16

Twenty-four hours passed without incident. Flint went home around noon, and Hardy tried to figure out how to pay the rent. Unable to find any clients, he settled on a high-stakes poker game.

He returned at 11:00 p.m., his financial hole dug even deeper. He gave Bear a big welcome, when his cell phone rang. The call originated from a number not in his contact list. He debated answering it—his mood wasn't conducive to a telemarketing call—but chose to pick it up.

"Hello, Nicholas. Any sign of the bad guys?"

Hardy stared at the phone, stunned. "Sara?"

"Of course, silly."

His mind raced. *Is she in trouble. Is she out of WITSEC? Is she on the run?* "Are you okay?"

"Great. You?"

"I'm fine. Did you leave WITSEC?"

"Not yet. Still debating."

Hardy didn't know whether to frown or smile. "Can you tell me where you are?"

"Afraid not," she said. "I have a new handler. She's okay, but I miss Garcia. So, no sign of the bad guys?"

"No." He'd almost forgotten about the mystery shadow from the night before.

"I figured as much."

Hardy rubbed his forehead. "Are you sure this is safe?"

"Probably not. But it's a one-time deal. I had to hear the story about killing your fiancée's father. I've spent a good part of my life around killers. I hope I'm not wrong about you."

Hardy stared at the floor. "That's a sore subject."

"Come on. I'm risking a lot here. Tell me what happened. And hurry. My handler will be back any moment."

Hardy tried to swallow, but his throat was dry. "It was an accident. He was beating his wife. I think my ex, Mona, knew. Anyway, I stepped in, and the guy attacked me. I defended myself, but he slipped and hit his head. He never regained consciousness."

"I figured it was something like that."

"Mona and her mother came after me with everything they had, trying to get me convicted of murder. It was going to be my word against theirs, and they had the home-field advantage. Big-money donors to Laguna Beach. Friends in all the right places."

"What happened?"

"Bret happened. He was on the force, and the first on the scene. He ditched his partner and beat the other cops there. Saved my ass."

"How?"

Hardy forced a swallow. "Let's just say he messed up the crime scene and made it impossible to gather evidence against me. Put his hands up by the guy's throat, pretending to give CPR. They couldn't be sure I hit him after that. Cost Bret his badge."

"Damn."

"Yeah. I'll never be able to repay him."

"He seems to have landed on his feet. He seems happy."

"He is," Hardy said. "But being a cop was his lifelong goal. He'll never complain, but I know what helping me cost him."

Sara paused on the other end of the line. "You're a good man, Nicholas. Justice was served. Don't forget that."

"I appreciate the sentiment, but I have a long list of people who don't agree."

Sara laughed. "I hear the garage. I gotta run."

"Will I hear from you again?"

"I'm sorry, Nicholas. I wish I could."

She hung up. Hardy stared at the phone, then pulled out his last bottle of Patrón, the tequila he was saving for a special occasion.

I guess getting ripped will have to do.

CHAPTER 17

Rivera Compound

Rivera stood on his second-story bedroom balcony, watching the ocean surf. His armed guards paced within the high walls of the patio below. He sported casual white slacks, beach sandals, and a loose-fitting island shirt. His phone buzzed.

"Sí."

"It's Matadamas. I'm outside Hardy's studio. The next time he leaves I'll install the bugs. Hopefully, we'll get lucky."

Luck, Rivera thought. *I haven't had much of that with Sara.*

He thought back to the killing in Texas, and the cascading events that irritated him, like the swarm of mosquitos dive-bombing his exposed skin.

Fucking bad luck. I risk going across the border to give Sara a birthday gift, to convince her to come back to the family, be part of the business. Then that nosey neighbor comes over. He flashed his shotgun at us. What was Victor to do? Just bad luck.

"It should never have come to this," Rivera said. "I saved your boy. Don't make me regret that."

"And I am so grateful, *patrón*. We couldn't have predicted Hardy saving her like that."

"I'll deal with Hardy later. Just find me my cousin."

Rivera glanced down into the patio and noticed one of his guards leaning back against the wall, asleep. He pulled a Beretta out of his waistband, took dead aim, and shot the guard in the head.

"What happened?" a panicked voice came across the phone line.

Rivera waved to the surviving guards below to remove the dead body. "Nobody sleeps on watch," he called down. He returned his attention to Mendoza. "One of my men disappointed me." He let that sink in. "You don't want to disappoint me, Matadamas."

Rivera hung up as the guards below scrambled to clean up the mess. Watching them reminded him of cleaning up in Texas.

Sara walks in to see Victor pull the trigger. Followed by that gringo husband, and her brother. Now we have three witnesses to deal with. How could we be so unlucky?

A breeze came in from the sea, and the curtains around the balcony puffed toward him, reminding him of the lace on the last week's porn star's nightgown. He grinned at the thought of it.

He watched Delgado's white caddy pull up to the guard post at the top of the hill.

Good. I wonder who he brings me this week?

Delgado's car entered the compound and cruised down the hill on the lone road in and out. He honked twice, and the guards let him drive into the patio and up to the front door.

Delgado scrambled out and retrieved a brunette from the backseat.

Rivera leaned over the balcony to get a better view. The Latina couldn't have been more than twenty-five, but had an air of assurance about her that promised maturity.

And experience.

She wore a sleeveless black dress, with slits down the side that exposed slim legs.

A little skinny, but she'll do.

Long legs followed Delgado toward the entry, when Rivera noticed her eyes.

Blue?

"Hold up," Rivera called down.

Delgado froze. "Boss?"

"What's with her eyes?"

Delgado glanced at her, and cringed. He stepped away from her, cowering. "They were brown when I picked her up."

The Latina gave them both queer looks. "I took my contacts out in the car. I can put them back if you want."

Rivera pursed his lips. "You are not pure."

"Pure? I'm Mexican. Not all of us have brown eyes."

Delgado took another step away from her.

"Mine do," Rivera said as he re-aimed his Beretta.

He fired two shots into her forehead. Delgado motioned for two guards to come clean up another mess. "I'm so sorry, boss. She fooled me. She always had brown eyes in the movies."

Rivera sighed. "An understandable mistake." He took his handkerchief out and polished the gun barrel. "But do not let it happen again. I'm weary of all this disappointment."

"Perhaps this will satisfy you," Delgado said, waving toward the car. "I brought one for me. Of course, she is yours now."

Another brunette cautiously slinked out. She was slightly thicker across the waist and legs, but had brown eyes.

Rivera smiled down on her. "You are exactly what I am looking for. You will spend the week, and be returned home safely."

"Thank you, Señor Rivera. You will not be disappointed." She scoffed at the carcass being carried away. "In fact, I'm twice the woman she is."

"How could I be so lucky?" he whispered as he waved her up.

CHAPTER 18

Monarch Beach, CA

The next morning, Hardy grabbed a rusting beach chair and drove down to the sand at Salt Creek Beach Park in the thick morning air to read the sports page and run his usual five miles.

Halfway through his paper he noticed black cowboy boots shuffling toward him. Deputy Garcia hovered over him, dressed in the same outfit of jeans, white shirt, and blue blazer.

Shit. Does he know about the phone call?

Hardy tried to look calm. "Deputy Garcia. What can I do for you?"

Garcia glared as he stepped in front of Hardy. "Just checking in. Anything unusual going on?"

"Nope. How did you find me?"

Garcia ignored the question. "Any sign of being watched?"

"Besides by you?"

Garcia leaned over, hostility raging. "I don't have time for your wise-ass remarks. Have you heard from Sara?"

Hardy tried to look incredulous. "Why would you ask that?" He cocked his head. "Isn't she someone else's problem now?"

Garcia increased the intensity of his scowl. "Just answer the fucking question."

Hardy's heart rate picked up speed, and he feared Garcia might notice some change in his face coloring. Hardy swallowed the last of his orange juice before continuing. "Of course I haven't heard from her."

"If you see or hear anything suspicious, you call me right away."

"I will. Say, did you figure out how they found her? How many of you knew where she lived? Where she worked? Where she'd be that night?"

Garcia's face turned red. "I don't much care for what you're implying. We're US marshals, for Christ's sake."

"Yet, someone who knew gave her up. Did you fail to vet anyone?"

"We did our job." He paused. "I want to find out how she was compromised as much as anyone. But we have to accept we may never know. Could just be bad luck. A chance encounter."

With that, Garcia walked back toward the parking lot. Halfway to the steps leading up to the snack bar, he turned back, stared at Hardy, then continued up the hill.

Was that really about his concern for Sara? Hardy wondered. *Or something else? Would they kick her out for breaking protocol?*

He ran an extra mile while he pondered too many unknowns.

CHAPTER 19

Hardy's Studio

Later that morning, between online poker hands, Hardy received a call from another unknown number. He stared at the cell phone screen, mulling over whether to bother.

She said she wouldn't call again. It's not her.

But what if it is? What if she's in trouble?

He started to answer, then wondered if Rivera's guys could be trying to locate him.

She's not going to call you if she's in trouble. You're not her go-to guy when she's got a crisis. Moron.

Besides, it's safer for her if she doesn't call.

Irrational hope won out over caution and valor. "Hello?"

"Nicholas," Sara said. "How are you?"

Hardy took a steadying breath. "Sara. What are you doing? This is reckless."

She didn't reply for a moment. "Nice to hear your voice, too. And here I was about to ask you out."

"What?"

"I know it's crazy, but how about we meet for dinner tonight. You know Geoffrey's in Malibu?"

Hardy sat up straighter. "I do. How can you get away like that?"

"I'm sneaky. My new handler promised to take Esteban to dinner and a movie to give me a break. I have just enough time to meet you."

"You're in Malibu?"

She caught her breath. "No. But I can get there by six. Are you busy?"

In Hardy's mind, his saint jousted with his devil. *This can't be okay, can it?* "That sounds risky. For you, and Esteban."

"Just don't get followed, and we'll be fine. You can do that, right?"

"That sounds like a challenge."

"Are you up for it?"

Hardy rubbed his forehead. "If you're sure."

"I'm never sure about anything these days. But, other than Esteban, you're the first good thing to happen to me in a long time. So good, that I took the chance to call you. And my handler doesn't make that easy. But I deserve to have a little life, don't I? Besides, I have something important to talk to you about. Best done in person, so I can read your eyes when you answer."

"My eyes?"

"Passports to the soul."

Hardy thought back to his sister. *I can't be the cause of another person's demise. I'd never survive it.* "I can't be putting you two at more risk. What if your phone can be traced?"

"Special burner phones provided by Presley. Encrypted. Can't be tapped or traced, in either direction. Except by the marshals, of course. So nothing to worry about."

Hardy remembered his morning conversation. "Hey, speaking of marshals, Garcia came to see me today, asking if I'd heard from you. You think he suspects we're in touch? Does that change your opinion about tonight?"

"What'd you tell him?"

"Nothing."

"Thanks," she said. "He was responsible for me since I went in to WITSEC. Great that he still cares, even though I'm someone else's responsibility now."

"I guess," Hardy said. "But he rubs me wrong. I can't stop wondering if he gave up your location."

"Garcia? No way. And, no, it doesn't change my mind. I'll see you at six. By the way, I plan to look pretty hot."

Hardy laughed. "You're a big tease, aren't you?"

"You have no idea."

He hung up and rubber Bear's head. "It'll be okay, right buddy? We'll be careful."

Bear looked at him like he was crazy.

CHAPTER 20

San Juan Hills Golf Club, San Juan Capistrano

Hardy found Flint, fresh off an early-morning round of golf, seated in the dining room, wearing a pink-and-blue flowered shirt. He was flirting with his server, a college coed and recent addition to the clubhouse staff. She appeared to find his jokes quite entertaining. She blushed as Hardy sat down and turned toward him with a huge grin.

"What can I get you?" she said, almost giggling.

"Bacon cheeseburger," Hardy said. "And a whiskey." He pointed at Flint. "My friend is buying, so make it the good stuff."

She gave Flint another big grin, and stepped away.

Hardy watched her disappear around the corner. "Didn't you date her mother last year?"

Flint furrowed his brow, clearly unsure. "Damn. You wouldn't be messing with a cowpoke like me, would you?"

"I believe you did. You might want to think about that one."

"Gracias for the tip."

Halfway through his bacon cheeseburger, Hardy's cell phone rang. He recognized Sara's number.

Flint leaned over, trying to see who was calling. "You always turn your phone off while you're chowing down. What gives?"

Hardy turned the phone away from Flint and accepted the call. "Hi."

Sara's voice sounded stressed. "Hey. Can you do me a favor?"

"Sure."

"Leave your phone at home. They could track you with it."

Hardy cleared his throat. "Okay. You sure about this?"

He waited for a response. After a few seconds, she said, "Yes." She disconnected.

"Who's that?" Flint asked.

"Just a friend of mine."

"Shirt or skirt?"

"None of your business."

He laughed. "Definitely skirt. Anyone I know?"

"No."

Flint watched Hardy, doubt and suspicion etched on his face. "Since when do we keep secrets about the ladies?"

Hardy started to put his phone away when Flint grabbed it and held it hostage. "If you don't tell me, I'm calling her back."

Hardy lunged for the phone but came up empty. "You don't want to do that."

Flint debated how far to go, then reluctantly handed the phone to Hardy. "You have a new girl I don't know about?"

Hardy exhaled, shut the phone off, and slipped the phone into his pants pocket. "I'm thinking about getting someone to clean the studio. Nothing to see here."

Flint laughed. "Y'all never cared about that." He gave Hardy a knowing look. "The mess bugged you when Sara was there, didn't it? You wanted to impress her."

Hardy smirked. "Right, Sherlock. I just thought it might help the business if the place looked nicer."

Flint stared at Hardy. "Maybe. But it was Sara who made you think of it. Am I right?"

"Would it do any good to tell you you're full of it?"

"I reckon not."

Hardy sipped his whiskey. "Garcia came by, asking me if anyone's watching us."

"I hate that guy. Acts like he's got a burr up his butt."

"Do you think he could have given Sara up?"

"A rouge marshal? Seems unlikely."

"I suppose."

Flint changed the subject. "Hey, guess what I bought this morning? A share in the plane."

"You're crazy, you know that? I understood getting the pilot's license, but a piece of your own plane?"

"A business jet. Seats twelve. Has a wet bar."

"Of course it does."

"The other owners hardly ever use it. Hey, let's go to Catalina tomorrow. Get ourselves a Buffalo Burger."

Hardy chuckled. "You really are too much. I guess business is good."

"Business is *muy bueno*. I found that woman Alice is pining for. She's now the CEO for an international investment firm, a real recluse. No public sightings in years. One fine lady. I can see why Alice is hot for her. Alice rewarded me handsomely. So I bought me a new toy."

"I'm happy for you." Hardy finished off his whiskey. "Any chance you can watch Bear overnight?"

Flint sat up. "The Bear? Sure. What's up?"

"I won't be around to feed him, and I might be out late. I can come get him in the morning."

"Nah, sleep in. I'll bring him by when I pick you up for the flight. The Bear can roll with us."

"Sounds great. Thanks."

Flint raised his drink and clinked Hardy's glass. "Here's to fun. And never having to deal with the Rivera cartel again."

CHAPTER 21

Geoffrey's Restaurant, Malibu, CA

Hardy met Sara as the sun set. She had claimed a table on the patio's edge, overlooking the ocean. The patio was otherwise deserted.

He'd dressed up in his white shirt and blazer, something he enjoyed but rarely found an excuse to do in laid-back Southern California. She wore a white dress and a large white hat with sunglasses. She lifted a glass of red wine in her right hand, as if to toast Hardy's appearance.

He smiled and sat across from her. "You're right. You do look hot."

She took his hand and shook her head, clearly pleased. "It's not easy to pull off hot and incognito at the same time. Nobody followed you, right?"

"Nope."

"And you left your phone at home?"

"I did." He pointed to her drink. "What are we drinking?"

"Chateau Margaux. Nineteen ninety-five. I just bought a few bottles."

"Nice. WITSEC must pay well. I should look into it."

"Ha-ha. We can thank Alice for making this possible. I wasn't with her that long, but she made me a serious chunk of change." She lowered her voice. "You're sure you weren't followed?"

"Positive." Hardy's guilt about seeing her bubbled to the surface. "But maybe this is too risky for you. Should I go?"

She shook her head hard. "No." Hardy could see the conflict in her mannerisms. He was sure they matched his own feelings. "I'm sorry. I'm sure it's fine."

Sara poured Hardy some wine. He swirled it around in his glass and took a sip. "Wow. You know your wine."

She smiled like his opinion mattered. "Since our dinner window is short, I took the liberty of ordering for us. I have some special dietary restrictions. I hope you don't mind."

"No worries. What restrictions?"

She waived his question off, as if it weren't a big deal. "I have too much iron in my blood, so I need to stay away from red meat, raw fish, alcohol . . ."

Hardy almost choked on his swallow of wine. "Alcohol?"

She grinned widely. "Yes."

"You are a *very* bad girl. Calling me. Meeting for dinner. Wine."

She chuckled. "I prefer to think of it as independent thinking. Or rebellious. Besides, I need you."

Before Hardy could ask what *that* meant, crab cakes appeared, and they nibbled, but Hardy imagined nibbling on something more enticing, which made him blush.

"What are you thinking about?" she asked.

Hardy cleared his throat. "Many things." He smiled. "So, why am I here?"

Now it was her turn to blush. She winked. "Not yet. If you're not interested, it'll ruin my appetite."

Hardy's muscled involuntarily shivered. *Damn. What's happening here?* He swallowed. *And do I want it to happen?*

"Want to hear my story?" she asked.

"Of course."

She paused, then dove in, keeping her voice hushed. "Born in Cabo San Lucas. Younger brother, Juan. By the time I was fifteen, my cousin Manuel became the local drug lord's right-hand man. Basically capitalized on the vices of the entire population. I'm not sure which offended me more—his behavior or the inability of his clientele to control those vices."

A stiff ocean breeze came up, and she shivered. Hardy stood and placed his jacket over her shoulders. "Go on."

"Victor and I became engaged when I turned seventeen. Meanwhile, Manuel had taken over the drug cartel in our region. I did computer stuff for him. Today we call it hacking. Back then, it seemed harmless to a naive girl like me. Then I found out what the business really was, and that Victor was in deep. I broke off the engagement. Neither Victor nor Manuel ever forgave me."

She paused. "I met my husband, Sam, in grad school here in the States. We married a few years later, and Esteban came along a year after that."

"Are your parents still around?"

"My mother suffered from the same disease that I do. Hemochromatosis. She passed away from it, and my poor dad died a few weeks later from a broken heart. After that, Juan moved back here with Sam and me."

Hardy felt a fresh wave of sadness for her. "Your disease is that serious?"

"If it goes untreated."

"But you're able to control it?"

"I have a phlebotomy once a week. They draw a pint of my iron-rich blood and replace it with iron-poor blood. My brother has it worse. He doesn't have the natural purging of a menstrual cycle."

She pulled her iPhone out. "Care to see what Rivera looks like? I found this on the Internet today."

"Sure."

Sara's iPhone displayed three powerfully built Hispanic men dressed identically in white slacks and black long-sleeve shirts.

"That's Manuel on the left," Sara whispered. "The shorter man in the middle is his second in command, Alberto Delgado. On the right, with the stud earring, is one of Manuel's thugs, Valenzuela."

Rivera had an acne-scarred face and an unsmiling, jagged mouth. Even in the photo his gaze promised an unforgiving and menacing persona.

"Presley says Rivera is expanding his operation throughout Latin America," she continued. "He now has investors who are buying into his operation."

"How did he amass such a big empire?"

She grunted. "He's mean and a murderer. He intimidates everyone. His thirst for power is off the charts. Power and beautiful Latina women. He can't get enough."

Sara flicked the phone off and sat motionless. "Then I witnessed a murder, my husband was killed, and I got jailed in WITSEC for the rest of my life. Yay, me."

"You really hate it, don't you?"

"That's what I wanted to talk to you about. I want out, and I'm willing to take my chances, but I can't risk Esteban's life." She paused, waiting on Hardy.

Hardy wasn't sure where the conversation was heading. He squinted, and put his palms up. "I'm not sure what you're asking."

Sara cleared her throat. "You've worked security. You provide protection."

"I run a martial arts studio. I teach people how to defend themselves. It's not the same thing."

Sara sagged. "Yeah. I know. I was just hoping, maybe, that you could help me get out of WITSEC."

Hardy sat up. "How?"

"Maybe I could hire you to protect us? We could disappear and you could come with us. At least until it's safe."

Hardy's visions of her wanting him around in a romantic way came crashing to the floor. "Like a security guard?"

"I don't know what to call it. More like a consultant. I need to trust someone to keep us safe. I need to land in one place and hunker down, instead of getting moved around all the time. I don't know why, but I feel like you're the one guy I can really trust."

"I'm honored, Sara, but I don't know I'm really qualified for that. The marshals have to be your safest bet, don't they?"

Sara stared out toward the ocean. "Yeah. I'm sorry. It was a crazy idea. I didn't even consider how dangerous it would be for you." She returned her attention to him. "This isn't your fight."

The flash of a nearby camera startled her, and she jerked back in her chair. She scanned the area, and, spotting something of interest, reached across the table and grabbed Hardy's hand.

Hardy turned to follow her stare. A man stood at the railing with a camera in his hand.

"I need to go," Sara whispered.

"Do you know that guy? Do I need to take his camera?"

She shook her head imperceptibly. "No. I just need to go. I'm sorry, Nicholas. It was selfish of me to ask. Please forgive me." She let go of his hand, focused on the photographer.

Hardy took a deep breath. "We should talk about this."

She stood and came around to his side of the table, handing him his jacket. She touched his cheek with her hand. "I was stupid to think I can ever get out. Please give me a few minutes to get away from the valet station before you head up. I'll destroy my phone as soon as I'm home. In case my willpower fails me again."

"I'll walk you to your car."

"No. It's safer this way. I'll be fine."

"No, really . . ."

She glared at him. "Please. Just let me go."

Hardy wanted to insist, but her glare won out. "Are you angry with me?"

"No. With me." She gave him a hug, turned, and walked briskly to the valet station without comment. Hardy slumped, then glared at the photographer, ready to pounce if he paid any attention to her, or followed her out. He did neither.

Hardy waited an empty ten minutes before paying the bill and leaving for the ride home.

I wasn't expecting that. Why would she think I can replace WITSEC? I'm not qualified to protect her.

He thought back to the attack at the party.

Maybe nobody is. Or, maybe I'm as good as anybody.

He chewed on that during the drive home. Once at the studio he considered doing the usual and logging on to a poker game. Instead he opened a bottle of Captain Morgan Spiced Rum, allowed his sister's memory to seep into his thoughts, and drank himself to oblivion.

CHAPTER 22

Rivera compound

Rivera's cell phone woke him at 2:00 a.m. The porn star was still awake, laying across his chest, her body still glistening from the sweat of their lovemaking. She smiled at him, eager to please.

He shoved her aside. "Not now, whore." He answered the phone while she cowered at the foot of the bed. "This better be important."

"Hardy talked to Sara, boss," Mendoza said. "Our man tapped his phone."

Rivera sat up. "Do we know where the bitch is?"

"The call didn't say. But I'm going in to squeeze him now."

"When did this happen?"

"Yesterday around noon." Rivera heard papers shuffling. "I've got it right here. She called him. She asked him for a favor. He said okay, and she asked him to turn his phone off and leave it at home. Then Hardy asked her if she was sure she wanted to do this, and she said yes. Then she hung up."

Rivera tensed. "They met."

"I think so, boss."

Rivera narrowed his eyes. "If you knew they were meeting, when why didn't you follow him?"

Mendoza shuffled more papers. "I just got the transcript of the call an hour ago. Our inside guy has to be careful."

Rivera exhaled and slipped on some flip-flops. "I see. Here's what you do. Watch the studio. Unless she shows up there, do not go in. I am coming. I want to question Hardy personally."

"But, boss, you aren't allowed back in the country. Your extradition deal."

"Let me worry about that."

He hung up and stared at his porn star. "We are done. Someone will drive you home."

"But, Manuel, I can make you so happy." She crawled across the sheets like a tigress. "Surely you have time for me before you go."

Rivera slapped her with the back of his hand, his ring cutting her face. "You think you are good enough for me? A whore? When I choose a woman, it will be a woman of class. Character. Beauty." He spit at her shivering body. "Not a whore like you. Get out before I change my mind and throw you in the sea."

CHAPTER 23

Hardy's Studio

Who gives a shit? Hardy thought through his drunken stupor as the clock struck five and his poker losses mounted. *No clients scheduled today. No clients scheduled tomorrow.*

He went to pour himself another drink, but found the bottle empty. He tossed it in the trash and decided to shower.

I miss the Bear. He never judges me. And even if I disappoint him, he stays by my side.

He thought about debating whether he deserved that from anyone, but decided to take the win and move on.

He puked on the way to the shower, just reaching the toilet bowl in time. He thought he could see writing in the chow (*you bailed on another one*), but chocked that up to his hangover. The shower helped wake him up and clear his head, but did nothing for the heavy-metal band pounding in there.

Sara needed your help, and you bailed on her. Just like . . ."

"Stop it," he yelled out loud.

He found his cell phone and turned it back on. No calls. *Screw it.*

He checked the last call received. *Don't do it. She told you not to call.* He dialed. *You know she destroyed the phone.*

Her groggy voice answered the call. "Yeah."

"Sara!"

"Nicholas, what time is it?"

Hardy glanced at the clock on the wall. "Five-thirty. I didn't expect you to answer."

"I didn't expect to answer either. I was so upset when I got home I forgot to get rid of this phone."

"I'm glad you forgot. I needed to know you got home safely. I wasn't happy with the way last night ended."

She sighed. "I'm so sorry. I let myself get caught up in how good you've been to me, and I made a horrible choice. For you, me, and Esteban. You need to forget I ever existed."

Hardy dropped his forehead into the palm of his right hand. "What if I want to take you up on your offer?"

Sara sighed, longer this time. "That's not smart. You were right. WITSEC is my best chance to stay alive. After I testify, Manuel will go crazy, and he'll never stop looking for me. I'll never be safe to be around."

Hardy made a fist and tapped it against his head. "What happened in Texas?"

She paused, and Hardy could hear her breathing harder. "I saw Victor kill my neighbor. Manuel was looking for me, and my neighbor was in the wrong place at the wrong time. My husband Sam told the police, and Manuel retaliated after he and Victor were arrested for the murder. Sam was assassinated by a sniper soon after. No evidence was ever found to link it to Rivera."

"I'm sorry. Rivera didn't do anything to you, your brother, or your son?"

"It's a family thing. He truly believed he could get us to come back into the fold. Eventually, he realized that's not happening."

"You're safe now."

"We'll see."

"How did Rivera get out of jail?"

"Manuel arranged for a prisoner exchange deal for an American the Mexican authorities had in custody. Even got immunity for this case. We didn't find out about the exchange until he'd made it home to Mexico." She paused. "Pisses me off."

Hardy felt his own rage. "There's no justice in that. At least you'll put Victor away."

"Listen, I'm going to destroy the phone now." Hardy could hear the crack in her voice. "Thanks for saving my life. I'll never forget you."

A loud crash was followed by a screech in the line, then dead air. Hardy dialed her number again. No answer.

He lay down to try to sleep, but kept starting a dream where he was playing poker head-to-head with Rivera. Rivera kept grinning and telling Hardy he owned him now.

Hardy gave up on sleep and logged back on to a poker website, looking for a game.

Before the flop on his first hand, as he made a big bet, he heard a scratching noise coming from the back exit. He stood to check it out just as the back door bust open, the sound of splintering wood echoing through the studio.

CHAPTER 24

Hardy stood, ready to strike. But the Hispanic man with the pencil-thin mustache and scar on his face appeared with a .357 magnum, too quickly for Hardy to budge. His teenage son followed him in, giving Hardy an "I told you so" grin.

Shit. Of all the nights for the Bear to be gone.

"Where is she?" the intruder demanded, brandishing his gun.

Hardy raised his hands slowly, wondering how his reflexes might be slowed by the alcohol. "Who?"

"I know you talked with her. Where is Sara?"

Hardy studied Mendoza's trigger finger. He had good pressure on it. Hardy decided against making a move just yet. "I don't know any Sara."

Mendoza pulled out a phone. He dialed, keeping the magnum leveled at Hardy. "I have him, boss. All clear."

Hardy knew what that meant. *Rivera.*

"You think I'm playing here?" Mendoza asked. "Do you know who you're messing with?" He handed the gun to his son, and pulled out a hunting knife.

Hardy gulped. *Great. First, I bring a fist to a gunfight. Now it's a gun and knife fight.*

"My knife worries you, does it? When my boss gets here you'll get to see it in action. We don't care about you. We just want the girl. Save yourself. Where is she?"

Hardy didn't respond, spending his energy trying to figure out a way to escape. And stay alive.

Mendoza grinned, exposing yellow teeth and bloodied gums. "Which finger would you like me to remove first?" He pointed the knife down at Hardy's crotch. "Maybe we should skip the hands and go straight for the cojones."

Hardy didn't hesitate. "Come and get 'em. If you're man enough. Or do you need Rivera to handle your business for you?"

Mendoza blanched. "*Hombre*, you talk big. You're in over your head. You'll tell us where she is. I promise you. We know she called. Garcia was right. She couldn't stay away."

Now it was Hardy's turn to blanch. He reached down to the desk to steady himself. "Garcia? I knew there was something off about him."

Mendoza turned pale. Hardy could see anger welling up in his facial features. "Shut up."

Hardy went on the offensive, hoping to bait Mendoza into losing his composure. "That's how you found her at the party. That's how you knew Flint was tailing you. I wonder what Rivera will think about you giving that info up." Hardy glanced toward the boy. "He'll gut you right in front of your son, won't he?"

Hardy heard someone step on broken glass. Mendoza froze, then straightened to attention. "In here, boss."

Manuel Rivera and his accomplice Delgado stepped into the room. Hardy recognized both of them from the Internet. Rivera wore a full-length camel-hair coat, and Delgado wore a business suit. A pistol bulged in Delgado's belt.

Rivera ignored Hardy and walked straight to Mendoza. "Where is my cousin?"

"She's not here, boss," he choked out, quickly adding as he pointed at Hardy, "but he'll talk. He knows how to reach her."

Rivera stepped in front of Hardy and slammed his fist into Hardy's face. Hardy's head crashed back against the wall, and his vision blurred.

"Let's simplify things," Rivera said. "You want to live? Tell me how I find Sara. Or we can start cutting off pieces until you beg me to kill her instead of you." He grabbed Hardy's throat and squeezed. "I always get what I want. I will get her."

Hardy squirmed and fought for breath, but his vision was swimming as the oxygen was being cut off. *Remind me not to drink the next time a drug lord is coming to kill me.*

Hardy grabbed Rivera's arm, but without enough torque to do any good. He realized his fate, and did the only thing he could think of to get Rivera to let go. He spit in his face, a splattering of saliva and blood sticking in a checkerboard pattern across Rivera's tanned complexion. "I'm HIV positive," Hardy choked out. "How do you like that, asshole."

Rivera released him, eyes bulging, and ran into the bathroom. After running some water he returned and glared at Hardy. He gave Mendoza a quick look, and Mendoza took Hardy's left hand and pinned his little finger on the desk with the knife pressing against it.

"Let's see how brave you really are, *amigo*," Rivera said. "She's dead either way. If we don't get her before the trial, we'll get her there. But you can choose to live. Where's the girl?"

Hardy smiled at Rivera. "Go to hell."

"You can't imagine the resources I have," Rivera said. "Do you really want to die for a hopeless cause?"

"You'll never find her," Hardy answered. "Hell, I don't even know where to find her."

Rivera signaled to Mendoza to start cutting. Hardy braced himself, hoping that he'd somehow handle the pain without giving them anything to go on, knowing deep inside that no amount of mental preparation could help him deal with losing a finger. Or worse.

Mendoza gave Hardy a huge grin and moved the knife across the base of his index finger, which started as a tingling sensation, and then escalated to pain, and fear.

CHAPTER 25

"I thought we were just going to take the lady." Everyone turned toward the boy. His hand was shaking. "Are you really going to cut his fingers off?"

Mendoza stiffened. "We do whatever Mr. Rivera says."

The boy lowered the pistol.

"What are you doing?" Mendoza lifted the knife a fraction from Hardy's hand.

Hardy saw his opening and took it. He slammed Mendoza across the nose with his forehead, and grabbed his wrist. The knife fell to the floor as Hardy jerked Mendoza's shoulder out of its socket. Mendoza screamed and slipped to his knees.

Hardy went for the knife, but Delgado clipped Hardy at the base of his skull. He fell to one knee, then propelled himself at Delgado, knocking him back into the wall. Before Hardy could go for the gun, he felt fresh steel against his neck.

"One move," Rivera said, "and I'll slit your throat."

Hardy froze. *Can I disarm them both in time?* He chose not to take the chance and raised his hands.

Mendoza rose to one knee in front of Hardy, his dislocated shoulder hanging like a soggy noodle.

Hardy grinned at him. "There's more where that came from, punk."

Rivera withdrew the knife from Hardy's throat as Delgado whacked Hardy across the chin. Hardy collapsed to both knees, his head a crescendo of pain. He expected to black out, but surprised himself. Part of him thought passing out would be easier. He could die without the torture, and Sara would be safer if he couldn't be coerced to talk.

"Watch him," Rivera ordered. He turned his attention to Mendoza. "Matadamas, I'm tired of your failures."

Through the fog laying across his mind Hardy watched Rivera jab his blade into Mendoza's neck, then slash it crosswise. Mendoza fell into his own pool of blood.

Mendoza's son yelled and raised the gun. He took jerky aim and fired it at Rivera. The bullet whizzed past Rivera and Hardy, imbedding itself in the wall.

Delgado dropped the boy with one shot to the forehead.

"Jesus," Hardy mumbled. "He's just a teenager."

Rivera sheafed the knife, grabbed Hardy by the chin with one hand, and lifted him up with the other. He threw Hardy back into his chair, saw Delgado had Hardy covered, and stepped away, wiping his forehead. "Fucking Christ. Look at what you made me do."

Hardy wiped some blood away from his mouth. "Me? You're the psychopath."

Rivera launched himself toward Hardy.

"No, boss," Delgado exclaimed. "Someone may have reported the shot. You can't be part of this."

Rivera turned on Delgado. "We can't leave a witness. We either kill him or take him with us."

"I don't know where she is," Hardy said. "Even if I did, I won't tell you shit." He spit some blood toward Rivera, hitting his shoes. "Why don't you put that gun away, and see if you're man enough to force it out of me?"

Rivera leaned over, fury etched on his face. "You really want me as your enemy?"

"I definitely don't want you as my friend. I saw what you do to friends."

Delgado squirmed. "It's time to go, boss. Do we kill him or take him?"

Rivera waived him to be still. He stepped up to Hardy. "You think I am a bad guy?"

"You don't?"

Rivera shook his head. "When I was younger, I tried to be a conventional hero to the people. I tried to expose the corruption in the government. I tried to give them a better life, through the law. Well, that was a waste of time. Now I give them what they want. I am their hero."

"You're no hero," Hardy said.

"Maybe I failed at being your kind of hero. I'm fine with that. Now I am the people's."

"I think you've been sampling too much of your own product."

Rivera's face turned red as Delgado stepped in. "Let's off him and go home. We'll get Sara another way."

Headlights appeared from the parking lot and a car pulled up outside.

Hardy took advantage of the momentary distraction and grabbed Rivera's arm. He kicked Rivera in the groin, Rivera doubling over in pain.

Delgado knocked Hardy to the floor with another blow to his head. Hardy barely held on.

"Boss, out the back."

Hardy tried to open his eyes, but couldn't.

"Nobody treats me like this," Rivera said, his voice barely a whisper. "Don't kill him yet. I want to torture him first. We'll come back for him later."

Bear barked out front as a car door opened.

The Bear. Flint. Help.

Another noise. An approaching siren.

"Now!" Delgado screamed.

Footsteps scrambled out the back as Hardy rolled over. Rivera's voice called out to Hardy from a distance, "This isn't over!"

Hardy heard a key in the front door. A moment later Bear was licking his face, whining.

"What the . . . ?" Flint's voice.

"Out the back," Hardy said, still trying to gain his equilibrium.

Footsteps scrambled past Hardy. A moment later he returned. "Nobody there. Rivera's posse?"

Hardy managed to get his eyes open. Bear wagged his tail and licked some blood off Hardy's cheek. "Rivera and his right-hand guy."

Flint whistled. "No shit?" He examined the dead bodies. "He do this?"

"Yeah."

"That's one mean sum-bitch."

"And crazy. Killed that guy right in front of me, and then the kid. Left me to ID him. He's reckless."

"That makes him even more dangerous, pard."

Hardy got to a sitting position. "Good thing you came by. Vegas had me at a thousand to one to keep my appendages."

"We need to get out of here. Looks like the marshals were right. I'll call 'em on the way to my place."

"About that," Hardy said, prepared to tell him that Garcia was working for Rivera.

The sound of steps through the entry interrupted him.

Garcia entered the room, pistol drawn.

CHAPTER 26

Garcia scanned the room, his gun raised. Bear barked and growled, ready to defend his master.

Oh, shit. Hardy met Garcia's gaze, trying to determine whether he planned to finish the job Rivera had started. Whether to sic Bear on him.

Garcia doesn't know that I know he's working for Rivera. Maybe I can get out of this.

He decided to play it out and gave Bear a "stand down" command. Bear sat and whined.

Garcia watched Bear, shifting awkwardly. "What happened here?"

Hardy took the lead. "Rivera and his thug just went out the back. If you hurry you might catch them."

Garcia squirmed. "Did you talk to him? What did he talk about? Tell you?"

"He wanted to know where Sara is."

"That all?"

"Isn't that enough?"

Garcia paused. "There's two bodies. You do that?"

"No," Hardy said. "Rivera and his thug killed them."

"Shouldn't you call for backup?" Flint suggested. "Get the police here?"

"Not yet," Garcia said.

"What about Rivera?" Hardy asked.

Garcia tensed. "You're sure it was him?"

"No doubt," Hardy answered. "The guy on the floor is the guy from the party, and his son."

Garcia paused for fifteen seconds, continuing to stare at Hardy. "Have you been in contact with Sara?"

"No," Hardy lied. He hoped Garcia couldn't tell.

Finally Garcia lowered the gun and holstered it. "I need to take you both in while we sort this out."

"What the hell for?" Flint asked.

"The police," Garcia said, "are going to show up soon. I need to take you in and control the situation. We need to leave now, before the police arrive." He glared at Bear. "Leave the dog."

Hardy shook his head, which triggered a round of nausea. He threw up into the trash can. After he wiped his mouth with an exercise towel, he scowled at Garcia. "No way. We can drop him off at a friend's house around the corner."

Garcia didn't look happy about that, but he didn't argue.

Hardy took a cavernous breath. *If we can get to their headquarters, at least we'll be surrounded by other marshals.*

A voice in his head countered. *If any of them can be trusted. And if that's really where he's taking us.*

CHAPTER 27

En Route

After dropping Bear off, Hardy got in the backseat of Garcia's sedan with Flint. He locked in on Garcia in the rearview mirror.

"I suppose the police will want to talk to me," Hardy said.

"It's been handled," Garcia said as the sedan pulled out and crept toward the freeway.

Hardy tried to stay relaxed, not wanting Garcia to sense the anxiety he felt being trapped in a car with someone on Rivera's payroll. He smiled at Flint, who was busy texting.

"Hand me your phones," Garcia said, his voice even deeper than normal.

"Why?" Hardy asked, his apprehension rising.

"Rivera probably found you through them. I need to confiscate them as evidence for my forensic team. Might be able to trace something back to him."

"We'll give them to you at your office."

"Now."

Hardy watched Garcia in the mirror. "Why?"

"Because I'm the fucking marshal, and you're the fucking screw-up that keeps putting my witness at risk. Hand them over."

Flint laughed at him. "You're delusional, pard. You're the ones who couldn't keep her safe."

The sedan cruised past the freeway on-ramp and stayed on the Ortega Highway.

"Hey," Hardy said. "You missed the on-ramp."

"Freeway's closed up ahead. We have to go around. The phones. I won't ask again."

"Yeah?" Flint said. "Why don't you come take it from me?"

The car swerved to a stop and Garcia was out the door faster than Hardy thought possible. The back door flew open and Garcia stuck a gun into Hardy's cheek. "I'm really not in the mood. Hand them over, so I can shut them off and make sure we're not being tracked."

"What the hell, man?" Flint said.

Hardy felt the cold steel against his cheek. *He's losing it. He sees his secret getting exposed, and he's freaking out. Better play along. For now.*

"Okay," Hardy said. "There's no need for the gun. We're all on the same side, right?"

Garcia bit his lip, staring at Hardy. Hardy handed him his phone, and Flint followed suit. Garcia pushed his gun into Hardy's cheek before removing it. "From now on, when I give you an order, you follow it. Or I'll throw you both in jail for obstructing a federal investigation. Am I clear?"

"Yeah, sure," Hardy said. "It's all good."

This is not good.

Garcia got back behind the wheel and shut off their phones. Then they continued into the darkness and seclusion of the Ortega Highway.

"Just how are you taking us back to Santa Ana?" Hardy asked. "Cutting up Rancho?"

They sped past Rancho.

Shit. He's not taking us to Santa Ana.

Flint leaned forward, a puzzled look on his face. "Where are we going, pard? Antonio? Seems like a long way around."

"Shut up!" Garcia exclaimed.

He's losing it. He's taking us into the canyon. Somewhere we won't be found.

Hardy checked the speedometer as they crossed Antonio. Forty miles per hour.

Too fast to jump out and survive?

Better chance than being shot and buried out here.

Flint fidgeted in his seat, grabbing the headrest in front of him. "You missed Antonio, pard. You need to turn around. Trust me, going straight is no good."

You got that right.

Hardy was about to get Flint's attention, to tell him they had to bail and run for it, when Garcia's car radio went off. "Deputy Garcia."

Presley!

Garcia flinched. His shoulders slumped. After a moment of thought, he reached for the radio. "Garcia."

"The police reported shots fired at Hardy's studio. They described your car as fleeing the scene. Two Hispanics are dead."

Garcia glanced at Hardy in the mirror. "Yes, sir. I have both Hardy and Flint. On my way back to you for debriefing."

Sure you are.

"You think it was Rivera?"

"That's what Hardy says."

"Get back as soon as you can. I'll be waiting."

"Roger that." Garcia swung the car around and drove back toward the freeway. "You say I passed the best way to get up there?"

"Yeah," Flint said. "You were headed for the middle of nowhere."

"I don't know these parts so well. Lucky you're with me."

Hardy sat back, but his muscles wouldn't relax.

Lucky.

CHAPTER 28

US Marshals Headquarters, Santa Ana, CA

The marshals office was tucked back in the corner on the top floor of the Santa Ana courthouse. After clearing the entry door they entered a cage. Garcia put in a key card, punched in a keypad combination, and ushered them into a small room equipped with a camera mounted in the ceiling. Straight ahead a door of shaded bulletproof glass with its own keypad protected the inner sanctum. Inside a young man in a blue suit sat alone in a sea of desks. Off to the side Hardy saw Presley in an office with a window facing the open room.

Is he part of it? Hardy wondered.

"Fancy office you have here," Flint wisecracked. Garcia grunted and shoved them into the room.

Presley motioned for Garcia to split them up into two conference rooms. Garcia made them empty their pockets into two trays and motioned for a young inspector to escort Hardy to one of the conference rooms. Hardy ended up with some newbie who looked like he didn't need to shave yet.

"You got any aspirin? My head's about to explode."

The inspector shook his head.

Hardy sat down and put his head on his arms on the cold metal table. He shivered, which caused a jolt of pain in his neck. "Seriously? In the entire office? Why don't I believe you? I have an idea. Why don't you come on this side so I can barf all over your shoes. It's not a pain-killer, but I'm sure I'll feel better."

The inspector kept at attention at his post. Hardy closed his eyes and waited.

Presley and Garcia came in a full hour later and relieved the inspector. Presley appeared to be stressed. Garcia just looked distant, a man distracted with other issues.

They sat down across from Hardy, Presley taking the lead. "Tell us what happened, Mr. Hardy."

Hardy inched up straight. "Like I told Garcia, I was home alone when the guy Sara saw at the party and his boy barged in and held me at gunpoint. Rivera and some muscle showed up, wanting to know where Sara is. Rivera killed the guy and his son, said they disappointed him, and that's when Bret showed up. They ran out the back."

"You didn't tell them anything about Sara's location?" Presley probed.

"How could I? I don't know where she is."

"Why do you suppose they thought you did?" Presley asked. "It seems odd Rivera would risk exposing himself in this country unless he was sure it would pay off."

"Beats me," Hardy said.

Another inspector knocked on the door and handed Presley a report. Presley glanced at it. "These are the findings from your studio. They found evidence consistent with the description you've given. They also lifted some prints, but none that place Rivera there. We did get prints from Sara, though."

Both agents turned back to Hardy.

"Care to explain that?" Presley asked.

"She was at my place that night I helped her escape," Hardy said.

"That was a long time ago," Presley countered.

"I suck at cleaning. Sue me."

Presley gave Hardy a suspicious look.

Hardy spent the next hour going over what he'd seen, repeating the same account until Presley was satisfied he hadn't left anything out. His head felt better, and his mind was clear again. After they'd exhausted their questions, Hardy decided to ask a few of his own. "Sara?"

"What about her?" Presley asked.

"Is she safe? Is she well-protected right now?"

"She's safe," Presley said. "That's all I can say."

"Like when they found her at the party?" Hardy countered. "Where were you then?"

Presley glared at Hardy. "If you haven't put her in jeopardy, she's safe." He turned to Garcia. "Bring Flint in."

Garcia left for a moment, returning with Flint in tow. They motioned for Flint to take a seat next to Hardy.

Presley cleared his throat. "Gentlemen, based on everything you've told me I think it prudent to offer you our protection. I can petition the US Attorney General to admit you as material witnesses to go after Manuel Rivera. You'd provide concrete evidence against him. I can get you new identities and have you on your way to new locations later today."

Hardy hadn't seen that coming.

"I know it's a lot," Presley continued, "but it's clear these people think you can help them get to Sara. You can testify that Rivera came into the country in violation of his exchange agreement. And he threatened to kill you."

Hardy's head swirled with so many disparate thoughts. He decided to ask the most basic question first. "Could Bret and I relocate to where Sara is?"

Flint threw Hardy a glance that showed plenty of confusion, but Hardy motioned for him to stay calm and let him talk.

Presley shook his head. "Only immediate family gets relocated together."

"How long do we have to think about it?" Hardy asked.

"The offer doesn't expire, if that's what you're asking. But the longer you delay, the longer you're exposed."

"If we accept, will we go in together?" Hardy continued.

"Nope," Presley answered. "If either of you go in you'll be restricted from getting in touch with each other ever again."

Flint exploded. "Enough with the whole Hotel California vibe. No way I'm going into WITSEC."

"I know it's a big decision," Presley said. "You should think it over before you decide. Either way, I'll need Hardy to testify against Rivera."

Hardy's focus moved from Presley to Garcia, who continued to keep his poker face. "Who will have responsibility for me? One of you two?"

Presley considered Hardy's question. "Deputy Garcia does have the advantage of knowing you both already."

Hardy tried to keep from reacting, but he could feel his face flush. Garcia continued to stare at Hardy, and Hardy saw a sense of recognition.

He knows that I know.

Hardy turned back to Presley. "Give us a day to think about it. Are we free to go?"

"You are. Deputy Garcia can take you both to a hotel and guard you until you decide."

Flint stood up. "I can take care of myself, thank you very much. Y'all just need to take me home."

Hardy knew they couldn't afford to be alone with Garcia, and stood as well. "Thanks, Marshal. We'll grab a cab. We'll call you later with our decision."

"I should come with you," Garcia said.

Hardy met his stare. "Thanks for the offer, but we'll be fine."

"I really have to insist," Garcia said.

Hardy turned to Presley. "We're free to go, right?"

Presley watched the interaction between Garcia and Hardy with more than casual interest. His normally stressed appearance now included squinting eyes and a furrowed brow. "Yes, you're free to go. Just remember, the people who are after you now aren't to be taken lightly."

Hardy glanced at Garcia. "I know."

CHAPTER 29

Hardy and Flint retrieved their possessions from an off-balance Garcia and rode down the elevator. Once the doors shut Flint couldn't keep his thoughts bottled up any longer. "What the hell? WITSEC? We'll *think* about it. Are you loco?"

"Relax," Hardy said. "I have no intention of going into WITSEC. I just don't want them knowing that. It might buy us the time we need."

"Time for what?"

"Find Sara."

The elevator doors opened and they stepped into the lobby, where a cleaning crew mopped the tile floor. Flint put his arm on Hardy's to stop him. "How do you plan to do that?"

"Working on it."

They exited the building. Flint pulled out his cell phone. "I'll get us a cab."

Hardy shook his head. "We need a rental car. Call Enterprise and have them bring us a car. A fast one. We may be on the road awhile."

"You mean *you* might be on the road awhile."

"Sara's in danger," Hardy said. "We met for dinner. I think Rivera had me followed. They might be able to find Sara."

"Isn't that against the rules?"

"Totally."

Flint glared at Hardy. "Why would you do that?"

"I don't have a good answer to that."

"And now I'm being asked to go into WITSEC? That's just great."

"Sorry, man."

Flint blew out a frustrated breath. "Isn't protecting her a job for the marshals?"

"We can't trust the marshals."

"What the hell are you talking about?"

"Garcia is working for Rivera. He's the one who told Rivera that Sara worked for Alice."

"Whoa. You sure?"

Hardy waited as someone passed by on the sidewalk. "The guy from the party roughed me up some before Rivera showed. He told me Garcia led him to her."

"You think *Presley* is dirty?"

"I don't know. Even if he's not, I don't know how he'd react if I told him about Garcia. I can't take the chance."

"Okay, let's say you're right about Garcia. He's her handler. He already knows where she is."

Hardy rechecked the entrance. "Sara told me she has a new marshal, and only Presley and her new marshal know where she is."

"We should tell Presley. If Presley knows where she is, that proves he's clean. Otherwise, Rivera didn't need us."

"That's true," Hardy said. "I just don't know if he'll believe me. I don't want him tipping off Garcia. Let's see if we can find her first."

"Pard, just how do you plan to do that?"

"I met her in Malibu. She has to be near there."

"You know how crazy you sound, right? How hard did they hit your head?"

Hardy put his hand on Flint's shoulder. "I'm good. I know finding her must sound impossible. If she's in trouble, I have to try to help her. I can really use your help."

"Suppose we perform a miracle and find her. Then what?"

"Warn her. Find a way to protect her."

Flint looked Hardy up one side and down the other. "I've asked you this before, but why do you care so darn much? Why is this your cross to bear?"

Hardy gulped, fighting to clear a dry throat. "I chose not to help someone once, when I knew I could've made a difference. My sister. She died. I'm not making that mistake again."

"You never told me." Flint shook his head. "We tell each other everything."

"I never told anyone."

Flint squinted. "I'm not just anyone."

"I'm sorry, man. It's hard to talk about."

"Is she the picture in your wallet? The one I thought was an old girlfriend? You never corrected me."

"Yeah. That's her." Hardy gave his friend the same look Bear gave him when he thought it was mealtime. "Can we get back on the task at hand?"

"Sure. We'll talk about this later. As for finding Sara, this is the dad-gummest idea you've ever had, and you've had some beauts."

"You're going to help me?"

"Of course I'll help you." Flint dialed a car rental agency. "If we're lucky we'll just get arrested."

"That doesn't sound lucky."

"It beats the hell out of getting killed."

CHAPTER 30

Enterprise delivered a white Volvo S80 with a V8 a few blocks away. "You drive. I have to do a search."

"For what?"

"Sara picked up a few bottles of nineteen ninety-five Chateau Margaux around her new place. There can't be many wine stores with that in stock."

"Fine wine in Malibu? They probably sell it on street corners. You know, instead of lemonade stands."

"Yeah, well, nineteen ninety-five was the best year in a hundred. The only way they got it was through an estate or auction. Not everyone will have it."

"Pard, that's much better than the needle in a haystack you made it sound like we were searching for. Why didn't you mention it earlier?"

"Just thought of it. Besides, it would have taken all the fun out of seeing you all worked up."

Flint jabbed him in the arm with his elbow. "You suck. Any other clever ideas you're holding back?"

"Nope."

A list of high-end wine stores along the coast came up on Hardy's Google search. He went through their websites to look for older vintages of Chateau Margaux, hitting pay dirt on the third try.

"Hey, I think I'm onto something."

"Yeah?"

"A wine store in Malibu. A wide selection of Chateau Margaux. Maybe we'll get lucky."

"If it turns out we can find her, why can't Rivera's people?"

"We know about the wine and they don't. So we have an edge. Garcia will eventually figure out a way to find out where she is. We don't have much time."

*****

They pulled up in front of the wine shop ninety minutes later. He pointed to the map on the car's GPS. "How do you want to search the area?"

"Door to door. No need to be secretive. We're going to pull her out anyway."

"Right."

They walked to the end of the block and turned inland into the neighborhood, where they found thirty-year-old homes lining the street. Hardy smelled the salt in the air. He could almost sense the parked cars rusting.

"You take this side, I'll take the other," Hardy said.

Hardy surveyed the street, looking for any sign that a young boy might live there. Not seeing anything obvious, he turned up the first walkway and rang the doorbell. After a short pause, the front door opened a crack. Hardy could see a tall blonde woman behind the screen.

"Good morning," Hardy began. "I'm looking for a friend of mine. Perhaps you know her. She's a medium-size brunette, looks Hispanic. Just moved here a month ago. Has a six-year-old son."

The screen door burst open, and the blonde shoved a gun into Hardy's forehead.

CHAPTER 31

She pulled Hardy into the house and swept his legs with one of hers, forcing him to the hardwood floor on his stomach. A sharp knee drove into his back and the gun barrel pressed against the base of his skull.

Son of a bitch. Taken down by a girl?

"If you so much as flinch I'll shoot you," she threatened as she jammed the gun barrel in deeper. "Is the guy across the street with you?"

"Yeah. Easy, now. Something tells me we're at the right place."

The blonde stood and put her foot in the small of Hardy's back, exerting excruciating pressure. "Who sent you?"

"Nobody. We came on our own."

She put more pressure on his back. "I asked, who sent you?"

"I told you. I'm here to warn Sara. She can vouch for us."

Hardy saw a pair of white tennis shoes appear from around the corner. "Nicholas?" Sara's voice. The shoes ran toward him.

"Stay out of sight!" the blonde exclaimed. "You know him?"

Sara fell down on her knees next to Hardy. "He's the one who saved my life."

The pressure on his back ceased. "This is Nick Hardy?"

"Yes," Sara said. "Nicholas, what are you doing here? How did you find me?"

Hardy studied the blonde. She was tall, thin, and deceptively strong. A face most guys could go for. "Can I get my friend in here?" *And can I get up before Flint sees you kicked my ass?*

"Who else is here?" Sara asked.

"Flint."

"Tricia, these are the good guys." Sara helped Hardy to his feet. "Nicholas, meet WITSEC Inspector Tricia Walker. She's my new live-in handler."

Hardy stretched his back out. "Inspector."

Walker glared at him. "How did you find us?"

Someone knocked. Walker wheeled around, her gun now aimed at the door.

"Bret?" Hardy called out.

"Did you find her?" came Flint's voice from the other side of the door.

Hardy checked with Walker, who motioned that he could open the door. Flint entered and regarded the gun pointed at his chest by Walker. "Whoa, now. Let's take it easy with that." He showed his empty hands to her.

"Close the door," Walker ordered. Flint obeyed, and she lowered the gun. Walker checked outside through the drapes. She seemed satisfied and returned her attention to them. "How did you find us?"

Hardy knew that telling the entire truth could get Sara in trouble. "I have reason to believe Sara's in danger here. Her identity and location may have been compromised."

"Obviously," Walker said. "How?"

Hardy glanced at Sara, questioning how she wanted the conversation to go. She cleared her throat. "I broke protocol and met with Nicholas."

Walker's face turned rouge. "You did *what*?"

"I'm sorry," Sara said. "I know it's against the security guidelines."

"Those security guidelines are designed to keep you alive," Walker scolded. "What were you thinking?"

"I don't know."

Walker returned her attention to Hardy. "She told you where we were?"

Hardy shook his head. "No. But she brought a bottle of rare wine, and I tracked it to the store around the corner."

"Christ almighty," Walker asked. She turned to Sara. "Do you have a death wish?"

"No," Sara murmured. "But you don't know how hard this is."

Walker grunted. "I know exactly how hard this is. That's no excuse."

Hardy found a chair and sat down. Everyone else did the same. "Rivera came to my place this morning. If it weren't for Bret they would've tortured me to get her location. I really didn't know then, and yet here I am. If they'd had more time to break me, they might have figured it out."

Sara went ashen. "Oh, Nicholas. What have I done?"

"I'm okay. Rivera killed the guy from the party. Then his henchman killed the boy."

Sara turned to Flint. "The boy?"

"Afraid so."

Walker gave Sara a look that said, "What did you think would happen when you broke protocol?" but resisted saying anything. She returned her attention to Hardy. "When did you meet?"

Sara put her head in her hands. "We met in Malibu last night. I also called him a few times."

"Jesus." Walker turned to Hardy. "Do Garcia and Presley know about this?"

"I didn't tell them," Hardy said.

"Well," Walker said, "they need to know. I'll call them and see what they want us to do. Sara, get Esteban ready. We're bugging out."

"Before you do that, there's something else," Hardy said. "The marshal's office has at least one person working against us."

"What are you talking about?" Scorn dripped from her words.

"Garcia is working for Rivera. That's how they found her in the first place."

Walker stiffened. "That's absurd."

Sara leaned forward, her stunned face flushed. "Nicholas, he's been protecting me."

"I know it's hard to swallow," Hardy said. "The guy at the party, he told me Garcia gave you up."

Nobody spoke. After a few minutes Walker rose and paced the room. "If that's true, which I doubt, he could have followed you here.

We need to move now. Sara, get Esteban into the car. Don't take time to pack anything."

Sara retreated. Hardy heard a muffled discussion in a back room.

Walker rechecked the scene out the front window again. Satisfied when she didn't see anyone, she turned back to Hardy and Flint. "What am I going to do with you two?"

"We're going with you," Hardy said.

"I can't allow that," Walker said.

"You don't know who you can trust right now," Hardy said. "Until we get some more answers, I think the safest play for Sara is for all of us to watch her."

"That's my call to make," Walker said.

Sara's voice from the doorway broke in. "It's my call to make." Sara stood there with Esteban holding her hand. "They come with us. I trust them."

"It's not your call either," Walker said.

"Yes, it is," Sara said. "They're coming."

Walker took a deep breath and stared at all three of them. Just as she started to respond she froze and threw her body in front of Sara. "Get down!" she said, as the front window shattered.

Hardy leapt back to Sara and ushered her and Esteban around the corner into the hallway, followed by the sound of more breaking glass within the front room. Then a devastating smell choked him, his eyes watering as tear gas rushed through the house.

CHAPTER 32

Hardy peeked around the corner and saw white smoke filling the room. Both Walker and Flint were hunched over with their arms across their eyes, trying to avoid the fumes.

"Bret, this way!"

Flint fell to his knees. Walker joined him.

Hardy started to go back for them when a gunshot split the door's wood trim next to his ear. He ducked back as a second shot plowed into the wall.

Sara pulled on Hardy's arm. "Follow me!"

"I can't leave Bret."

"They don't care about him. It's me and Esteban they want. Hurry!"

Hardy looked back. *I can't leave him.* He coughed as the gas thickened in the hallway. Another voice made the case for helping Sara and Esteban. *If you go back in there, the gas will wipe you out. You're Sara and Esteban's only chance.*

He heard the front door crash open.

Shit! He checked Sara and saw her desperation. He picked up Esteban and motioned toward the back. "Go!"

She led them down the hall past the last bedroom door, toward a dark, dead end. Esteban sobbed on Hardy's shoulder.

"Where are we going?" Hardy choked.

"Escape route," Sara gasped.

She reached down and pulled up the edge of a rug at the end of the hallway, exposing a door built into the floor. She pulled it open and stepped aside while Hardy put Esteban on his feet.

"Go ahead," she urged. "Just as we practiced."

Esteban stepped down the stairway that led into a lighted room below. Hardy held the door as Sara followed him in. He noticed the rug was attached to the edge of the door, so that when they closed it, the rug would be pulled back tight on the floor.

Before entering he turned to see if Flint or Walker had followed, but found the hallway deserted.

If you hurt him, I'll find every one of you.

A door in the back of the house crashed open. Men shouted in Spanish. He recognized *Senorita* and *Gringo*, but the rest sounded like, well, a foreign language.

Hardy slid into the opening and shut the trap door behind him just before he could be seen. He found himself in a ten-by-ten-foot room with no doors or windows and a single light hanging from the ceiling. His claustrophobia kicked in, and he felt a recognizable sense of panic. *Can this get any worse?*

"Is there another way out of here?" he whispered, his tongue clogging his mouth.

Sara stood at the far end of the room. "Back here."

Hardy joined her and saw a hole, pitch black inside, just large enough to crawl through. Sara removed a cover that kept anyone from gaining access from the other side.

Why, I believe it can get worse.

"Where does this go?" Hardy asked.

"It dumps out onto the hill behind the house," she answered, choking back panicked tears. "Once there, we can scale down the hill to the shopping center. I don't know what to do from there."

"I do. Our rental car is down there."

If you can get through this tunnel to hell.

Sara went first into the blackness. Esteban followed, and then Hardy. He couldn't see Esteban even though he could hear him scrambling forward just inches away. They crawled this way for about twenty yards, in quarters so tight that Hardy's shoulders rubbed the edge of the tube as he shimmied his way along. He fought his demons, following Esteban's panicked breathing, until he could see light as the tunnel ended.

Hold it together. Just a few more feet.

They dumped out into the sunshine on a steep incline composed of small rocks and clay. Hardy's clothes were soaking wet, and he could feel the flush in his face.

"You okay?" Sara asked. "You don't look so good."

"Never better. Let's get out of here." Hardy picked Esteban up again, and cautiously started the precarious climb down. Each step was like walking a tightrope.

He reached the asphalt parking lot and helped Sara with her last step. Now on level ground, Hardy led them around the building to the front of the wine store and the parked Volvo.

A stark reality hit Hardy, and he froze.

Flint has the keys.

"Nicholas?" Sara inquired. "What's wrong?"

"Bret has the keys. We're going to have to hoof it."

She tried the door and found it unlocked. "Climb in. I'll hot-wire it."

You'll do what?

Hardy grabbed Esteban and loaded him into the backseat of the Volvo. He grabbed the passenger seat next to Sara, who popped off the plastic covering and fiddled with the wiring below the steering wheel. Seconds later the engine coughed and they pulled out northbound onto the Coast Highway.

Hardy pulled out his phone and dialed 9-1-1. "Shots fired. US marshal Walker and a PI in distress. Call US Marshal Presley in Santa Ana for the address." He hung up and bowed his head. "I can't believe I left Bret back there."

"Want me to turn around?"

Yes. "No. Too dangerous."

"Do you really think Garcia sold me out to Rivera?"

"I know he's dirty. He knows I know. I could see it in his eyes."

"Do you think they followed you?"

"Bret would've noticed," Hardy said. "They must have found you another way."

"How?"

Hardy shook his head. "I don't know."

"Do you think Bret and Tricia are okay?"

Hardy gave her a sideways glance and saw the concern etched into her face. "They're both well trained. I'm betting on them."

"You'd all be safe if I'd just followed the rules." She sagged into her seat. "I told you I was dangerous."

"We can debate that later."

"I still don't understand how he found us if you weren't tailed."

Hardy jerked in his seat. "Oh, shit. Pull over."

Sara stomped the brakes and pulled over onto the dirt. "What?"

A city bus pulled in across the street. Hardy signaled to Sara to get herself and Esteban onto the bus. She took Esteban by the hand and raced across the road.

Hardy climbed out and pulled all of his personal possessions out of his pockets—the ones Garcia had confiscated earlier at his office. A quick perusal didn't uncover anything but he decided to discard everything. He threw it all into the front seat and joined Sara.

The bus driver's queer look worried Hardy. At least there were no other passengers. The driver drove back south toward the house they had escaped from.

"Stay down," Hardy said to Sara. "Don't let anyone see you."

"What are we doing?"

Hardy eyed the road ahead, looking for a good exit point. "When I was in the marshal's office, Garcia took both Bret's and my personal possessions around the metal detector. He had them the entire time we were in there."

"You think he tracked you?"

"It would explain how they found us. I ditched everything in the car."

Sara stared at him, her eyes wider than he'd ever seen them. "How can we get away without a car? When they find the car they'll see the bus stop and come after us."

"Yeah, we need to get off and find someplace to hide until Presley tells us what to do."

A large black Mercedes came roaring around the corner and flew past, going north. Hardy couldn't see inside the blacked-out windows.

"I think that's them," he said. "We only have a few minutes."

Hardy stood up and jetted to the front of the bus.

"Hey, buddy, you can't stand while I'm driving," the driver said.

"I need you to stop the bus," Hardy said.

"I can't do that."

Hardy stepped past him and hit the button that opened the doors. The driver slammed on the brakes, bringing the bus to a halt. After the three of them climbed down they turned back to the driver. Sara handed him a C-note.

"Thanks, man," Hardy said. "You're saving a life."

"Godspeed, folks," the driver said before pulling away.

Hardy took Sara by the arm and led them down a path between two majestic homes to the beach, hidden from the highway.

We need to find somewhere hidden and call Presley for help. That bus driver can't be expected to hold his tongue under pressure.

Hardy's heart raced as they reached the shore. They were about out of time and options.

CHAPTER 33

Hardy, Sara, and Esteban removed their shoes and walked in the ocean until they found a rock outcropping. The surf was up, and the incoming tide took care of their footprints.

"We better call Presley," Hardy said.

"Can you talk to him? I'd like to talk with Esteban."

"Of course."

She handed him her iPhone. "In my favorites list. His cell, bypassing the receptionist."

Hardy punched Presley's name and walked down the beach a few yards, turning his back on them so little Esteban couldn't hear. The marshal answered on the second ring.

"Sara?" He sounded anxious.

"It's Nick Hardy."

Presley paused before replying. "What the fuck are you doing with Sara's phone? Where is she?"

"She's safe, but we need your help. Rivera's people attacked the house. Sara, Esteban, and I managed to escape. Bret and Walker didn't get out."

"Jesus. How did you find them? I should have locked you up when I had the chance—"

"Shut up and listen," Hardy interrupted. "Garcia is working for Rivera. He planted a tracking device on me. He's the one you need to lock up."

"That's insane." Presley's voice dripped with scorn.

"Rivera's guy from the party told me. Garcia knows that I know."

"You're crazy."

"It's true. He's been watching me. Must of needed another way to find her."

"Why would he? You didn't know where she was."

"Yeah, well, we met for dinner just before they showed up last night."

"Are you fucking kidding me?"

"We need to focus on what's important. Garcia is dirty, and we're in a tough spot."

"Why didn't you tell me this when you were in here?"

"Garcia didn't leave us alone. Honestly, I don't know who to trust in your office. If Garcia's been turned, who else might be dirty?"

"Where are you?"

"On the beach about a mile north of the house in Malibu. They drove up the coast after us, and they know we ditched the car. We doubled back on a bus."

"A friend of mine heads up Malibu PD," Presley said. "She'll grab you. I'll get there as soon as I can. No one else here will know."

"All right. What's her name?"

"Chief Knight."

"What about Garcia? And Bret and Walker?"

"I'll get a team out to the house," Presley said. "I pulled the 9-1-1 call up on my computer. No info yet. I'll look into your allegation about Deputy Garcia."

"You need to arrest him. He's orchestrating all this."

"You just keep your heads low and keep Sara and Esteban safe. Knight's on her way."

Hardy hung up and went back to Sara and Esteban, busy playing a word guessing game about ocean animals. "Help's on the way. Presley knows the local chief, a woman named Knight. Should be just a few minutes."

Sara twitched nervously. "Was he mad?"

"You could say that."

"I don't blame him." She stared down at Esteban. "What if he throws me out of WITSEC? What happens to us then?"

Hardy sat down next to them. "They need you."

"Only until the trial. What if I've screwed everything up?" She ran her fingers through Esteban's hair. "He's all I have left."

Hardy winced inside, another reminder she wasn't interested in him the way he was interested in her.

"Anything on Walker and Bret?" she continued.

"He's also sending someone to the house."

"I can't believe Garcia was behind all this. I trusted him."

"I know."

"I feel so . . ."

Hardy reached over and took her hand. "It's all going to be okay. I promise."

The sound of shouting down the beach, in Spanish, interrupted them.

CHAPTER 34

Hardy rose to peek through the rocks. Three Hispanic men dressed in black, each wearing long pants, long-sleeve shirts, and bulky jackets, stood on the beach, speaking in excited voices.

"Do you know what they're saying?" Hardy asked.

"They found the bus," Sara said. "The driver gave us up."

Hardy knew to expect that, but the reality still hit him in the gut. *I might not be able to get us out of this. Is this really how it all ends?*

Hardy looked back the other direction. He didn't like their chances of outrunning them on the sand. He checked up the hill. It would be a tough climb for him, let alone Esteban.

"Three voices," Sara said.

He turned back to watch them. "Yeah. I don't think we can outrun them. Or their bullets."

One of them walked in their direction. One moved the other way, and one stayed put.

"There's one heading toward us," Hardy told her. "We have two minutes, tops."

She pulled Esteban closer to her. "What do we do?"

"I'll jump him when he comes around the rocks, take his gun, and hold off the others until help arrives."

"Can you really do that?"

I have no idea.

"Yeah." He motioned for Sara and Esteban to stand. "Once I move, you and Esteban run as fast as you can."

"I can't just leave you here."

"I'll be fine."

The man approaching them had a hand inside his jacket, ready to draw and fire.

Hardy took a steadying breath. It didn't work. "Get ready. Just another minute now."

He peeked back through the rocks. Fifteen feet. Ten feet. Five feet.

The man in the middle yelled something to the approaching thug, words Hardy didn't understand. The assailant stopped and turned.

If Hardy moved now, he'd be seen by the other two, which might cost Sara some time in her escape. If he waited, he might lose the element of surprise on the closest adversary. He weighed those options and decided to pounce.

He crouched down. Just as he started to spring forward, the closest gunman began jogging back the other way. Hardy lunged around the corner, exposed, as the adversary ran away from him.

No, no, no.

Hardy skidded to a stop in the sand. *Now what, dumbshit. Chase him down? Duck back behind the rocks?*

That internal debate was rendered moot as the man on the far end of the beach spotted Hardy and started yelling.

The man closest to Hardy stopped and spun around. His eyes scanned past Hardy.

Sara.

The assailant squared up and pulled his gun out. Hardy lunged to his right, trying to shield Sara.

A gunshot exploded, followed by a searing pain in Hardy's shoulder. He fell to one knee as several more shots rang out.

CHAPTER 35

An adrenaline rush overcame the pain and Hardy jumped back to his feet and lunged as the thug raced past him toward Sara and Esteban. He grabbed the assailant's jacket with his good arm and spun him around, catching him by surprise and off balance. He threw him into the sand at the surf's edge, jumped on him, and grabbed the wrist that held the gun, directing it toward the ocean.

More gunshots were fired down the beach. Using that distraction to his advantage, the gunman rammed Hardy's forehead with his.

Hardy fought to retain consciousness, but lost his grip on his wrist. The assailant swung the gun to point-blank range at Hardy.

I screwed up, Sara. Sorry.

Dazed, Hardy waved at the gun as a shot rang out.

He didn't feel any impact or pain. Instead the man went limp, blood pouring from the side of his head.

What the hell . . .

Hardy saw a female police officer arrive and kick the gun away. She checked the man's pulse as Hardy fought to stay conscious. "Help's on the way."

Hardy shook his head. "Sara and Esteban. Up the beach."

"They're fine. Coming back."

"Two more are down the beach."

"They split when they saw my men. We'll pick them up."

"Black Mercedes," Hardy slurred, his head starting to spin.

"I saw it. Presley says to get you all somewhere no one will look for you, so my station's out. I have friends vacationing in Monte Carlo. Asked me to keep an eye on their place. You'll be safe there."

Sara fell down at Hardy's side, tears draining down her face. "Nicholas, are you okay?"

"I'm good," he choked.

The police chief tore open Hardy's shirt to take a look. "You're going to need a doctor. I think the slug's still in there."

"No hospitals," Hardy said.

The chief contemplated that for a moment. "Presley will know what to do."

The sound of sirens interrupted them. Minutes later, a half dozen police officers swarmed the beach.

"Tell me," Hardy whispered to the chief, "how did you know who to shoot?"

She smiled. "You didn't exactly fit the profile Presley described for the cartel gang." She laughed. "I'm glad I wasn't wrong. Would have been a lot of explaining to do. So much paperwork."

Hardy wanted to mention that paperwork would have been the least of his problems, but lost consciousness.

CHAPTER 36

Safe House, Malibu

The pain in Hardy's shoulder startled him awake. He forced his eyes open, and saw Sara seated next to him in a small bedroom. Children's toys were stacked on a teal bureau. She smiled and brushed his cheek with her fingertips. "You're back. I've been so worried."

Hardy wet his parched lips. "Esteban?" He barely recognized his own, croaking, voice.

"We're both fine," Sara said. "Thanks to you."

"Don't know about that. Almost got you killed."

"You saved our lives."

"Bret? Walker?"

Her smile widened. "They're sleeping down the hall. Beaten up, but they're going to make it."

"How'd they get away?"

"The police found them stuffed in the trunk of the Mercedes. The doc says you just had a flesh wound. It will sting for a day or two, but nothing to worry about."

"I passed out?"

"Sí. Doc says that can happen from the shock. He'll want to know you're awake. I'll go get him."

She left the room. Hardy followed the pain and glanced down at his bandaged shoulder.

She returned with a tall, elderly gentleman shuffling behind her in slow motion. He could have been eighty. "Nicholas, this is Dr. Unger."

Hardy didn't know whether to thank him or ask him when he last practiced medicine.

"He's a friend of Presley's," she continued. "Retired and off the grid. Handles some sensitive cases for him."

"Thanks, doc," Hardy said. "Can I get some water?"

Sara helped Hardy drink from a water bottle. He took a sip while Unger checked the bandage.

"It just grazed you," Unger said. He sounded older than he looked. "It'll be sore for a few days, but you'll have full range of motion in a day or two."

Hardy watched Unger's shaking hand. *Jesus. I'll probably lose the arm. Presley's revenge?*

Hardy took another sip and let Sara take the bottle away. "Garcia?"

Presley came into the room. Sara shrunk. Unger ambled his way out, leaving Presley at Sara's side. He didn't smile, but managed a gruff, "Welcome back."

Hardy didn't smile either. "Thanks. What's the deal with Garcia?"

The lines in Presley's forehead deepened. "He's gone."

"I told you," Hardy said. *Oops. Don't get yourself kicked off the team. Sara needs you.*

Presley glared at Hardy. "We haven't seen him since you left our office. No sign of him at his apartment. We have a nationwide manhunt."

"Maybe Rivera has him under his wing in Mexico."

"He could be anywhere," Presley said. "The chances of us ever catching him aren't great. He's a pro at hiding, blending in, leaving no trail."

"No clues?" Hardy asked. The pain in his head was neck and neck with his shoulder.

"No," Presley said, shaking his head. "Checked on his finances. No big deposits. For now Walker and I are the only ones who know what happened or where you are. I'm taking over Sara's protection detail. Until the trial."

"Here?" Hardy asked.

"Not sure. This place is off the grid. The owners won't be back until May. I have a lot to think about."

Hardy turned to Sara. Her features were blurred, and she had a cloudy halo behind her head. Hardy blinked, but couldn't focus any better. "Whatever you decide, consider me part of her detail." His speech slurred that time.

"Nicholas?" Sara said. "Are you okay?"

"A little woozy."

"I'd love to be rid of you," Presley said, "but you aren't in any condition to be moved. So you stay for the time being. At least this way I'll know where you are." He glared at Sara. "Excuse me. I need to check on Walker." He stormed out.

Sara reached out and held Hardy's hand. "He's really pissed at me. I don't blame him."

Hardy shook his head, which sent a bolt of pain, special delivery, from his shoulder. "My guess is he's more angry about Garcia. Working right under his nose. Probably figures he should have seen something."

"I know he's really upset about that. I think part of him hopes Garcia will turn up and it was all a big misunderstanding."

"Don't bet on it." Hardy closed his eyes, hoping the dizziness would stabilize. *Fail.* "I wonder when Rivera turned him?" He opened his eyes again.

Sara moved a step closer. "You don't look so good."

Yeah. That's what I was going for.

Presley stepped back in with a piece of paper in his hand, a grim expression on his face. "I know what Rivera has on Garcia," he announced.

Hardy and Sara both waited for him to clarify.

"Garcia's brother lives in Mexico. He vanished a month ago. Rivera must be using the brother as leverage. That helps explain the timing. Garcia is trying to save his brother."

"That's totally like Rivera," Sara said. "He tries to exploit family bonds all the time."

Presley paced around the room. "Maybe we can find Deputy Garcia's brother. If we can take his brother back, Garcia has no reason to work with Rivera anymore. We could even get them to testify against Rivera. Finally get something that will put that bastard away for good."

"Good luck with that," Sara said. "The local police down there aren't going to lift a finger against him. They're scared of him."

Presley rubbed his chin as he thought more about it. "I have some contacts down there in our Mexican field office who owe me a favor. I should pay them a visit."

Presley reached into his pocket and pulled out a large cell phone.

"What's that?" Hardy asked.

"It's new, made just for WITSEC. State-of-the-art encryption. Internet access. Can't be traced. It's the only way I'm communicating with the office, or anyone else for that matter, while we're here."

"Technology advances must be hard to stay out in front of," Hardy said.

"You can't imagine," Presley said. "GPS tracking of cell phones, texting, Facebook, Twitter, search engines, face recognition. All making it harder to hide people and stay out of the limelight. I miss the old days. Now, they can come at you from so many different angles. We have to update the guidelines every month now."

"It's only going to get worse," Hardy said.

"We have a team working to leverage new technology. They're the best in the world at what they do."

The phone gave a short burst of noise that startled them all. He picked it back up and pushed the answer button. "US Marshal Presley." He pulled the phone away as a loud voice blurted words at a machine-gun pace. "Hey, calm down. What happened?"

Hardy and Sara exchanged furtive glances. *This can't be good.* Hardy tried to reach for her, to grab her hand, but his body didn't go for it.

Presley's face flushed, and he moved to a chair next to the bed. He sat down with a thud and held his head with his free hand. "How sure are you?" He slammed his hand down on the nightstand. "Now you listen to me. I don't care who you have to put on this, or what it takes. You find him. You find them both."

The person on the other end continued. Presley fidgeted, interrupting after ten seconds. "Hey. I don't care whose branch is to blame. I'm sorry about your inspector. Let's just get him back. What do you need from me?"

After a few moments, Presley continued. "I'll have it sent right over. Keep me informed. Finding him is priority number one. Agreed? Good."

He hung up the phone, but didn't look up. "I have some tough news," he choked out.

Sara leaned back against the wall. "What now?"

"Your brother, Juan, was kidnapped."

CHAPTER 37

"What?" Sara asked. "He's being protected. How could Manuel find him?"

"They don't think Rivera did it," Presley said. "They think Garcia did."

"Oh my God!" Sara exclaimed. "He turned another agent?"

"No," Presley said. "Juan's inspector was drugged. Found incoherent a half hour ago. Your brother's the only witness missing."

Sara slid down the wall. Presley helped her to a graceful landing. He turned back toward the door and yelled for the doctor to come back in before sitting down next to her. "We're putting every available resource on finding him. They can't have gone too far."

Sara didn't respond, but Hardy had plenty to say while he hovered over Presley. "What kind of messed-up organization are you running? Corruption. Incompetence. How can you let this happen?"

Presley stayed seated, but Hardy knew he'd hit a nerve. "Hey, shut the fuck up. That kind of talk isn't helping her."

Hardy choked back a response, mindful of Sara's fragile state. "Why do they think it was Garcia?"

"Someone from Juan's apartment building in Eureka came forward with a description that matches Garcia."

Sara stirred. "Juan was in Eureka?"

"Yeah."

"How did Garcia know?" she asked. "You were the only one in your office who knew."

"I don't know," Presley said.

"The inspector just gave Juan up?" Hardy asked. "Aren't you guys trained to protect your witnesses?"

"Garcia is trained to find people's breaking points. The drugs may have been a factor."

Unger eased back in and saw Sara and Presley seated on the floor. Sara's coloring leaned toward a light yellow. The doctor leaned over, took a syringe out of his bag, and gave her a shot in her arm. "She'll need her transfusion soon."

"Can you handle that for her?" Presley asked.

"I can, but I'll need more blood. I can call in a favor, but after that we'll need to find her a doctor who has access to the blood supply."

Presley exhaled. "That will put her on the radar screen. Garcia will be watching for any patient getting transfusions, starting with any with Sara's condition, so using a new alias won't buy us anything. Even if we alter the condition in the medical records he'll look for any blood work with her type."

"You could move her around," Unger said, "with a prescription that can be filled at any lab or hospital in the country. I can help arrange that. I have several folks who'll do it for me. Garcia doesn't know her identity here in Malibu, right?"

"He shouldn't."

"We can use that name for the prescription," the doctor continued. "If she stays on the move, in no clear pattern, maybe he'll always be one step behind her. You'll have to have someone travel with her."

"I guess that's what we need to do," Presley said.

"I can take her and keep her on the move," Hardy said. "He won't be expecting that."

Presley eyed Hardy with clear annoyance. "If it weren't for you—"

"I'd be dead," Sara said.

Hardy leaned forward and gestured toward Presley. "I know it's not by the book, but you know you can trust me with her."

"It's more complicated than that," Presley said.

"What are you worried about?" Hardy asked. "Your career? How it will look to your boss?"

Presley's face flushed. "You think I care about my career right now?" He looked at Sara, still motionless, and Hardy could see the admiration.

No, he doesn't care about his career right now.

"I'm sorry," Hardy said. "I know keeping her safe is all you're concerned about."

Sara jerked, and made eye contact with Hardy. "Nicholas? They have my brother."

"I know."

Unger sighed and turned to go. "I'll see to one more transfusion here. That should give us at least five days. We'll need to take her in and get her that prescription."

Sara stiffened. "The transfusions. Juan."

Unger stopped. "What about Juan?"

Presley grabbed his forehead. "Shit. He has the same condition. More advanced. He's been getting the same medical treatment all along."

"Juan needs those transfusions twice a week," Sara said. "We have to find him right away."

Hardy could see the concern on Unger's face. "Does Garcia know about his condition?"

"No," Presley said. "Only his inspector and I knew."

"Garcia knows Sara needs them?" Hardy asked.

"Yeah."

"So he knows what to do," Hardy said.

Sara rose to her feet. "We don't have much time. Even if Juan tells Garcia about the treatment, Garcia won't risk the exposure. He knows we'll be looking for it."

Presley rose. "Just as he'll be looking for you."

Sara waived away the idea. "Forget about me. We have only a few days to get Juan back. Let's go figure out how we're going to do that."

Hardy sat up on the edge of his bed. That brought Unger, who'd been standing in the doorway, back in. "Where do you think you're going?"

"You heard her. We need a plan and we need it now."

CHAPTER 38

They assembled in the spacious living room, comfortable with its rustic twenty-foot ceiling, wood paneling, and massive fireplace. The home was high in the canyon, and Hardy could see the curves of the sagebrush hills leading down to the ocean. He sat next to Sara on a leather couch. She held his hand as they settled into the soft cushions. Hardy fought the urge to glean more of that than she intended.

Flint and Walker were escorted in by Unger. Flint made a beeline for the couch, and tried to wedge himself between Hardy and Sara. Hardy ignored Flint's cuts and bruises and playfully tossed him to the side, where he sat next to Sara.

"Smartass," Hardy said.

Flint winked at Hardy, then turned to Presley. "Y'all sure know how to throw a shindig."

Hardy smiled, knowing the head wound hadn't hurt Flint too badly.

Presley started. "Okay, new info. The assailants were all captured. There's no way Garcia or Rivera know. We're safe here."

"What if they get to Knight?" Hardy asked.

"Nobody knows about the connection between me and Knight," he said. "Her report says she responded to the 9-1-1 call. That's where she found the three guys."

Hardy cocked his head. "Isn't one of them dead?"

"Didn't report it," Presley said. "Next, there's been no sighting of Garcia or Juan. We'll keep looking. Finally, we went through all of Garcia's records. Nothing there. We need to work together to get the outcome we all want."

Sara cleared her throat. "I'm not sure we all want the same thing."

Presley leaned toward her, his elbows resting on his knees. "What do you mean?"

"I just want to find Juan before his condition gets worse. Get him and Esteban to safety. I don't care what happens to me. I'll give Manuel what he wants if he'll just leave my brother and my son alone."

"Rivera wants you all dead," Presley said. "I see no reason to believe he'll spare your brother and son if you turn yourself over to him. Juan is still a witness, even if he didn't see the shooting. He can place them both there, and describe the threats after the killing. It might be enough to put Ortega away."

"What else is there?" Sara asked. "Rivera holds all the cards."

Hardy leaned forward so he could see everyone. "Just because Garcia took Juan doesn't mean he's turned him over to Rivera."

"What else would he do with him?" Presley asked.

Hardy cleared his throat. "Garcia's motivation is to get his brother back. To do that he needs to deliver Sara to Rivera. Juan isn't going to be enough."

"I don't see how that helps us," Sara said.

"Garcia will be looking to make a deal," Hardy said. "With us."

"If he needs us both to satisfy Rivera," Sara said, "he has nothing to trade for me."

"There's one more option," Hardy said. Everyone turned to him. "Presley said it a few minutes ago. What if we help get his brother back?"

"That's awfully dangerous, isn't it?" Sara asked. "What makes you think we can find him, let alone free him?"

Hardy stood and paced. "All true. But we have some leverage. And skills. Garcia wants to capture Sara without losing Juan. He knows that's almost impossible. He's gotta be desperate. Without any leads on Sara's whereabouts, he has to contact us."

"Presley," Flint said, "how will he go about that?"

Presley rubbed his chin. "He won't risk anything through the marshals. He'll expect me to go to Eureka, so he'll leave a clue there. He'll want to set up a meeting. Insist Sara be there. He'll have Rivera's guys there, and they'll try to take her. Or kill her."

Sara let out a deep breath. "We don't have much time. Juan is very sick."

"Garcia will be in just as big a hurry as we are," Presley said.

"So you go to Eureka looking for him?" Sara asked Presley.

Hardy shook his head. "No. We need to save Garcia's brother while we look for Garcia. I think Presley and Flint need to go to Mexico. You and I need to go to Eureka."

Presley shook his head. "No way Sara leaves my protection."

"Think about it," Hardy said. "When we talk with Garcia we have to have something to offer him. You and Flint are the most qualified to find his brother. I can go look for Garcia's clue without you."

"Why do I need to go?" Sara asked.

"Because we may need you to reason with him. My guess is he still has some loyalty to you."

The room went silent as everyone pondered the situation. Sara broke the silence. "Let's go get Rivera, too. Let's take him out."

"What do you mean 'take him out'?" Presley asked. "We're not the mob."

"I'm done being a target," Sara said. "Let's go on the offensive. Take away his resources. His influence."

"I like that," Hardy said. "You must know his vulnerabilities."

Walker turned to Presley. "Sir, I have to agree."

"Do you understand the magnitude of what you're suggesting?" Presley asked. "We have enough on our plate without trying to put Rivera out of business at the same time."

Now it was Sara's turn to stand. "I'll try anything to get my life back."

"Sara," Presley said, "you're always going to need protecting. Remember, the program is for life."

"The program sucks," came her terse reply.

Presley's shoulders slumped. Sara noticed and gave him a hug. "I do appreciate all you're doing for me. I wouldn't be alive today without you. But it does suck."

"I know," Presley said, "but I don't intend to be the first US marshal to lose a witness."

"I didn't follow the security guidelines. It's my fault."

Presley shook his head. "I'm not into fault. I'm into winning. That means you testify, put that bastard Ortega away, and we get Juan back safely."

Sara bolted upright. "I know what could cripple Rivera. You guys ever heard of the Lust Gambit?"

"I did," Hardy said. "At Alice's party. It's an investment con."

"Right," Sara said. "Alice told me about it as part of my training. It's been successful a few times in the last several decades. Rivera is a perfect mark for it."

Hardy leaned forward. "It sounded kinda dated. What would we need to pull that off?"

She pursed her lips. "It is dated, so he won't know it. As for what we need, just a big pile of money, a team to run the con, including a point person Rivera doesn't know but can't resist, opportunity, and a shitload of luck."

They all stared at her until she chuckled. "Okay, I didn't say it would be easy."

"Tell me about this Lust Gambit," Presley said.

"It's a financial scam based on the target having an ego and a lust for power so big that he sees himself as invincible. Willing to take risks. Rivera is perfect. We offer him something in exchange for that power, and when he takes the bait, we take his money. Put him out of business."

"How do we get clear of him after the con?" Hardy asked. "He's going to be pissed, and he'll have muscle with him."

"Yeah, we'll have to do something about his muscle. And we'll need Alice."

"Do you think she'll help?" Presley asked.

Flint laughed. "After the invasion of Rivera's guys on her home, and what he's doing to Sara, she'll help." He gave Sara a knowing smile. "Right, Sara?"

Sara grinned. "I'm pretty sure I can convince her."

Presley, Flint, and Hardy exchanged eye contact. Presley broke the silence.

"Let's get to work."

CHAPTER 39

Rivera Compound

Rivera threw his glass against the wall of his kitchen, shattering it and splashing ice and tequila across the paver flooring. "I don't give a fuck that you have Juan. Until you bring me Sara, your brother stays with me."

One of Rivera's housekeepers came in and starting cleaning up the mess, showing no sign of being startled or surprised.

"And where are my men that we dispatched to Malibu?"

"I don't know," Garcia answered, his voice tired. "But we can assume they didn't get her, or you'd know by now."

"I don't understand why this bad luck keeps happening to me. You planted the tracking device on Hardy. How could they escape? My men are well trained."

"So are the marshals."

Rivera made a fist. "Really? Then why haven't you given me what I need?"

"I'm doing my best. I need a crew here in Eureka. They'll come looking for Juan. They know about my brother by now. They know I need Sara. They'll come."

Rivera grunted. "I'll send Valenzuela and his men. But do not test my patience, Garcia. If I don't have Sara soon, I'll slit your brother's throat, and then come get you."

CHAPTER 40

Ferndale, CA

Sara pulled out a small slip of paper from her purse. "Shaw House Inn B&B in Ferndale. Restored Victorian, built in eighteen fifty-four. Five miles off the one-oh-one, ten miles south of Eureka."

Hardy saw the exit for Ferndale ahead. "Almost there."

"Presley booked us two of the eight guest rooms. I think our cover is better as a married couple, don't you?"

"Garcia may be looking for a single woman checking in. Probably just one bed per room, though."

"That's okay. I brought a chastity belt."

Hardy laughed. "Ah. Guess you don't trust yourself with me, huh?"

She lowered her voice. "I don't, actually. But I could never act on it."

"I bet you could."

"If I slept with you I'd want to do it again, and again, and again. And that's not possible. I'm leaving when this is done and we'll never see each other again. How can I do that if I'm sleeping with you? If I'm falling in love with you?" She sighed. "I hope you weren't expecting anything different."

"I wasn't expecting anything."

"You sure?"

Hardy gulped. "I'm good." He chose to change the subject. "Anything we need to go over?"

She shook her head as she leaned back in her seat, letting the wind blow her hair around through the opening in the window. "I don't think so. You go to the courthouse and look for clues. I'll check the local newspapers. Nothing to it. Under no circumstances do we announce our presence to the marshals in Eureka."

"Right."

Sara pointed at the dazzling reflection the moon cast over the ocean. "Beautiful, isn't it?"

"Yes. The ocean's not bad either."

She elbowed him gently. "I wonder how Bret and Presley are doing?"

"They should be at Alice's by now. Then they fly to Mexico in Bret's jet. I hope Alice will do what we need."

Sara squeezed his knee. "Don't worry about Alice. She'll help."

"That must have been weird, her being interested in you like that."

"Yeah. She wasn't pushy about it, and respected the fact I don't play on that team, so I could handle it. She's actually really nice. But I don't miss that part."

"Hopefully Presley will get a lead on where Garcia's brother is being kept. We could use that when we talk with Garcia. Maybe form an alliance."

"What strange bedfellows that would turn out to be."

"Yes. In an odd way, we may both want the same thing."

"Except for Presley wanting to throw him in jail for several lifetimes."

"Except for that."

"Look at the sky. It reminds me of my hometown in Mexico."

Hardy gave a quick glance. "Amazing."

Suddenly a shooting star lit up the sky.

Sara almost jumped for joy. "A shooting star. I love shooting stars. They bring good luck."

"Yeah?"

They followed the star's path down the night sky, and were rewarded with several more.

She reached out and grabbed his hand. "Quick, make a wish."

Hardy smiled at her and complied.

After a few moments she nudged him. "Okay, what did you wish for?"

"For you to get your life back."

She squeezed his hand. "I like the sound of that."

"How about you?"

She smiled coyly and shook her head. "Sorry. I'm not at liberty to say."

"What?"

She leaned over and lay her head on his shoulder. "Please don't let Manuel get me."

"You have my word."

CHAPTER 41

Alice Polk Estate

Flint, dressed in shorts and a loose-fitting Tommy Bahama shirt, rang Alice's doorbell as Presley fidgeted. Presley wore beige slacks, a matching polo shirt, and a Bass Pro fishing hat.

Alice answered on the second ring. Her hair had been tinted with red streaks.

"Alice," Flint said. "You look great."

Alice eyed him. "I didn't look great before?"

Flint blushed. "That's not what I meant." He squirmed and pointed at Presley. "This is Marshal Presley, the man I mentioned on the phone."

Alice swung the door open, revealing a size-four brunette in the foyer with long hair and a dark tan. "Mr. Flint, this is Raquel, the colleague you found for me. She jetted over from Mallorca for the week."

Raquel gave Flint a firm handshake, and then smiled at Presley. "Nice to meet you both." She gave Flint a second look, and Flint sensed a flicker of interest.

Presley cleared his throat. "If we may, Ms. Polk, we need a moment of your time. Better to do it inside."

"Of course," Alice said, keeping her stare fixed on Flint and Raquel. "Let's be seated in the living room. May I offer you something to drink?" She stepped between Flint and Raquel and led them inside.

"No thanks," Presley said. "We can't stay long."

They seated themselves, with Alice grabbing the seat on the white couch next to Raquel. Flint and Presley sat across from them in yellow armchairs. Flint forced himself to look at Alice, fighting an instinct to imagine escaping to a deserted island with Raquel.

"Do you need some privacy?" Raquel asked. "I can wait outside."

"No," Flint blurted out. He saw Alice's frown and took a breath, "I mean, this may actually involve both of you." He turned to Presley. "Don't you see? She's perfect."

"You're right. But . . ."

"Perfect for what?" Alice demanded.

Presley leaned in. "Ms. Polk, Sara is in trouble. She needs your help." He lowered his voice. "I'm told you know a con named the Lust Gambit. We want you to pull it on Sara's cousin, Manuel Rivera."

Alice blinked. "Sara needs me?"

"She does," Flint said. "And we'll need a Hispanic beauty to play the lead role. A Latina he can't resist." He switched his gaze to Raquel. "Someone exactly like Raquel."

Raquel straightened up. "Oh, this sounds like fun."

"It's a dangerous ploy," Presley said. "Rivera is bad news. If we don't fool him completely, it could go very badly."

"I've heard of this Rivera fellow," Alice said. "Vindictive as hell. Kills for fun."

"That's him," Flint said. "He's trying to kill Sara. It was his guy at your party. The only way we save Sara is to make him vulnerable to his enemies."

Alice shifted her attention to Raquel. "And you think Raquel can lure him in."

"She fits the profile." Flint gave Raquel an extra oomph in his smile. "Perfectly."

"No," Alice said. "Find somebody else."

Flint turned to Alice. "You're Sara's last chance. Only you know the con, and can orchestrate it in real time."

"I can't ask Raquel to put herself in harm's way," Alice said.

Raquel stood. "I'm going to get that drink. Then you'll explain this Lust Gambit thing to me."

Alice's head swiveled. "No. It's too dangerous."

Raquel reached down and stroked Alice's cheek. "Since when did we withdraw from a worthwhile risk. When we were younger we did all sorts of crazy things. Dangerous things."

Alice shook her head. "That was different."

"Your friend needs you," Raquel said. "Needs us." She smiled at Flint. "Will you come along?"

"Presley and I will be there to protect you."

"Then I'm in."

Alice sighed, conceding. "The Lust Gambit is a complex con. We'll need his attorney on our side."

"His attorney?" Flint exclaimed. "Just how do we do that?"

"I don't know," Alice said. "But we'll need him to sign papers. Raquel's charm can only go so far. He'll be investing money that doesn't belong to him. He'll expect assurances that only his trusted attorney can provide."

After a long silence she continued. "Perhaps this is a bad idea."

"No," Presley said. "I can offer the attorney protection. A new life. I just have to get to him. I know some influential people down there. They can get me a meeting."

"You sure about this?" Flint asked. "Sounds mighty risky."

Presley laughed. "Hell, kid, we blew past risky when we decided to go after him. Besides, Rivera can only kill me once."

CHAPTER 42

Shaw House Inn Bed and Breakfast

Hardy and Sara checked in to a cozy and well-heated room. Raindrops beat against both the wood roof and the metal rain gutter above the top-floor setting, sounding like a percussion set. They just needed a few more instruments to round out the band.

Sara showered first. When Hardy returned he found Sara had built a barricade of pillows around her. She snored.

Great. No sex, and no sleep.

He climbed in and covered his head with a spare pillow.

Hardy woke at six to the same sound of a steady drumbeat on the roof. Sara still slept with her back to him.

He contemplated the day ahead, feeling a sense of foreboding, and decided to take his mind off the impending search. He pulled out the cell phone Presley had provided, discovered it had Internet access, and joined an online poker game. He found a high-stakes game, just the ticket to take his mind away from reality.

I wonder if Presley can track where I've been on this? He thought about shutting it down, but decided to press on.

Sara rustled after a few hands and rolled over. "Hey."

"Morning," Hardy mumbled, his voice raspy from its first words of the day. "Sleep okay in your little fortress there?"

"Great. Whatcha doing?"

"Playing poker. Trying to relax."

She leaned over to see the poker game, the hint of a frown forming. "Really? Gambling? I'm relying on you today."

Her tone reminded him, vividly, why he had sworn off romantic relationships. "It's just a card game," he said, not meeting her gaze but making certain the edge in his voice was unmistakable. "Don't worry about me. I'll be ready."

She lay silently for a few moments, then grabbed her bag and shuffled into the bathroom. The door closed sharply.

Hardy went back to his game, playing even more aggressively, and losing faster, than usual. "Courthouse opens at eight. You hungry?"

"Whatever."

CHAPTER 43

Ensenada

Flint landed his jet at first light and taxied to an open space along a back fence. Presley sat behind him. Flint could hear him whispering on his phone.

Flint shut the engines down and unbuckled himself. He slid into the aisle and opened the door. Stairs eased to the ground. "We're here, boss."

Presley hung up, unbuckled, and went down the stairs first. Flint followed, noting the soldiers walking the grounds. A large stucco arch announced they were in Mexico. "What's with all the guns?"

"This airport is run by the Mexican Air Force."

"That a problem?"

Presley turned to him. "You planning an attack? Come on. My contact will take us to the station."

"Doesn't Rivera own the police?"

"Jeez, stop being such a girl. My guy can be trusted. We're just two guys on a fishing trip."

Flint saw a beat-up Chevy Vega approaching, with the ocean as a backdrop. A warm breeze tipped some palm trees. "I could get used to this."

Presley grunted. "You live in Laguna Beach. You really want to live here?"

"The breeze is warmer. Feels good."

The car pulled up and they piled in. The driver, stocky in his uniform, wore a wide hat rather than a police cap.

"*Hola*," Presley said. "This is Flint. Flint, Rodriguez."

"Howdy," Flint said. The driver pulled away before Flint could close his door.

They rode to the station in silence, where they were escorted through a back door into a small room with chipped white paint and linoleum floors.

"Sit," Rodriguez said. He grabbed a rolled up sheet of paper from the top of a file cabinet as Flint and Presley took seats in wobbly, wood chairs, and unrolled it on a square, wood table. Flint pulled a splinter out of his ass.

Rodriguez pointed at a red X inland on the map. "This is where Rivera keeps his prisoners. Two kilometers southeast of here. A kilometer from his home."

"Where's his compound?" Presley asked.

Rodriguez pointed to a stretch of coastline. "Here. But he won't keep your man there."

"Prison guards?"

Rodriguez scratched his head. "We don't know how many. We don't interfere with him. It's bad for your health. *Comprende?*"

I comprende plenty, buddy. I drew the short straw and landed in hell with Deputy Dog here while Nick and Sara are sharing . . . He stopped himself, knowing they were also taking risks.

Flint exhaled. "What's the plan, boss?"

"We break in and get Garcia's brother." Presley turned to Rodriguez. "Any intel on the layout? Guard shifts?"

Rodriguez shook his head. "No, señor."

"When does he change guards at his compound?" Presley asked. "I bet it's the same at this place."

Rodriguez paused, then acquiesced. "Twelve-hour shifts. They change in an hour."

Flint checked his watch. "Not much time."

Presley stared at the map. "I can't get a team here that fast. Looks like it's just you and me."

Great. "Giddyup."

Presley turned to Rodriguez. "I'll need some equipment. Guns."

"Sí, señor." As Rodriguez shuffled out, Flint saw him cross himself.

CHAPTER 44

Ferndale

Sara and Hardy feasted silently on typical Bed and Breakfast fare—pastries, pancakes, bacon, sausage, eggs, and freshly squeezed juices. Hardy was quiet due to contemplating the formidable task ahead. He thought Sara's silence went beyond her concern for her brother. *She's pissed.*

After breakfast, they walked back to their room, single file.

"Are you okay?" Hardy asked as they entered their room.

"I'm fine."

"You sure?"

"Nicholas, your life is none of my business. I'm sorry if I seemed judgmental. Gambling and drugs are such a sore point for me. Like an open wound that won't heal."

"I'm not like those people that Rivera manipulates."

"I hope not. For your sake." She smiled. "I'm a little anxious, I guess."

He turned and started for the door.

"Hey, aren't you forgetting something?" she said.

He turned back and tried to hug her.

She held him off. "I meant, don't you need a jacket? It's cold and wet out there."

Hardy stepped back. "Right." He found his jacket and slipped it on.

"Did you take your pain pills?"

"Yeah," he lied. "No worries."

"Be careful," she said. "Don't underestimate what they'll do to win."

Hardy winked at Sara and closed the door quietly behind him.

*****

It rained all the way into town. Hardy parked in a two-hour lot across from the Humboldt County Courthouse and dodged puddles as he ran to the main entrance and stepped inside.

The courthouse hummed with activity.

He put his keys, belt buckle, and money clip in a bowl for the X-ray and passed through the metal detector under the close watch of an armed marshal. After retrieving his belongings, he started his search.

Presley had given him some clues on what to look for. Garcia's message would be written on a formally posted note, so it would receive little scrutiny, using initials rather than names.

On the second floor Hardy found the message meant for them. At the bottom of a flyer was a lightly written note in pencil.

MR Enterprises. 1-866-555-6666.

Presley had tipped Hardy off that "MR" might be used to indicate Manuel Rivera. Hardy jotted down the number quickly and walked away.

Once outside he sprinted down the block toward his car. The rain continued to fall from the dark sky, and the wind had grown stronger, piercing his jacket.

He stopped halfway there. A dark-blue Honda Civic SI passed him on the far side of the street, creeping by.

Hardy slowed his pace and watched the Civic move along until it came to the end of the block and pulled into the left turn lane. A moment later it turned the corner, giving Hardy a side view of the driver. He couldn't recognize him from that distance.

Hardy scanned the area. The streets shimmered from the rain, with just a few people going to and from the courthouse.

He jogged across the street, climbed into his car, and pulled out onto Fifth Street, the Redwood Highway as the locals referred to it, which doubled as Highway 101, checking his rearview mirror for any sign of a tail.

No one, he thought, as he envisioned a hero's welcome at the B&B.

Still, the Civic bugged him and he decided to take a circuitous route, driving north for about five miles, passing an airport on the right. When he found a spot with a good vantage point of the road in both directions he pulled over to the side and parked.

Across the road to his left, with railroad tracks separating the high-way from the water, raindrops pelted Humboldt Bay. A high hedge ran along the road to his right. There was no way to sneak up on him.

He relaxed. Feeling a sense of accomplishment at finding the clue without being spotted, he put the car back in drive.

The same blue Civic splashed around the bend behind him.

CHAPTER 45

Hardy swung the car around until he was going back toward the on-coming Honda. The Civic slowed down as he passed it and Hardy saw the face of the driver staring at him.

The driver's diamond earring studs sparkled in the raindrops linger-ing on the side windows. He'd been in the photo on Sara's iPhone.

Valenzuela. Rivera's man.

Hardy floored it. He watched the Civic screech into a power turn in his rearview mirror and momentarily lose its grip on the wet pavement, skidding sideways off the road toward the railroad tracks. It regained its equilibrium as Hardy made it around the first S-curve in the road, which temporarily shielded him from view.

Hardy figured he had about a two hundred yard head start. Leafy trees and high vegetation dominated the road on his left. He needed to get to a place where multiple curves would keep Valenzuela from knowing he'd veered off.

The car sped around another bend and the Civic still hadn't appeared in his mirror. He scanned the street for a side road of any kind. Up ahead to the left there was a gap in the greenery along the road.

Paved. Go for it.

He swung the car hard to the left, but the tail end shimmied as he aimed for a one-lane driveway with a wooden rail fence on each side. The driveway angled to the right behind some hedges after about twenty feet.

He fought for control, knowing that any crash would give his po-sition away. The tires skidded along the road as he careened toward the fence on the right side of the driveway. Just before he barreled through it, the tires caught hold and the car straightened out. His front fender scraped the fencing but didn't knock the railing off. He regained control and raced forward around the L in the driveway. An old Victorian home sat about a hundred yards ahead, with no signs of occupation.

He pulled over, shut the engine down, and waited. Seconds later he heard a car pass by on the highway at breakneck speed.

The road straightened out just past his turnoff. *Valenzuela will know I got off.*

He considered his options.

Go back to the highway and head the other direction, hoping I'm out of range by the time Valenzuela doubles back. Follow the driveway to the house and ask for help. Or leave the car and start running.

He noticed level terrain inland for a few hundred feet. Beyond it a ridge of hills led up into Rocky Gulch.

He didn't like his chances back on the highway. If he chose the house he'd be trapped inside. There was good cover up the mountain, and he would have the high ground.

The hills it is.

CHAPTER 46

Rivera Compound

Delgado answered his cell phone on the first ring. He hung up after getting the message.

"Presley is here."

Rivera smiled. "Right on cue. I love having predictable adversaries. Are we ready?"

"It is done. You'll have Sara soon."

CHAPTER 47

Rivera Prison Complex

Flint checked his watch. "Any second now."

He and Presley lay prone behind a mound in a sea of sand, which surrounded the walled-in complex that housed three buildings. Their car was parked behind them, out of sight.

"You ready?" Presley asked.

"Y'all kidding me? I was born ready."

"Mighty cocky for a guy who almost peed his pants at the airport."

"You just handle your end. Don't worry about me."

One guard stood at the only entrance. Two others were seated within the walls, smoking and laughing. Each building had one door, and the windows were all barred. The wall was eight feet high, solid concrete, and covered with barbed wire.

A van came around the corner, pulling up to the front entrance. The two guards inside the walls stood and stamped out their smokes before joining the guard at the entrance. The van's side door opened, and three new guards jumped out. The three on-duty guards piled in, and the van drove off, leaving a smoke screen of dust and exhaust while the new guards huddled over some smokes.

"Now," Presley said.

He and Flint charged down the hill. They ducked behind the wall to the south side of the east entrance and leaned back.

"Clear," Flint said. He held out his hands and Presley hopped on, climbing to the top of the wall. Presley used metal cutters to slice through the barbed wire, and created a space large enough to pass through.

Once Presley disappeared over the wall Flint stepped around and walked toward the three new guards, who were still milling around the entrance. "Howdy," he yelled.

The guards raised their weapons. Flint recognized automatic rifles. He slowed down and raised his hands. "Hold on there, partners. I'm just looking for the highway."

One of the guards stepped forward. "On your knees, señor."

Flint complied. "I don't mean no trouble. I'm just trying to get to town."

The lead guard approached, his weapon pointed at Flint's head. "How did you get here?"

"Was out for a ride on my horse, and ran into some bandits. Took my money, my horse, left me to die. Lucky I ran into you guys, eh?"

The guard rubbed his chin. "That depends."

"Oh yeah? On what?"

"Whether you have anything to trade for your life."

"They didn't take everything. We can make a deal."

The guard hesitated. "What kind of deal?"

"I have some money in my shoe. How about I trade it for water and you point me toward the highway?"

Flint pulled the cash out of his shoe and held it out.

The guard smiled through grisly teeth. "Toss it over."

"How about that water?"

"You don't need water where you're going."

Flint eyed the front entrance. *Presley. Where are you?* "Yeah?"

"*Uno*, you'll dig a grave. Then you'll get in. Then we'll bury you. If you don't make it hard on us, we'll shoot you before we bury you."

Flint let out a deep breath. "Doesn't sound too fair. Think I'll keep my money and be on my way."

The guard aimed the rifle at Flint's chest. "*Adios, amigo.*"

Flint gulped. *Presley? Need some help here.*

CHAPTER 48

A metallic crash from inside the prison complex saved Flint's life. The lead guard turned back toward the entrance, giving Flint the chance to get on his feet.

Another crash.

The guard bolted to the front entrance, joining his compadres. Gunshots rang out in their direction, and they ducked behind the wall.

Flint heard a grunt around the corner, and scrambled back to where he'd boosted Presley over. A heavyset man in tattered clothes fell to the ground on his side of the wall.

"Are you Garcia's brother?" Flint asked as the gunfire accelerated.

"Sí. Ernesto Garcia. I knocked over the ladder by mistake. The marshal is trapped."

Flint helped him to his feet. "We have a car over that hill. Hurry. I'll be right behind you."

Ernesto did his best jogging imitation, rambling across the sand.

Flint returned to the corner and peeked around. The three guards were firing into the complex.

"Presley. Let's go."

"I'm pinned," came his response. "Fly Garcia's brother out of here. I'll get there another way."

"I'm not leaving you here."

"We can't lose the chance to save Sara. Go. That's an order."

Flint glanced at Ernesto, who had reached the top of the hill. "I don't work for you. Toss me one of those guns."

A pistol flew over the wall. Flint lunged for it, but a bullet dusted up the dirt behind him. Flint dove back behind the wall as automatic gunfire riddled the stucco just inches away.

"I can't get to it," Flint yelled. Peeking around the corner, he spotted one of the guards racing toward him. "I've got company."

"Hang on. When you hear all hell break loose, run to the car and get Ernesto out of here. I've got this."

Flint imagined multiple scenarios, but in none of them did Presley "got this."

He braced himself for the guard to turn the corner, automatic weapon blazing, when Presley screamed like a wild man. The gunfire stopped, momentarily, and Flint glanced around the corner.

The guard was frozen, apparently mystified by the primordial screams. Flint used the commotion to charge, and tackled him as the gun went off, firing rounds at their feet. Flint stepped behind the guard and cut off his oxygen with a tight grip, until he released the trigger and passed out.

Flint grabbed the rifle and prepared to charge the entrance, but found it deserted. "Presley?"

Presley was escorted out the front by the two guards. His fingers were interlocked behind him, and one guard had a pistol to the base of his neck.

"I told you to go," Presley yelled.

The guard with the pistol knocked Presley to his knees. "Drop the weapon and surrender, or I shoot your friend in the back."

Flint considered his options. *They all suck.*

"Marshal," Flint yelled. "Do me a solid."

"What's that?"

"Duck."

CHAPTER 49

Rocky Gulch, Eureka

Hardy climbed up the hill. The rain came down harder and the visibility stunk. Rivers of mud streamed down the hill between the foliage. He took each step carefully and was a third of the way up the hill when he heard a screech below.

He could only see vague shapes in the storm, but saw Valenzuela getting out of the Honda. He moved to Hardy's car, and, finding it empty, scanned the area. Hardy didn't budge, and Valenzuela didn't act like he saw him. Valenzuela opened the hood of Hardy's car and tooled around inside.

So much for doubling back to my car, Hardy realized. *With the ocean behind him, it won't take a rocket scientist to know which way I've gone.*

Hardy didn't have the luxury of watching and ran back up the hill as fast as he could.

The higher he ran the more uneven the terrain became, with large roots and tree branches jutting out every few feet. He knew that one turned ankle might be the end for him, so he slowed down a little to make sure he stayed on his feet.

He hit a gap in the brush halfway up the hill and glanced back. Valenzuela stood at the base of the hill and now carried a rifle of some kind. The large scope mounted on top sent a clear message. Valenzuela was a serious sharpshooter.

Hardy turned and hustled to get back into the brush when he slipped and fell to his knees. Just as he fell a shot rang out from below and whizzed past his right ear.

"Stop!" came a shout from down below. "One move and I'll kill you."

Hardy froze and considered his options. *Valenzuela probably can kill me where I kneel, but he needs me alive to find Sara.*

"Stand up and walk slowly back toward me," Valenzuela called out. His voice sounded closer.

Hardy needed to go another ten feet uphill to get to cover, and another hundred feet to the top of the ridge. He debated his options, but kept returning to the only viable solution. For Sara's sake he needed to get away, or be killed trying.

"Okay," Hardy yelled down to Valenzuela. "Don't shoot. I don't want to die."

He rose, hands raised. At the same time he braced his right foot against a tree root and pushed off. He managed a good lunge and scrambled up the hill and into the brush.

Another shot blasted into the ground near his feet as he ran into the forest.

"There is nowhere to run, señor," Valenzuela called out again. "You're surrounded on all sides. Make it easy on yourself."

Hardy reached the top of the ridge and checked out the terrain in all directions. The ridge continued to rise to the Northeast, with falloffs on each side. He continued along the ridge, hoping the uphill running might tire Valenzuela faster than it tired him. It also kept him on the highest ground, and allowed him better vantage points.

After a dozen yards he found a gap in the foliage. A hiking trail ran along the ridge, with better footing and decent cover on each side. He sprinted up the trail, leaving obvious tracks, but creating more separation from Valenzuela.

Off to the ocean side of the hill he heard the sound of dogs barking.

"Señor?" Valenzuela called from behind. Hardy couldn't judge the distance, but he sounded just as close as before. "Do you hear my friends? They're here for you. You better hope I get to you before they do. They'll tear you apart."

He has dogs? Hardy wondered.

Given the low cloud cover, the rain, the uneven terrain, and the howling wind, Hardy couldn't tell how far away those dogs might be. They knew where he was and the direction he was running, so they could intercept him. He figured he had no more than fifteen minutes before they caught up to him.

I can't outrun them. I need to make a stand.

CHAPTER 50

Hardy's shoulder pounded like he'd power lifted his car. *You picked a fine time to go all macho and skip the pain pills.*

A wide, tall redwood loomed off to the right about ten feet from the trail. He decided to duck behind it and wait.

A few minutes passed, the only sound the deep, angry barking of the dogs. Getting closer. They were clearly determined to cut him off to the North. He tried to tune the dogs and the pounding rain out, listening for footsteps coming up the trail.

He heard panting, along with sloshing through mud. The tip of a rifle came into view first. Once Hardy saw it he slid back around the tree and approached Valenzuela from behind.

Just before Hardy reached him, Valenzuela wheeled around, leveling the rifle at Hardy's chest. Hardy grabbed the barrel and tilted it to the side just as the blast went off, sending the bullet over his left shoulder.

Hardy grabbed the rifle with both hands and jammed the butt into Valenzuela's face, drawing blood from the corner of his mouth. Valenzuela held on as Hardy pulled the butt away from him, then shoved it into his nose as hard as he could.

Hardy heard Valenzuela's nose split open over the sound of the dogs, which were going crazy after the gunshot. Valenzuela instinctively reached for his battered face, and Hardy took the rifle from him.

Hardy stepped back. "How'd you find me?"

Valenzuela reached into his jacket for the pistol he'd flashed earlier, and Hardy knew he had no real alternative.

Hardy tossed the rifle aside and grabbed Valenzuela's arm before he could get the pistol, then yanked his shoulder out of its socket. Valenzuela screamed almost as loud as the gunshot. He dropped to his knees as Hardy took the pistol from Valenzuela's jacket and put it in his own.

Hardy's shoulder begged for mercy. "Let's try that again. How'd you find me?"

Valenzuela glared at him as he fought his own debilitating pain. "You think you can hide from us? We know every move you make."

"How?"

Valenzuela smiled and spit some blood in Hardy's direction.

Hardy didn't have any more time to mess with him, so he slammed the gun into the side of Valenzuela's head. Valenzuela fell limp to the ground as Hardy released him. Hardy checked his pockets, but found them empty.

The dogs were getting closer with every falling raindrop, and the gunshot had given Hardy's location away. *They could be on top of me at any moment.* As much as he wanted to rest his shoulder and get some strength back, he knew he had no time to spare.

He ran back toward the cars as fast as he could. The rain poured down harder, and the visibility worsened. Whenever he thought of slowing down, owing to the conditions, the sound of the barking dogs reminded him every second counted, and he pressed on at full speed.

What if they have someone at the cars, waiting? That's what I'd do.

If someone was waiting for him down there he'd have to deal with it. To escape he needed to get to the road in a vehicle.

He made it to the gap in the trees and saw the cars below, but the driving rain and wind coming off the ocean limited his visibility, and he couldn't make out anything other than their shapes.

The rain started to crystalize into tiny hailstones. Each stone felt like a painful jab with a knife tip.

A strong river of mud flowed to his left and had a clear path to the bottom. He made a command decision and jumped into the mudflow, allowing it to take him down the hill at breakneck speed. He immediately lost control, and shot down the hill without any chance of slowing down or avoiding jagged rocks and tree roots in the way. He tumbled down the hill at the mercy of the mudflow, and the flow didn't seem to be in a merciful mood.

Even with the powerful swishing sound of the flowing water, he could make out the sound of rabid barking behind him.

Two-thirds of the way down the hill his left ankle caught a rock and twisted on the way by. A searing pain ran up his leg as the rock ripped into his calf muscle. He turned just in time to avoid ramming it with his head.

He'd saved himself several minutes by going down the mudflow. The question was whether he could walk when he hit level ground. The canines roared, only minutes behind him.

The temporary river dumped out onto the field just south of the parked cars. Hardy slammed into the massive mud pile at the bottom of the hill and turned over on his side. He needed to traverse about thirty feet to reach the blue Civic. He couldn't see inside it because of the weather but was encouraged he didn't see anyone standing there.

That has to be a rental car, with keys he's not used to carrying. They weren't on him. Maybe he left them in the car.

The barking grew suddenly louder. He turned and saw two Rottweilers barking at him from the top of the ridge.

He struggled to his feet, unable to put much weight on his left ankle. He had to limp, knowing that if he lost his balance and fell over, the dogs would be all over him.

A loud voice boomed behind him, commanding the Rottweilers. "*Fass!*"

Hardy limped as fast as he could toward the Civic, losing his balance on the slick surface, but always managing to stay upright.

Fifteen feet. Ten feet. Five feet to the Civic.

The driver's side door flew open and a man with a handgun appeared.

CHAPTER 51

Ding, ding, ding.

Hardy realized the keys were in the ignition.

He slammed the car door into the assailant, pinning his arm and forcing the gun to aim over his head. The pistol's shot whizzed above him as the shooter screamed in pain.

Hardy joined him with a guttural cry of his own.

Hardy kept the pressure on the door with his hip so the attacker couldn't get free, grabbing the gun in both hands and twisting it away from his slippery grip. Hardy hopped back, and the nemesis tumbled out onto the mud as his weight threw the door open. Hardy leaned over and drove the pistol butt into the side of his head. He whimpered and lay still in the slop.

The barking reached a crescendo and Hardy could hear paws splashing behind him. He wheeled around and raised the pistol.

Two angry dogs, larger than life and black as night, bore down on him from less than twenty feet. A man ran behind them, carrying a rifle.

Hardy aimed the pistol and fired it out of self-defense at the feet of the lead Rottweiler. It was just enough of a shock to halt them in their tracks. Hardy knew their imbalance wouldn't last long and he had only a moment to get in the car.

He swung himself into the driver's seat and slammed the door shut just as the two dogs appeared at the window, clawing the glass.

He set the pistol on the passenger seat, turned the key in the ignition, and heard the joyous sound of the engine starting to turn over.

His joy turned toward panic as the engine didn't start and continued to grind in a futile effort to catch.

The Rottweilers stopped scratching at the driver's side window and retreated just enough to get a full head of steam and charge at him. They hit the glass simultaneously, and the force of the impact cracked it in several spots.

Hardy reset the key and tried again, with the same result. The dogs backed up and charged again.

A collage of cracks spread across the window. The surreal image, with the wind blowing the rain and hail around the cracked window, made the Rottweilers look like some sort of horror movie poster.

A rifle, pointed at Hardy's head, replaced the dogs through the same window.

"Shut it down, señor, or I'll blow your head off," the man yelled, trying to be heard over the elements.

Hardy's right hand moved toward the pistol on the seat.

"Don't even think about it," the man threatened.

The Rottweilers put their paws on the doorframe at the window's edge, growling and showing off razor-sharp fangs.

Does he know they need me alive? Hardy wondered. *Maybe he no longer cares.*

A flash of lightning struck a nearby tree. The dogs whimpered and dropped temporarily out of sight. The man with the rifle spun around at the explosion at the tree, lost his balance in the mud, and fell backward onto the ground, the rifle slipping out of his hands.

Rather than going for the gun, Hardy went for the keys again.

The engine turned over.

The Rottweilers charged the window again. Glass shattered around Hardy's left cheek just as the car shifted into gear and lurched forward. He leaned away from the window as giant jaws snapped at him, just missing his ear. Their foul and angry breath lashed at his cheek. He floored the car and the dogs fell away from the window even as the tires spun and fought for a grip. He managed to turn the Civic around in the slop and aim for the highway.

The man with the rifle had regained his footing and stood in his path, with a clear shot at Hardy through the front windshield.

He floored the Civic and aimed it straight at him, which seemed to catch him off guard. He chose self-preservation and dove to the side as Hardy drove past him. But the acceleration caused Hardy to lose control when he veered left toward the highway, and he had to slow down to keep from fishtailing.

One of the Rottweilers leapt for the open window and sunk its teeth into Hardy's left arm, tearing at it with all its strength and rage.

Stunned and bleeding, Hardy tried to yank his arm clear as he swerved the car to the right. Neither action freed him from the death grip of the dog. He could feel its teeth digging in and gripping muscle, tendons, and bone as it used his arm as leverage to try to climb into the car and tear his throat out.

Hardy picked up the pistol on the passenger seat and put the muzzle against the Rottweiler's forehead.

"Let go!" he screamed, hoping the dog understood, and he wouldn't have to kill him.

Hardy leaned as far away from the window as he could as he started to pull the trigger. That extra three inches saved his life as the second Rottweiler lunged up into the window, trying to grab his face, and missing by less than an inch.

The second Rottweiler knocked the first dog's paws off the door and he let go of Hardy's arm to get his footing again. Hardy pulled his mangled arm back in and punched the accelerator. The second Rottweiler also tumbled from the window, barking and growling.

Once I make the left turn around the corner I'll be safe.

He spun into the turn too fast, and the tires lost their grip on the perilous road. The Civic lost control, careening toward the post-and-rail fencing that bordered the property. He reversed the steering wheel, but the car's momentum carried it crashing into the fence.

The Rottweilers bounded toward him with a renewed sense of urgency and fury.

The engine still ran, and he floored it. There were just twenty feet left.

The combination of the hail, rain, and wind made it nearly impossible for him to see. He slowed down to get a clear look.

If I can turn onto the highway the wind will be blowing crossways, and against the passenger side window.

Ten feet to the highway.

A figure flashed into his peripheral vision. The man was back, but he'd dropped the rifle. He reached out to grab the exposed doorframe, failing to notice the glass shards protruding across the bottom. He released the door and cried out in pain as the glass sliced his hands open.

Hardy made the left turn. Halfway through, the car lost control again and he braked to keep from slipping off the road into the railroad tracks. Both Rottweilers converged on him and the exposed window. His good fortune continued when his braking caused them to misjudge their jump and crash onto the hood of the car.

The dogs whimpered and fell off the slick hood onto the ground on the other side of the car. Hardy saw smears of their blood being pelted by driving rain and occasional hail on the hood of the car.

The car settled on the highway and pointed south, the way back to Sara. Hardy edged the car forward again when the man reappeared at his window, grabbing Hardy's shirt collar with both bloody hands.

"Where do you think you're going?" he screamed at Hardy as he tightened the grip on his shirt.

Hardy hit the gas hard, and the car lurched forward, dragging the assailant along. After a dozen steps his legs lost the ability to keep up, and he let go with an angry jerk, falling to the ground.

"Home, you son of a bitch," Hardy said as he sped back toward the inn.

CHAPTER 52

Rivera Prison Complex

Flint fired as Presley crouched down. The bullet struck the guard square in the chest, and he crumpled to the ground without getting off a shot.

"Let's go!" Flint yelled.

Presley grabbed the guard's automatic weapon and slogged toward Flint in the sand.

Flint could hear the sound of an engine approaching over the hill, in the direction of his car. "I think someone's coming."

"Go," Presley ordered. "Don't wait for me."

Flint ran over the hill and found Ernesto standing next to the car. "Climb in," he yelled as he closed the gap.

A helicopter appeared over the ridge beyond the car. It flew straight at him. A man with a rifle hung out the passenger side.

Rivera's men.

Flint waved frantically at Ernesto to get in the car. He dropped to one knee and fired at the sniper. The sniper returned fire, and the sand around Flint exploded. Flint rolled to his side, spinning in the sand to stay just beyond the path of bullets.

"Gun in the glove box," Flint yelled to Ernesto as he dove to the side to dodge another round.

Ernesto retrieved a pistol from the glove box and fired it toward the sniper. The sniper jerked back and grabbed his shoulder. The helicopter spun away, moving toward the prison.

Flint charged ahead, pulling the key out, and dared a glance back at Presley as Ernesto climbed into the backseat.

Presley popped over the hill just as Flint got in the driver's seat. The helicopter was almost directly above the marshal.

Get out of there, Marshal.

Automatic gunfire broke out. Flint turned in his seat and saw Presley firing at the helicopter. The gunfire turned into empty clicks. The sniper was still grasping his shoulder, his rifle limp in his hand. Presley turned and disappeared back over the hill.

Flint started the car. *Marshal, what are you doing? You can't outrun a helicopter.*

He shifted into drive and watched the helicopter dive over the hill in Presley's direction.

"I should get out," Ernesto said. "They want me, not you. You can still escape."

Flint looked at Ernesto in the rearview mirror. *Shit. What would Nick want me to do?*

Save Sara.

But Presley?

He wants the same thing. Save Sara. He knew the risks.

Flint slammed his open hand on the steering wheel, then hit the gas and fled for the airstrip.

CHAPTER 53

Ferndale

Hardy pulled up to the inn and parked in the back as close to the rear entrance as possible, keeping the engine running.

"Nicholas," came a call from an upstairs window. Sara leaned out their bedroom window, shock etched in her expression. "Where's our car?"

"I'm okay. We need to get out of here. Grab everything. I need to keep the engine running."

She paused as if needing to ask a dozen different questions before nodding and disappearing.

Moments later Sara came out the back door in sweats with their two small bags in hand. She tossed them in the backseat and sat down in the passenger seat. "What happened? Whose car is this?"

"Rivera's men. They disabled our car so I swiped theirs."

She reached out and brushed his cheek, staring at his arm and leg. "Oh, Nicholas, you're bleeding. We need to get you to a hospital."

He shook his head. "No time. Do you have the cell phone?"

She reached back and retrieved it from the nearest bag. "They were expecting you?"

He pulled the soaking-wet note he'd taken on MR Enterprises from his pocket and handed it to her. "Yeah. I found Garcia's note in the courthouse. I was tailed after I left. Armed men with Rottweilers. I was lucky to get out of there."

"I'm so sorry." She reached across to hold his hand. "You really need a doctor. Those gashes need stitches. You've lost a lot of blood. Is there anything else? Dizziness? Internal pain?"

Hardy tried to shrug off her concern. "Tweaked my left ankle. I'm fine." He turned onto a road that paralleled the coast. "Let's call Presley."

She dialed Presley's number and let it ring. "No answer."

"Try Bret."

That also got them nothing but empty ringing. She gave him a questioning shrug and hung up.

Hardy drove along the coastal road. "We'll try later. We need a new ride. There's plenty of cash in the bag. Just need to find a car."

Around the next bend he saw a beat-up white Toyota pickup parked on the side of the road with a "For Sale" sign in the back window.

"Hey, look," Sara said. He pulled in behind it.

They saw a middle-aged man cutting wood and a younger man stacking it next to a run-down house. She winked at Hardy and stripped off her sweat-suit top, revealing an outfit meant for a hot day at the beach. She reached back and took out the satchel with their loot. "Sit tight. Be right back. With the car."

She bounded out of the car and down the driveway to where the two men worked. They saw Sara in her halter top, and looked at each other as if the answer to their prayers stood before them.

She moved her hands and hips around, pointing, before shaking the older man's hand. The young man ran into the house and came back with a pink slip and key, and Sara handed the elder man a stack of bills. She returned with the young man in tow.

She put her arm around Hardy and helped him out. "You're still bleeding. I better drive."

She escorted him to their new ride while the young man moved all the bags over to the truck bed. Hardy climbed in the passenger side, Sara thanked the young man, and they drove off.

"The Civic?" Hardy asked as they sped down the road.

"He's going to move it off the highway and into a garage they have in the back. They'll keep it there for a few weeks."

"How'd you swing that?"

Sara flashed Hardy a mischievous grin. "Two single men, one an adolescent. How do you think?"

"You're bad."

"You haven't figured that out yet?"

"Slow learner."

She winked at him. "I have faith you'll catch on. They also told me where the nearest doctor is. She works out of her home. We can get your wounds cleaned and stitched up."

Hardy considered the risk involved. "Is that a good idea? Rivera's men will check all the local doctors and medical centers."

"We'll have to chance it. You need medical attention."

CHAPTER 54

The doctor, a brunette in her thirties wearing a white coat, opened the door, took one look at Hardy, and ushered him in. A waiting area had several pregnant women waiting. Several had infants in tow. The doctor stitched Hardy up, injected him with rabies and tetanus shots, wrapped his ankle in ice, and gave him some pain-killer. When she asked how he'd been bitten he told her he'd been hiking and attacked by strays. She didn't press the issue.

Sara and Hardy went back to their pickup and she pulled out the phone number. Water and bloodstains had made a mess of the slip of paper.

"Can you make out the numbers?" Hardy asked.

She leaned down and studied them. "The first three look like eight six six. The next three look the same. I'm thinking five five five. Then more sixes. See how they match the first ones?"

Hardy dialed the number from their cell phone and put the phone on speaker. After some clicking the phone on the other end started to ring.

"MR Enterprises," answered a female voice on the other end. She could have been from India based on the accent. "How can I direct your call?"

Hardy gave Sara a nod that they had the right number. "I'm calling in response to an ad I saw today," he said.

"Your name?"

"Nick Hardy."

He heard a shuffling of papers on the other end. "Hold, please."

More clicking sounds. He pictured being transferred around, perhaps by way of an elaborate switching network to keep from being traced. After several minutes of clicking a man with a gravelly voice and Southern accent came on. "MR Enterprises. Please state your business."

"I have some urgent business with Mr. Garcia," Hardy said.

"Your name?"

"Nick Hardy."

A pause. "Just a moment, Mr. Hardy."

We heard more clicking, and a different voice came on. British and feminine. "Mr. Hardy, I have some instructions for you."

"Go ahead."

"There will be a teleconference in one hour. In addition, there will be a video feed at a website, and you'll get to see the merchandise you're looking for. Understand?"

"Yes."

"Excellent," the voice said. "Here's the website to log on to. It has the phone number for the call as well." She told him the web address, and hung up.

Hardy turned to Sara. "We need to get some food. A place with a wireless signal."

"Any coffee house will have free Wi-Fi."

They settled on a diner next to a coffee shop, parking the truck just around the corner as a precaution. Sara picked up a specialty coffee to satisfy her craving while Hardy ordered some food and logged onto the Internet from their cell phone, picking up a wireless signal from the coffee shop.

While they waited, he told her all about the trip to the courthouse and the chase that ensued. She sat in rapt attention, unable to move as he explained every detail.

"That must have been awful," she said.

"No worries. It's ten minutes till the webcast. Let's try to reach Presley one more time."

That resulted in more endless ringing.

"Maybe they're in a bad location," Sara said.

"Maybe, but it seems odd."

"Do you think something happened to them?"

He finished the final bite of his cheeseburger before answering. "After today, we have to consider every possibility. Rivera's network obviously extends further than we imagined. But Flint and Presley can handle themselves. We can't jump to conclusions."

He brought the website up and they both stared at the empty screen, still a few minutes early. Then he switched over to the phone and dialed the teleconference line.

"Can they track us?" Sara asked.

"Maybe. Need to keep it short and get moving when we know what he wants."

Sara took his hand. "We know what he wants. He wants me."

There was a beep on the line, followed by Garcia's voice. "Check the video feed. He'll be on for ten seconds. Then we'll talk."

Hardy switched back to the Internet. Juan wore a blindfold and a gag. His skin was orange. After a few seconds he faded away, and Hardy switched back to the phone line.

"You bastard, if you hurt him I'll kill you," Sara said.

"Sara, when did you get so emotional?" Garcia said. "After a year of holding your composure?"

"What do you want?" Hardy asked.

"Ah, if it isn't the irritating Mr. Hardy. I should have finished you off on the beach that morning, when I had you in my sights from the hill. It would have been so easy, and it would've saved me so much trouble. You cost me my career."

"I said, what do you want?"

"Oh, it has nothing to do with what I *want*," Garcia said. "It's what I *require*. I need to hand Sara and Juan over to Rivera. I know you two are here. Sara, I can guarantee safe haven for Esteban in exchange for you. I can pick you up tonight."

Sara paused. "Just how can you guarantee Esteban's safety?"

"I can tell Rivera that I killed him as part of capturing you. Then I'll hide him with a good family where no one will ever find him. There'll no longer be a record of him in WITSEC, and Rivera won't be able to coerce another inspector to divulge his location. I'm his best bet at a safe life."

Sara shook her head. "You don't even know where Esteban is."

Garcia laughed. "I bet you thought that about Juan as well. I know the system inside and out. I found Juan, and I can find Esteban. You know I'm right."

She gave Hardy a concerned look. "Why should I trust you?"

"What choice do you have?"

Hardy realized his hands were clenched and the muscles in his wrist were burning. He forced himself to relax and keep his voice steady. "No way we turn Sara over to you. It's a death sentence for her and her brother. And since you don't have her, you have nothing to offer Rivera. You need us as much as we need you."

Garcia cleared his throat. "If you don't cooperate tonight I shall turn Juan over to Rivera and you can deal with *him*. I think you'll find me much more reasonable. Besides, maybe he'll spare them both. Once the trial is over he has no reason to kill them."

"That's not a chance we're willing to take," Hardy said. "You won't turn Juan over without her. That does you no good. Your bargaining power is a mirage. With us or Rivera."

"Sara, are you willing to take that chance?"

Hardy held his hand up, asking her to resist the urge to reply. "We have an alternate proposal. We can get your brother back, and no one has to get hurt."

"You think I'm an idiot, Hardy?"

"I'm dead serious. We can save your brother. I know you don't really want to turn Sara and Juan over to Rivera."

"That's irrelevant. We'll meet tonight, or Juan gets shipped to Rivera. Sara, I'm giving you your only real chance to save your son."

"Where and when?" Sara said, her voice steady.

"That's my girl," Garcia said. "Before we get to the specifics, put Marshal Presley on."

"He's not here," Hardy said, unsure of how much to say on the subject.

"Don't give me that," Garcia said.

"He went to find your brother," Sara said. "He wants to help you get him back."

"How touching," Garcia said. "Even if that's true, it's a big waste of time. My team will meet you at eleven p.m. Call this number again at ten-thirty. I won't be at the exchange, so don't think Presley can use the meeting as an opportunity to capture me."

Hardy started to say something, but Sara put her hand on his arm and shook her head. "I'll be there."

The phone line went dead. Hardy leaned back in the booth. "You shouldn't go. He can't get his brother back without you."

"You saw Juan. He doesn't have much time left. We have to meet and see what happens. The status quo will kill him."

They heard a shout through the wall, coming from the coffee shop next door. It sounded out of place on this lazy evening in this quiet community.

A horrifying realization hit Hardy like a sledgehammer to the gut. He shut the phone off. "We gotta go."

"What's wrong?"

"Garcia must have traced us. Those must be his men next door, where the Wi-Fi signal originates. They'll expand the search when they don't find us there."

They walked out the back door and down the alley toward the truck, thankful they'd thought to park it around the corner.

They turned the corner onto the street. Hardy saw no one on their path to the unlocked truck. They hustled to get there and Sara fired it up.

They sped down the road in the opposite direction as two men came around the corner. Hardy recognized the men from that afternoon. They didn't seem to notice them, instead focusing on the alley.

"That was too close," Hardy observed.

She gave him a concerned look. "If they found us now they can do it again tonight when we call back in to get the location of the meet. I might be able to hack the signal, keeping us off their search grid."

"Yeah. The skills Rivera taught you might come in handy after all."

She stared ahead as she drove, lines etched on her forehead.

CHAPTER 55

The road took them toward the beach, and a few minutes later they pulled into a turnout. The surf, influenced by the storm, crashed down with a violence rarely seen in Hardy's home waters. Sara melted into him, and they sat listening to the raw power before them.

The cell phone rang. Hardy flipped it open on speakerphone. "Hello?"

"Howdy," Flint's rushed voice said.

"Boy, is it good to hear from you," Hardy said. "Any luck down there?"

"We found the package we were looking for."

Sara and Hardy exchanged wide-eyed glances.

"Did you get him?" Hardy asked.

"I'm in my jet just short of the border. But Presley didn't get out."

Sara almost vaulted herself into the windshield. "He's dead?"

"I don't know. He and a helicopter were going at it. He ordered me to get Ernesto back to you, and I did. But I don't feel good about it."

Sara sagged back into her seat. "You have to go back."

Hardy took a deep breath. "We heard from Garcia. He wants to meet. Tonight."

"You can't do that," Flint said. "We're not ready."

"We know," Hardy said. "We haven't come up with any decent alternatives, though. If you get Garcia's brother up here tonight maybe we can change the game. How long will it take you to get here? There's an airport at the north end of Eureka."

"It'll take me over a couple hours," Flint said. "They'll allow flights in until nine or ten if it's a typical regional airport."

Sara cleared her throat. "We don't know where he wants us to meet, but it may be my only chance to get Juan back to safety."

"When's the meet?"

"Eleven," Sara answered.

"You know," Hardy interjected, "he's going to want to get Sara to Mexico in a hurry. He has to be flying. My guess is the meet will be there at the airport."

"Agreed," Flint said.

"Here's what we'll do," Hardy continued. "We'll get to the airport right now, and find a place to hide. I bet they won't be tracking everyone who goes in and comes out. We can set up and provide surveillance. Maybe get the drop on them."

"Okay," Flint said. "I'll get up there as soon as I can."

Sara brushed away a tear. "What about Presley? Should we call the marshals?"

"No. He made it clear we can't trust anybody. I'll go back after I deliver Ernesto. Let's get you and Juan safe first. It's what Presley wants."

"He's right," Hardy said. "It sucks, but he's right."

Sara bit down on her lip. "If Rivera hurts him . . ."

"Yeah."

CHAPTER 56

Hardy left for the airport with a sense of unease.

"Sara?"

"Yeah?"

"Remember when Garcia said he won't be there?"

"Yes."

"It's all Rivera's team up here. And they won't care that we have Garcia's brother. Even if Flint gets him up here, unless we can deal with Garcia, rather than Rivera's hired muscle, we have no bargaining chip."

"Let's hope Garcia lied about being here personally. Maybe he can even help us neutralize Rivera's men at the meet."

*****

The airport featured one runway that could handle the business jets and props that dominated the local action. They made it through the security checkpoint and entered the waiting area. Private pilots walked back and forth between the building, the airstrip, and a large maintenance and storage hangar midway down the runway. A whiteboard listed incoming and outgoing flights, with the last shuttle flight out scheduled for 8:00 p.m., in another hour. The airport closed at ten.

"I think that hangar out there is our best bet to hide out," Hardy whispered, pointing to the structure fifty yards down the runway.

Sara pointed to a note pinned to a bulletin board. "Look at that."

The note advertised a plane for sale, and to get in touch with Bob, who could be found at the plane inside the maintenance hangar. Sara took the flyer off the bulletin board. "If anyone asks, we can tell them we're here to look at the plane."

They walked to the hangar, seeing no sign of any of the men from the morning. They found two small planes inside, each attended to by someone with a cart full of tools and parts. They walked to the back of the building and leaned back against a tool bench, scanning the scene in front of them.

"What do you think?" she asked.

Hardy pointed to a storage closet to their right. "Plenty of room in there. There's no guarantee someone won't go in and find us, though."

"Do we have a wireless signal in here?"

"Good question. Let me check."

Hardy took the cell phone out and verified he had a strong wireless signal. Just as he was about to put it back in his pocket, it rang, causing them both to involuntarily flinch. He turned the volume down as they both leaned closer to hear.

"Hello?" Hardy answered.

"Hey," Flint's said. "Should arrive just before they lock up at ten. The tower knows we're coming. They asked me to hurry so they can get home—sounds as if it's slow up there after eight."

Sara beamed at the news. "That's awesome. We're inside. Hiding out in the hangar."

"Any word from Presley?"

"Nothing," Hardy mumbled. "We'll keep an ear out for him while you're in the air."

"Roger that, pard. See you soon."

Sara gazed off into the distance with an ashen face as Hardy hung up the phone. "What if Manuel has him?"

"Let's stay focused on getting Juan back. Flint is right. Presley knows how to take care of himself."

They ducked into the maintenance closet, a large room full of parts on metal racks from floor to ceiling. They hunkered down in the corner and held each other on the floor before exhaustion overcame them both and they dozed off.

*****

Hardy awoke to the sound of a jet engine approaching. He straightened up, feeling the stiffness of sitting on the hard concrete floor. He nudged Sara awake, and they eased to the hanger door.

A business jet taxied off to the side of the runway. A lone man with a headset on and glowing orange lights in his hands waved it to its spot and the pilot cut the engines. The door to the jet opened and Flint appeared. Hardy waved, and Flint acknowledged him.

"Thanks for waiting, man," Flint said to the man who helped him park.

"No worries," the man said as he went back to toward the main building, his night officially over. "They'll be locking the front doors in ten minutes, so you'll need to hustle up."

"Who watches the planes at night?"

"Our security guard. You won't have anything to worry about. Nothing ever happens up here."

The man vanished into the dark and Flint stepped down the stairs, surveying the surroundings. Hardy could make out a pistol in Flint's right hand. He signaled back up the stairs, and a bull of a man dressed in a torn shirt, pants ripped down the seams, and bare feet emerged from the jet. He resembled a shorter version of Garcia.

"There's Garcia's brother," Hardy whispered to Sara. Moments later Flint and Ernesto joined them in the hangar.

Sara jumped into Flint's arms and hugged him. Hardy approached Garcia's brother and shook his hand. Ernesto winced at the handshake.

"Hi. Nick Hardy."

"Hello." Ernesto spoke in a thick Mexican accent. "I am Ernesto. Mr. Flint tell me all about you on flight."

"Sit down," Hardy said. "You've had quite an ordeal."

Ernesto looked Hardy over from head to toe. "I not only one."

Sara stepped up to him. "Ernesto, I'm Sara. We're so glad you're free. We'll get you back with your brother."

Ernesto shook her hand without any hint of recognition. That struck Hardy as a little odd—Flint must have told him about her, even if Rivera hadn't—but he shrugged it off.

"Any word from Presley?" Flint asked.

Hardy sagged. "Nothing."

"Shit. I need to go back and find him. Let's get this done."

If there's anything left to find, Hardy thought, keeping it to himself. "It's time to call Garcia."

"He said he won't be here at the meet," Sara said to Flint. "We need him here if our trade offer is going to work."

"He'll show," Flint said. "I wouldn't trust anybody else."

The cell phone beeped as the conference call connected.

"Airport," Garcia said. "Eleven p.m."

"Garcia," Hardy said, "we have Ernesto. He's with us now."

They waited for a response. Ten seconds. Twenty seconds.

Sara clamped down on Hardy's arm. It hurt plenty, but he let her dig in. He tried again. "Garcia, we can give you Ernesto. There's no need to turn Sara over to Rivera. All we want is Juan back safely, and you and your brother can leave."

More silence. Nerve-wracking, gut-wrenching agony disguised as still, peaceful air.

Garcia finally responded. "Let me talk to him."

Hardy pulled Ernesto closer to the phone. "Luiz?"

"Ernesto! You're really free?"

"Sí, *hermano.*"

"*Cómo?*" Garcia asked.

Hardy muted the phone and whispered. "In English, please. Don't mention the plane. Just say you're here. Okay?"

"I try." Hardy undid the muting and Ernesto leaned toward the phone. "Señor Presley and Señor Flint find me and escape me."

"Is Presley there now?" Garcia asked.

"No," Hardy said. "Presley is still in Mexico and doesn't even know we're meeting. You have my word. All we want is Sara's brother. You and Ernesto can walk away."

"Why should I trust you?" Garcia countered.

Ernesto rubbed some sweat off his forehead. "Luiz, is true. They save me. I trust them."

"Have you been taking your meds, Ernesto?" Garcia asked.

"Sí." Ernesto glanced at Hardy. "Rivera provided them. I'm under control."

Hardy wondered what meds Garcia referred to, but ignored the question for the moment.

"So, do we have a deal?" Hardy asked. "Ernesto for Juan?"

Rather than answer, Garcia cautioned them. "Rivera's men will be at the meet."

"How many?" Hardy asked.

"Two," Garcia said. "Three would have been three, but I understand you put one in the hospital."

"Will the Rottweilers be there?" Hardy asked.

"Yes."

Flint leaned forward. "This is Bret Flint. I have a few ideas on how to neutralize them. Tell me how you set it up and we can figure out how to disarm them."

Garcia explained the specifics of the meet, and Flint said, "We'll be ready."

"So," Hardy asked, "do we have a deal?"

"Deal."

CHAPTER 57

Hardy checked the time. Quarter to eleven. They were alone except for the security guard, who they could see with his back to them in the terminal building.

Showtime.

Flint retrieved two pistols from his plane and gave one each to Ernesto and Hardy, keeping one for himself. He pulled out a rifle and slung it over his shoulder. Sara held her hands up in mock frustration.

"You get two, and I don't get one?" she said.

"Sorry," Flint said. "I need both. The rifle's a tranquilizer gun. One dart at a time. Used it for hunting in Africa last year."

"Isn't there a delay with those?" Hardy asked.

"Different darts. These are made to knock humans out pronto." He turned back to Sara. "You and Nick will have to sort out who should have the pistol."

"Chicken," Sara said.

Hardy considered the gun in Ernesto's hand. "Your brother talked about meds. Anything we need to know?"

Ernesto grunted. "Ulcers. I'm fine now." He smiled and went back inside Flint's jet and hid out of sight.

"You trust him?" Hardy asked when Ernesto was out of range.

"He saved my life in Mexico. He's solid."

"Okay. You sure about the rest of this?" Hardy asked.

"Pard, I'll take care of the dogs. You just stay out of sight."

*****

Flint moved over behind the main building near the airport's main gate, being careful to stay out of the security guard's sight. He set up under an open window with a clear view of the guard, who sat inside with a sandwich and his iPod earphones. Flint fired a tranquilizer dart into the guard's leg. The reaction was instant. The guard flinched, reached for his leg, then fell limp in his chair.

Flint reloaded a fresh dart into the chamber, climbed in through the window, and moved the guard behind the ticket counter, out of sight. He moved to his next vantage point behind the building.

*****

Hardy and Sara held their position in the shadow of the hangar entrance, watching the delivery gate, the only way a car could get in, just off the terminal building. The wind had died down and the moon made a move to be seen through the scattering cloud cover. Hardy figured they'd have the element of surprise on their side, and the moonlight would help them see Rivera's men more clearly.

A car approached the gate with its headlights off. The man in the passenger seat eased out with bolt cutters in his hands, cut the lock, and reached down to catch the chain before it crashed to the ground. He swung the gate open, keeping a keen eye out for the guard, and the car cruised inside the gate, parking off to the side. The man closed the gate behind them.

The sturdy driver climbed out, his hands bandaged from the afternoon's tussle, with the two Rottweilers in tow on leashes. The dogs sniffed the wet runway, starting to get agitated. Hardy could make out silencers on both guns.

"Uh-oh," Hardy whispered to Sara. "The dogs still have my scent. They know I'm here."

"Bret's ready for that," she reminded Hardy. "It's just two of them. He'll handle it." She pointed out at the two men. "Shouldn't we have silencers, too?"

"Nothing we can do about that."

The pair of men and Rottweilers started toward the main building. One of the men took out a handheld walkie-talkie. Hardy made out the words "all clear," probably giving Garcia the go-ahead to bring Sara's brother in.

The Rottweilers strained against their leashes to move down the runway toward Hardy.

"Smell the guard?" the man holding the dogs asked.

"They can't have his scent," the second man said. "Must be a wild animal down there."

"*Aqui?*"

"Well, if it's not an animal, whose scent could they have?"

A fresh thought seemed to hit them simultaneously. The man with the leash reached down and undid the clasps connecting the leashes to the dogs' collars.

"*Voran!*" he commanded, and the dogs broke toward Hardy, barking as they charged.

"Get behind me," Hardy told Sara as the Rottweilers closed in. He aimed his pistol at the lead dog and waited for him to come closer.

"Do you have to kill them?" Sara asked.

"Them or us."

Just as he prepared to pull the trigger, the lead Rottweiler yelped, a red tip of a dart in its hindquarters. The dog whimpered and lost its balance, collapsing to a heap.

The second Rottweiler stopped for an instant, then charged again, barking frantically, drool dripping from its muzzle.

Hardy took dead aim. Before he fired, Flint sank the second Rottweiler with another tranquilizer.

Hardy let out all the air he had. *Too close.*

The two men heard the rifle shots, ducked behind the hood of the car, and aimed their pistols in Flint's direction. The corner of the building protected Flint for the moment, but he'd lost the element of surprise. He needed these men disabled before Garcia arrived, which could be at any moment.

Hardy knew if he could distract the two men, Flint could get behind them unnoticed and drop them without having to use the pistols.

"Hey!" Hardy yelled out to them. "Remember me?"

Both men swirled in Hardy's direction, and the Rottweiler's owner moved toward Hardy until his partner grabbed his arm and pulled him back down out of sight.

"I'm going to kill both of these dogs," Hardy continued, "unless you surrender right now."

That initiated a heated debate behind the car's hood.

"We have no beef with you," Hardy pressed. "Put your weapons on the hood of the car and come out with your hands locked behind your head."

"Fuck you!" yelled the man with the bandaged hands.

*****

Flint made it to the other end of the building and crouched down at the corner behind the two men. If he could traverse another ten feet along the fence he'd have a clear shot.

The Rottweilers' owner scanned the area for Flint as the second man climbed back behind the wheel. Whether he planned to charge them or try to make a run for it, Flint didn't want him in there.

Flint reacted quickly. He ran along the fence until he was in firing range, and nailed the dog owner in the thigh with a dart. The man crumpled to the ground.

The man behind the wheel jerked and shifted the car into reverse, flooring it. It closed the twenty-foot gap before Flint could reload a dart.

Oh, shit.

Hardy jumped out of the hangar into the open. *Any shot could hit Flint.*

"Hey. Over here!"

The driver ignored and plowed toward Flint.

Hardy ran toward them, looking for a better angle. "Hold on, buddy!"

Flint jumped backward onto the fence, losing his grip on the rifle, which fell onto the asphalt. He scrambled up the links just high enough that the back of the car missed his feet by inches.

"A little help here."

He jumped on the trunk, pulling his pistol out. The driver threw the car into drive and accelerated. Flint lost his footing and fell backward onto the pavement, slamming his shoulder and losing his grip on the pistol. The car screeched to a stop and the driver leaned out the window with his pistol aimed at Flint, now a sitting duck.

Hardy had closed to about ten feet. "Hey!" he yelled, trying to distract the driver. But the driver was having none of it, and Hardy braced himself to kill a man.

A dual-propeller airplane swooped down out of the clouds and fog and hit the runway with a screech of tires. The driver swung his head to check on that noise, which gave Flint just enough time to retrieve his gun and vault behind the car, out of sight.

The driver put the car into reverse and gunned the engine, barely missing the diving Flint. Flint bounced to his feet, even with the front passenger window, and took the shot. The driver screamed in pain, dropped his gun onto the pavement, and grabbed his shoulder.

Hardy rushed forward and kicked the dropped gun away, holding his own at the man's temple.

"That's enough, *amigo*," Hardy told him. "You're all done here."

"We will keep coming until you and your friends are all dead," came the rebellious reply.

"It must really piss you off to get your ass kicked twice in the same day by a group of amateurs, eh?"

"Die, *cabrón*," he said.

Hardy drove a blow into the man's neck, rendering him unconscious. "After you."

CHAPTER 58

Hardy and Flint joined Sara and Ernesto a respectful distance away from the small plane and waited for the door to open.

Garcia sat in the pilot's seat. Juan, silver tape across his mouth, sat in the copilot's seat. Garcia held a pistol up against Juan's temple. He stared at the scene in front of him, but mostly at his brother.

"It's okay, Luiz," Ernesto said. "They are keeping their promise. No one will hurt us."

After a few seconds Garcia wedged open the tiny window at his seat. "Are you armed, Ernesto?"

Ernesto pulled out his pistol. "I am, Luiz. We are safe."

"I'll be the judge of that," Garcia said. "Watch all three of them. I need to escort Juan off the plane. If any of them makes a move, I want you to shoot. Can you do that?"

Ernesto shifted uncomfortably. "I don't know, Luiz. They rescue me."

"Just do what I say. Who else is armed?"

"The men," Ernesto answered.

Garcia waved to Hardy and Flint. "Lay them on the ground in front of you and kick them toward the plane. Slowly."

Hardy and Flint did as he asked.

"Jesus," Sara said, "just let me come get Juan. You and your brother can fly away and the nightmare will be over for all of us."

"Stay where you are," Garcia commanded. "None of you comes near us. Understand?"

"Yeah, we get it," Hardy said. "We'll do it your way. Let's just get to it. Sara's brother needs help. Every minute counts."

Ernesto aimed his gun in their general direction, looking at them sheepishly. "Sorry."

The plane's door popped open and slim stairs unfolded. Garcia and Juan appeared at the opening. Juan's skin tone approached a faded bronze.

Juan's eyes lit up at the sight of Sara. He pushed on Garcia to let him go. Once he was on solid ground he stumbled to her.

Sara ripped off the tape. "It's all going to be okay now." They held each other on the runway, both speechless.

Garcia stepped up to his brother. "It's good to see you, Ernesto. I'm so sorry you were imprisoned. Can you ever forgive me?"

Ernesto smiled at him in a way that made Hardy uncomfortable. "Don't worry about that, Luiz. You didn't have anything to do with my *capture*."

Garcia's expression turned to confusion. "What do you mean?"

Ernesto reached out with his free hand and grabbed the pistol from Garcia, shifting his handgun toward his brother and placing it over his heart. "I mean I've been working for Rivera for years."

CHAPTER 59

"I thought up the *kidnapping* as the way to get you to help us."

Garcia stared at his brother with a horrified expression. Sara turned Juan away, murmuring "Oh, no," while Hardy judged how fast he could get to the weapons on the ground.

Maybe Ernesto won't be fast enough to kill both of us, but he'll get off at least one close-range shot.

"Why?" Garcia asked. "We are *family*."

Ernesto grunted. "Rivera pays for my kids to get an American education. He pays for my wife's plastic surgeon and keeps her in blow. He pays for my women and tequila. He is my family now."

"You're off your meds, aren't you?"

"What meds?" Hardy asked.

"My brother is a sociopath. Very dangerous when off his meds."

Hardy exhaled. "That would have been good to know."

"Shut up!" Ernesto commanded.

"I don't understand," Garcia said. "What made you think the kidnapping would get you to Sara? How did you know I was her inspector?"

"That was just luck. We figured you could find her since you were a marshal. We had no idea it was you protecting her. A small world, eh, Luiz?"

Hardy looked again at the guns on the ground.

"So what now?" Garcia asked his brother.

"You fly the four of us back to Rivera. He is quite excited to be seeing his cousins again. There will be a big celebration, and a big reward."

"What about me?" Garcia asked.

"I'll put in a good word for you. Your future can be bright, *hermano*."

Ernesto motioned for Sara and Juan to board the plane.

Sara refused to budge. "My brother isn't going anywhere with you. Take me, but he stays here."

Ernesto waved his gun toward the plane. "I'm afraid I must insist."

"No," Garcia said, catching them all by surprise. "I would have done anything to save you, Ernesto, but you can't put them in the hands of that madman."

"Still playing the big brother, eh? Still trying to control me. You haven't changed a bit. At least Rivera treats me like a man."

"A man doesn't side with a lunatic like Rivera."

"You're in no position to bargain," Ernesto said. "Keep your mouth shut if you want to retire in comfort. Rivera will do that as a favor to me. Don't be stupid."

"You can't fly the plane without me," Garcia said. "I *can* bargain."

Ernesto stared at Garcia, nodding reluctantly. "You still have loyalty to her. That's a shame. Now I see how it must be."

Ernesto pulled the trigger and Garcia's chest exploded, blood spraying several feet in all directions. His body jerked from the impact, dropping to the ground. His chest cavity was an open wound, like something had gestated from it.

Hardy leaned forward toward the weapons on the ground, but Ernesto's handgun pivoted and took dead aim at him. "Fortunately, we have another, faster plane, and a pilot for it. I guess we'll all be taking a trip to Mexico now, won't we?"

CHAPTER 60

The night turned much darker as the moon dodged behind some clouds. Ernesto trained his pistol on Flint as he leaned down in the darkness and gathered the rest of the weapons.

"Ernesto," Sara began, "just take me. I'm the one Manuel wants. You'll still be a hero."

Ernesto glared at her. "Save it, woman. You're both going. And I need Flint to fly the plane."

He shifted his gun toward Hardy. "You, however, are no longer needed. I think I'll take care of you right here. One fewer person to worry about on the plane. Step away from them."

Hardy took a few steps to the side to keep Sara away from the line of fire.

"You can't kill him!" Sara yelled at Ernesto. "Manuel will want him, too."

Hardy appreciated the sentiment, but he knew he was expendable.

Flint stepped in front of Hardy. "He comes with us or I don't fly the plane."

Ernesto laughed and reset his aim on Sara. "You're all so melodramatic. If you won't fly the plane I'll just have to kill you all right here, starting with Sara and Juan. Rivera would prefer to do it himself, but I'll still be the hero if I come back with their severed heads. Is that what you want?"

"No!" Hardy exclaimed, stepping back in front of Flint.

Sara's brother moaned, and started to sag again.

"Ernesto," Sara pleaded, "I need to get Juan seated right now. Manuel will be much happier if he gets us all back alive, and you know it. He's been looking forward to taking care of us personally for years. Let me take Juan to the plane. You can tie all of us up, and none of us will be able to bother you. He'll want Nicholas as well. He tried to interrogate Nicholas a few days ago and Nicholas escaped. Even beat Manuel up. You know how Manuel feels about that. He'll want the chance to get even."

"I have some rope on the plane in my emergency kit," Flint said. "Plenty for each of them while I fly the plane."

Ernesto gave that some thought. "Maybe we'll take Mr. Hardy along after all. Having your friend on board may help insure you don't do anything stupid up there."

Ernesto studied Juan. "What's with your brother?"

"He has excessive iron accumulating in his internal organs. He needs a hospital."

"We'll be in Mexico in a few hours."

"He might have less than a few hours. He could go into cardiac arrest any time."

Ernesto waved them toward the plane again. "That's a chance we'll have to take. Get him on the jet."

He leaned down, and placed the handgun used to kill Garcia in the hand of one of the unconscious men.

"You stupid prick," he said to the unconscious man. "Couldn't even handle these losers without my help. You deserve to get caught, and killing a US marshal to boot. You're lucky though. It's probably a better fate than what Rivera would have done to you for failing him."

He rose and followed the others to the plane, another pistol aimed at them. Hardy stood firm.

"The doctor," Hardy began, "that treated my wounds is only a half hour away. She could do Juan's transfusion in the privacy of her office."

"What is it with you people?" Ernesto said, his irritation obvious. "We're getting out of here now, before some police officer on his rounds happens to drop by. Move."

Everyone boarded the plane. Sara helped Juan up the stairs and into his seat, sitting down next to him, whispering words of encouragement to him. Hardy went in next and sat in the back. Flint took his seat in the cockpit, waiting for further instructions.

"Where's the rope?" Ernesto asked.

"In a box under the copilot seat," Flint said.

Ernesto retrieved it. He pulled a knife handle from his jacket and switched it open, exposing a four-inch blade. He cut the rope into several long pieces.

"Okay," he said to Flint, "come back here and tie them up. Tie their wrists, their feet, and their upper bodies to the chairs. Move very slowly. I'll be watching, so do the bonds tight. There aren't going to be any mistakes on this trip. Do you have any tape for their mouths?"

"No tape," Flint said.

"All right," Ernesto said. "I expect absolute silence. Understand?"

Everyone nodded.

Flint walked back and started with Hardy. He bound Hardy's hands behind him. Hardy hoped to see a message in Flint's expression, something similar to, "Hey, don't worry, I have a plan," but he didn't see anything other than concern.

Flint bound Hardy's wrists, feet, and upper body and moved on to Sara and her brother. "I'm sorry," he whispered to Sara. "He fooled me."

She smiled as best she could. "How could you know?"

"Shut up!" Ernesto commanded.

Sara's smile evaporated as she shifted her gaze to Ernesto. "What did you do with Marshal Presley?"

Ernesto raised his gun as if to strike some compliance into her, but stopped short. "Ah, yes, your beloved Marshal Presley. We played him as the arrogant fool he is. We were alerted the second he and Flint entered the country, and we knew he'd come looking for me. So we made it possible for him to find me. Just hard enough to be believable, mind you. We orchestrated Flint being able to escape with me, and kept Presley behind. Once I was in the air, we removed Presley from the equation."

"What did you do to him?" Sara repeated.

"I imagine there are pieces of him spread out all over the Mexican desert by now." He smiled at her and winked. "Is that what you wanted to know?"

Sara glared at him, but refused to give him the satisfaction of a reply.

Flint finished tying all three of them and turned back to Ernesto. "Now what?"

"Where are your parachutes?" Ernesto asked.

Flint pointed above them. "There are two parachutes and eight life jackets, one for each seat."

"Get them," Ernesto instructed.

Flint retrieved those from several overhead compartments.

Ernesto strapped himself into a parachute after waving Flint back to the pilot's seat. He took the other parachute and the life jackets and tossed them out the door before closing it behind him. "If you deviate from my instructions at all I'll blow the door and I'll be the only one to get out alive. Understand?"

"Got it," Flint said.

"Now fly us out of here. Back to the airstrip we took off from in Mexico. I'll be sitting in this seat right here, keeping an eye on you. I can see the instrument panel and I know how to read it. Just because it's dark out doesn't mean I won't know if you veer off course. If you do anything I don't like, I'll kill your friend first."

Flint strapped himself into the pilot's seat. "You might want to be careful with that gun. A bullet could rip through the plane's skin and we could lose cabin pressure. That would be unpleasant for all of us."

Ernesto pulled his knife out again. "Oh, if you make a mistake, he'll wish he'd taken a bullet. I'm quite creative with my knife. Now shut the plane's radio off. We'll turn it back on and use it to call them when we get close."

Flint shut off the radio and started the engines. Ernesto strapped himself in the seat diagonally facing Flint, which allowed him the keep an eye on everyone. Flint maneuvered the plane down the runway, turned it around, and prepared for takeoff.

Hardy's skin was drenched in sweat. In a little over two hours they'd be in Mexico, in Rivera's clutches.

CHAPTER 61

Flint cleared his throat. "We should fuel up."

"What are you talking about?" Ernesto asked.

Flint pointed to the fuel gauge. "Look for yourself."

Hardy leaned over. The fuel gauge read less than half full.

"No," Ernesto said. "We need to get out of here right now."

Flint opened his hands, imploring Ernesto to listen to reason. "Think about it, Ernesto. We have no approved flight plan, so how are we going to get approval to land and get refueled later without unwanted scrutiny. We need to stay under the radar all the way down. If we run out of fuel en route it will be too late. The only safe move is to get it here. Now."

Ernesto glared at him. "You just figured this out now?"

"My plan was always to get fuel here," Flint said.

"Can you even get fuel now?"

"The security guard should have the key that starts the pumps," Flint said. "He's unconscious back in the terminal building."

Ernesto flashed Flint an expression of disbelief. "You're telling me we have to go all the way back in there. Dragging all you out there and back? Fuck it. We'll take our chances."

"That's a dumb move, man," Flint said.

"You're flying us out of here right now," Ernesto said. "Figure out how to make it work." He flashed his knife in Hardy's direction. "If it will help, I can always cut your friend loose now and lighten the load."

Flint shook his head and returned his attention to his checks for taking off. "No. I'll figure it out."

Ernesto glared at him. "I thought you might."

Hardy heard a sudden pop, and the plane shuddered. Ernesto jumped out of his seat and peered out the window.

"What the fuck was that?" he said.

Hardy looked out his window but couldn't see anything in the pitch-black night.

Flint pointed to the front tire pressure gauge. "We're losing tire pressure. I think the front tire must have blown."

"What the fuck?" Ernesto said. "What'd you do?"

"It wasn't me," Flint said.

"Bullshit!" He took a step toward Hardy and put the knife up against his throat. Hardy could feel the tip dig in enough to draw blood. "Tell me what you did or I end him right here."

"I didn't do anything," Flint said. "I'm in here with you. What could I do?"

"Leave him alone," Sara said.

Ernesto slapped her hard with his free hand, drawing blood in the corner of her mouth. "I said no talking, bitch." Ernesto twisted the knife at Hardy's neck again, and the pinch of blood became a small stream.

"Take us out of here right now," he told Flint.

Flint shook his head. "I can't take off with a flat front tire. We need to replace it."

Ernesto's face turned a shade darker. He shifted his gaze back out the window, looking for any sign of trouble. "Fuck what Rivera prefers." Ernesto returned his attention to Hardy and grinned. "He'll just have to take my word for it that you're all dead."

Hardy could see the muscles in Ernesto's hand tense. Ernesto started to move the knife deeper into Hardy's throat.

Flint swung around, preparing to vault himself at Ernesto. Ernesto heard him shift, and realized his mistake. He'd taken his focus off of the one man who could hurt him. Ernesto spun around, knife in front of him, and growled at Flint.

"Where do you think you're going?" Ernesto asked with a sneer.

Now that Ernesto was standing between Flint and Hardy they had him where they wanted him. Hardy brought his legs, still tied at the ankles, up into his midsection and rammed them into Ernesto's lower back.

Ernesto was caught off guard and stumbled forward toward Flint. Flint sidestepped the knife and grabbed hold of Ernesto by a parachute strap and pulled him forward. Ernesto lost his footing and fell, meeting Flint's knee in his abdomen. Ernesto collapsed to the floor, holding his gut and fighting to breathe.

Flint slammed his interlocked hands on Ernesto's exposed neck, and the knife slid away from his limp hand. He didn't budge.

Flint reached in and secured the pistol in Ernesto's pocket. He took the knife and cut the ropes binding the three others.

A sudden commotion outside caught Hardy's attention. He saw a dozen men wearing US marshal jackets surrounding the plane. Someone pounded on the door.

"US marshals! Lay down your weapons and open up!"

Presley.

Hardy looked at Sara, who continued to hold her brother. She closed her eyes and let out a deep breath of relief.

"Is that you, Marshal?" Flint called out as he moved toward the door.

"Yes. Is everything okay in there?"

"Yeah. It's under control. I'm going to open the door now. Tell your men to stay cool."

Flint reached for the handle and twisted it open. Fresh air and a stiff breeze came pouring in, exchanging the stuffy air of the cabin for the natural pine scent of the region.

Presley stepped into the plane, pointing at Ernesto on the floor to another marshal who came in to secure him, going straight to Sara and Juan, and leaning on one knee in front of them. "Are you injured?"

Sara shook her head. "He needs a doctor bad. He's way overdue on his treatment."

"We have two ambulances pulling up outside," Presley said. "One for each of you. Let's get you both out of here."

"I don't need one."

"I insist," Presley said. "You've been through a lot, and we need to get your vitals and make sure you're stabilized."

"Nicholas needs it more than I do," she said.

"We'll take him and Flint with us and we'll get you all checked out."

"I'm fine," Hardy said to Presley, grinning at his total focus on his witnesses. "Thanks for asking."

Presley grinned back, but didn't say anything.

Presley helped Sara get Juan down the stairs. Hardy and Flint followed. The dozen US marshals made a human wall from the plane to the ambulances, making sure Sara and Juan were loaded in safely.

"How did you get here?" Sara asked Presley as she climbed into one of the ambulances. "How did you know where I was?"

Presley took her hand and squeezed it. "You can't hide from me. I'm always watching, always looking out for you."

"You were in Mexico." Then she lowered her voice. "We thought you were dead."

"I'm tougher than I look." He winked to the nurse inside and she helped Sara climb in.

Flint and Hardy walked to the car parked in front of the ambulances.

"Did you see that move to take Ernesto down?" Flint asked Hardy. "Pretty sweet, huh?"

"It was okay. A little awkward."

"No way. I nailed it."

"If you say so."

CHAPTER 62

"Where are we going?" Hardy asked Presley as they pulled out.

"Local hospital. They're waiting to do the transfusions on both of them."

"Is that safe? They won't come looking for her there?"

"Every available marshal will be there protecting them. Three agents in each room. Once Sara and her brother are stable we'll move them. Even if Rivera has any more men up here, which I doubt, they'll both be protected."

"Why didn't you just shoot Ernesto instead of blowing the tire out? If he reacted a little quicker we might all be dead."

"We could see Ernesto moving around through the window," Presley said, "but we couldn't see the rest of you. So we went for the tire to buy some time. We were about to give the order to take the shot when Flint took matters into his own hands."

"It looks as if you went through hell up here," Presley said.

"We all did," Hardy said. "How did you manage to get away? Ernesto made it sound like they caught you."

Presley looked off into the distance, as if reliving the experience. "I shot their sniper, and the pilot got out of there."

Flint whistled. "You're one lucky cowpoke."

"Luck had nothing to do with it," Presley said. "After I got rid of the chopper, I hitched a ride to the border. I commandeered a faster jet and received confirmation en route that your plane was scheduled to land in Eureka. What I didn't know was where you'd go after you landed. We landed at a private strip south of here and headed into town to gather our team at the courthouse. A satellite feed told us Garcia's plane was landing, and we rushed in."

Presley turned back around and watched the road ahead.

"You should know Garcia stood up to his brother about Sara," Hardy went on. "It's why his brother killed him."

Presley didn't respond, continuing to stare straight ahead. Hardy decided that wasn't a subject to delve into.

They pulled into the hospital's ER lot and the marshals jumped out before the cars settled. Orderlies wheeled Sara and Juan inside as marshals watched attentively.

An orderly came over and offered Hardy and Flint assistance. Flint waved him away, and helped Hardy past the ER counter and directly into an area cordoned off for them, where a nurse took Hardy by the arm and set him up in his own curtained-off space. Hardy could hear the activity around him as they tended to Sara and Juan. The hushed and serious tone permeated the hallways, typical for a hospital. The nurse told Hardy to lie down, and he fell asleep moments later.

*****

Hardy slept through the rest of the night, awakening to a nurse moving a cart with a squeaky wheel up to his bed. An IV poked out of his arm, and she connected it to the bag on the cart. The room reeked of medicinal smells.

She flashed pearly white teeth when she saw Hardy open his eyes. "Good morning. How are we feeling?"

Hardy stretched his neck to loosen it up. "I can't speak for you, but I feel great. What are you giving me?"

"Antibiotics and a pain-killer."

"How is everyone else?"

"Still asleep. We completed the transfusions on your colleagues, and they're both going to be fine."

Hardy closed his eyes and exhaled. "Is Marshal Presley here?"

"Oh, yes. He stayed at the young woman's side the entire time."

Presley came around the curtain holding a candy bar. He approached Hardy. "Sara told me what you did yesterday. Very impressive."

"Not a big deal. Everything under control?"

"I wouldn't go that far, but we should be able to leave this afternoon."

"Back to the original plan?"

"Yeah. We'll have Juan relocated to Malibu to join Esteban until the trial. Flint and I will meet Alice and Raquel in Costa Rica to set up the sting, and you and Sara can drive to Dallas for the trial."

"I know Garcia is a sensitive subject, but are you sure there won't be any more corrupted marshals?"

Presley turned red, but acknowledged the fairness of the question with a nod.

"Until a few days ago I thought it impossible. The truth is people are vulnerable to all kinds of weaknesses, and blackmail has been effective in turning people against causes they believe in. Look at the FBI, the CIA, the NSA, the Armed Forces."

Presley took a bite of his candy. "The practical reality is that Rivera had unique leverage on Garcia and there's no reason to believe it can be repeated. In addition, Rivera had no reason to target any marshals up here."

He finished chewing before continuing. "The trial in Dallas is more complicated. Rivera knows we'll be coming. We have to accept that he'll try something there, and turning a marshal would make that a lot easier for him. So we're vetting those marshals again. Truthfully, I don't expect another breach to happen in my lifetime."

The nurse stepped up and interrupted. "We should let Mr. Hardy rest. His body has some healing to do."

*****

Hardy slept through the rest of the morning. A nurse woke him for lunch, an altogether forgettable experience.

"Any chance I can go visit my friends?" he asked the nurse.

"I think that can be arranged. After lunch we'll put you in a wheelchair and you can go for a spin."

"I don't need a wheelchair."

"Sorry. Doc's orders."

Hardy wolfed down his meatloaf, corn, and jello, and washed it down with what he could only hope was apple juice. That taken care of, he called for the nurse and asked to go for his ride. She wheeled him into Sara's area and discreetly vanished.

Sara sat up. Her normal coloring had returned. "Nicholas."

"Hey. How you feeling?"

She was beaming. "Fabulous. My iron levels are back to normal, so I'm good to go."

"How's Juan?"

"He's good. He's out for tests now."

Flint came walking around the corner on his own.

"Bret," Sara cried out. "You're up and about."

Flint came over and hugged her, then came to Hardy and gave him a high five. "They just released me," he said with a grin.

Presley joined the party next, a half-eaten Almond Joy in his hand. He gave a nod while unwrapping the remainder of the candy bar. "Lunch," he muttered as he took a ravenous bite.

"Nicholas, guess what?" Sara asked.

"What?"

"I just talked to Esteban," she said. "He's fine, and having big fun with Walker. It's all coming together. We testify in a week, and my family will be back together."

"That's awesome," Hardy said. He turned to Presley. "Are we still getting out of here today?"

"That's up to the doctors to decide, but I hope so. The sooner the better."

"I spoke with Alice," Flint said. "They'll meet us in Nosara."

"And I have a makeup specialist from Hollywood all set to go," Hardy said. "I've worked with her for years on the sets. She guarantees that Rivera won't be able to recognize us."

Hardy raised his eyebrows toward Presley. "How about the money to lure him in?"

"All set," Presley said. "I have approval to tap into the Marshal Service Asset Forfeiture Program. There's over a billion dollars in the fund now from seized property and assets. Getting five hundred million to front our operation was easy."

"Does Raquel really understand what she's getting herself into?" Sara asked.

"She does," Flint said.

"I'll be with her all the way," Presley said. "I'll make sure she's safe."

"What else is there to do?" Hardy asked.

Presley cleared his throat. "Flint and I will fly Juan back to the safe house. Then to Mexico to convince Rivera's attorney to help us, in exchange for his freedom and safety. Assuming we're successful, it's on to Nosara to get everything set up. We'll meet you in Dallas in five days."

"You think the attorney will cooperate?" she asked.

"I believe he wants out," Presley said. "This will be his chance."

"When will we know the verdict?" she asked.

"Hard to say," Presley said. "Your testimony is the morning of day two. The prosecution plans to rest that afternoon, and the defense will start the next day. Maybe they'll take a day or two, but they really won't have much. So it should get to the jury a day or two after you testify. You'll be long gone, relocated to what we expect will be your final stop. With Juan and Esteban."

Sara smiled and closed her eyes. "It's going to be all right."

Hardy heard the squeak of wheels around the corner and a nurse appeared with Juan in a wheelchair. His complexion was now a healthy light brown, and he had a big smile on his face.

"Juan." Sara exclaimed. "How are you feeling?"

"Very well. They took me out to the garden in the back. It's beautiful out there. Sunny and warm."

Sara took Hardy by the hand.

"Juan, I want you to meet someone. This is Nicholas Hardy. Nicholas, this is my brother."

Hardy leaned forward and shook his hand. "A pleasure. We're all relieved you're feeling better."

Juan sized Hardy up and down and smiled, then leaned around him so he could see Sara and gave her a thumbs-up. Then he looked back at Hardy. "You are the man who keeps saving her?"

"One of many."

Juan shook his head. "From what I hear, you've done most of the heavy lifting. We owe you more than we can ever repay."

Hardy felt a little embarrassed by all the attention, and everyone staring at him. Sara pulled him toward her so she could whisper in his ear. "Don't get a big head. I say that about all the guys."

Hardy smiled back.

CHAPTER 63

Amarillo, Texas, Three Days Later

Hardy woke up in the middle of the night to a sound he didn't recognize, bolting upright and realizing Sara wasn't in the bed next to his. Other than the light from the clock he couldn't see anything.

"Sara?"

No answer.

Shit. Rivera took her, and I slept through it.

Panic assaulted him and he lunged toward the room's only exit, which led to the parking lot where he'd parked their truck.

He found the door still bolted from the inside.

She's got to be here.

A retching sound came from the bathroom.

He went to the door and knocked. "Sara? You okay?"

Another retch.

"Sara, I'm coming in," he announced as he opened the door.

She'd installed a small night-light in the outlet by the sink and he could see her on the floor, leaning back against the tub with her head hovering over the toilet, her face grimacing in obvious discomfort and her right arm holding her stomach. She wore one of his shirts as a nightgown of sorts. He'd been sleeping in a pair of boxers, and the bathroom was cold, causing him to shiver. Her coloring was more yellow than tanned.

Jesus. She'll never make it to Dallas like this.

He sat down next to her and put his arms around her. She titled her head away from the toilet long enough to give him just a hint of a smile, then threw up into the bowl again.

"It's okay, I have you," he said as he held her.

She pointed to a washcloth on the towel bar and he leaned up to grab it, ran some warm water on it, and handed it to her. She first used it to wipe down the back of her neck and face, finally using it to clean around her mouth. Once she finished she tossed it into the sink.

"Sorry you had to see that," she said.

"Don't worry about that. What can I do to help?"

The pretense of a smile. "I feel better now. Thanks."

"Did you get some bad food?"

"No. It's my condition."

"What can I do?"

She drew a deep breath. "I need a transfusion."

"Let's go to the hospital."

She reached out and held his hand. "What time is it?"

"A little after four."

"Yeah, let's pack up and go now."

"I'll pack everything up. What do you want to wear?"

"Anything clean."

Hardy went back to get her some clothes. "Do you feel up to a shower?"

"My legs are too weak."

"I can take one with you and keep you steady."

"You're just trying to get your hands on my body," she teased.

"With that body of yours, who can blame me?"

She laughed a little. "We've made it this far without breaking our rule. Let's not screw it up now."

He decided it wasn't the time to argue with her again about her rule.

Instead, he went back in and turned the shower on. "You have to do me a favor."

"What's that?"

"Stop using words like screw if you want me to get through this."

204 - **STEVEN G. JACKSON**

She gave him an unconvincing smile.

He lifted her off the floor and helped her step into the tub. He stepped in behind her and held her tight, leaving her shirt on. She let him wash her thoroughly, even making a slight moan as he scrubbed her.

"Nicholas?"

"Yeah?"

"I'm sorry I'm such a pain."

He swept a moist mound of hair away from her forehead and lifted her chin. "Don't be silly."

She put her head on his chest and held him with a grip that lacked her usual strength.

"C'mon," he said, "let's get you cleaned up and to the hospital."

After I turn the water temp to freezing and calm myself down.

*****

They made it to the hospital's ER, which enabled him to see her in a brightly lit room. Her face, more bronze than yellow now, scared the hell out of him.

The nurse at the ER desk took one look at her and rushed her into a room ahead of half a dozen other patients, mostly youngsters with various cuts and abrasions. They began her phlebotomy right away. Hardy passed the time reading some magazines in the lobby. The doctor came out a few hours later with Sara's status.

"She completed the treatment and is resting now," he began, motioning for Hardy to stay seated. He sat next to him. "Her serum ferritin level is back under fifty. Her organs are functioning fine, so she didn't suffer any permanent damage, but it may have been close. Too close. We probably caught a break that she started her menstrual cycle when she got here. How long has it been since her last treatment?"

"Three days," Hardy told him. "She thought she could go five."

The doctor pondered this for a moment. "We'll need to keep a close eye on her. These things have a way of accelerating. The nausea and cramping were a result of the intestines absorbing the excess iron, but to be honest with you, she may have come close to going into cardiac arrest, one of the byproducts of the iron accumulation in her blood."

Hardy didn't know what he should tell him.

"We'll keep her here and monitor her until her next treatment, see how she does. If it accelerates, we'll know and can get out in front of it. When her condition reverts to normal I will release her."

Hardy shook his head. "We have an important engagement in a few days, and we have some driving to do to get there."

The doctor grunted. "That's an extremely sick individual in there. She can't go anywhere."

The doctor stood, gave Hardy a look meant to put him in his place, and returned to his domain, leaving Hardy to hang out with the room half full of banged-up kids and sleeping adults.

*****

They let Hardy in to see her after her breakfast. She was still a little yellowish.

"No way," Sara said to him after he told her the doctor's plans.

Hardy squeezed her hand. "He says it's dangerous to leave. Maybe he's right."

"I'm fine. Really."

"Maybe they can delay the trial a little."

"No!" Sara screamed at him, her face turning a dark shade of crimson. "It's been delayed enough. What's the matter with everybody?"

Her outburst caught Hardy by surprise, and he immediately regretted his suggestion. "Sorry. I'm just trying to do what's best for you."

She glared at him another moment, then relaxed and reached out for him.

"I'm sorry," she said. "You didn't deserve that."

Hardy could see her exhaustion. "Don't worry about me."

"I'm so tired, Nicholas. I need to get the trial over with."

"Then that's what we'll do." Hardy put her hand back in her lap. "You rest up now. If we leave tonight we'll still be fine getting to the trial on time."

"Thanks. I think I'll sleep for a few hours before we get back on the road."

He watched her doze off.

*****

She slept all day and into the evening. The doctor came by every two hours to check on her, giving Hardy a sharp glance in case he'd forgotten who was in charge.

They woke her that evening to get some solid food in her. She smiled, stretched, and took some water before speaking. "Hey."

"Hey," Hardy said. "You okay?"

"Better, thanks. What time is it?"

He read the clock on the wall. "Almost eight. You've been out all day."

She looked stunned. "Wow."

The nurse brought her some dinner and slid it in front of her. Sara grimaced at the sight of it. Hardy laughed as the nurse shuffled off. "Need me to go find some real food?"

She shook her head. "Don't bother. I'm full anyway. What I need to do first is call Juan and Esteban. Before we hit the road."

Hardy pulled out their cell phone and dialed Walker's number for her. It rang twice before Walker answered. "Walker."

He handed the phone to Sara, accidentally hitting the speakerphone button. Sara said hello and they could both hear Walker's reply blast throughout the room.

"Oops," Hardy said, and pointed to the button to shut the speaker off.

Before Sara could turn it off a loud crash came over the line. Sara froze, looking at Hardy with uncertainty.

"Tricia?" Sara said. "What was that?"

Another loud crash followed, and then a shout. From a young boy.

"Walker," Hardy yelled into the phone. "What's happening?"

They heard Walker yell, "Leave him alone!" and then the phone line went dead.

CHAPTER 64

"Chief Knight found no sign of them," Presley said over the phone an hour later. "There was obviously a struggle. She found signs of a helicopter landing outside in the mud."

Hardy and Sara sat in her hospital room. She hadn't spoken since the call to Walker had been disconnected.

"They left a note," Presley continued.

"What'd it say?" Hardy asked.

"It said, 'Wanna trade?'"

Sara shook her head, almost imperceptibly.

Hardy slammed his open hand against the wall, which aggravated his sore shoulder. "How could they have found them? You said they'd be safe."

"I know."

"We've underestimated Rivera at every turn," Hardy said. "Why should I take Sara into the trial, where they know she'll be? When you've proven you can't protect her?"

"I can and will protect her," Presley yelled. "Don't lecture me on how to do my job."

Sara interrupted. "Guys, arguing isn't doing us any good. We all made mistakes. We need to focus on what to do next."

"Sorry," Hardy said. "What can I do to help?"

"I'm sorry, too," Presley said. "Right now the best thing you can do is keep Sara safe. When she's well enough you need to bring her to Dallas. I'll work on finding her family and Walker."

"Okay," Hardy said. "Did you see the attorney?"

"Yeah. He's on board. The place in Nosara is almost ready. It's coming together."

"You need to find my family," Sara whispered.

"I will," Presley said.

Hardy hung up. He watched helplessly as Sara bit her lip and choked back a flood of emotions that he, as a man with no children, could only guess at.

He half expected her to shut down and curl up into the fetal position. Instead, she threw off her covers. "Get me the hell out of here."

Hardy considered whether to risk another outburst, but decided the question needed to be asked. "Do you feel up to it?"

"I'm fine. We need to go to Dallas. That's where this all gets resolved."

He retrieved Sara's clothes from a dresser and set them on the bed. "We need to get a nurse in here to disconnect you from everything. They might refuse. The doctor was adamant."

"I worked at a free clinic while in school. I know how to safely disconnect myself." She disconnected the sensors and removed the intravenous line in her arm. "There, all done." Blood dripped down her arm and she grabbed a few tissues, stuck them into the wound, and folded her arm at the elbow.

Two nurses ran in, panic etched on their faces. "What are you doing?"

"I'm leaving," Sara said.

"You can't leave," the lead nurse said.

Sara slipped on her clothes as more nurses joined them. Just as she finished getting dressed the doctor arrived in a huff.

"What's going on here?" he bellowed.

Sara glared at him. "I'm leaving."

"You'll leave when I give you a clean bill of health," he insisted. "I need you to get back in that bed."

"Just try to stop me," Sara said as she challenged them with a fiery stare.

No one tried to stop them. Minutes later they drove off, heading for the trial and whatever else awaited them in Dallas.

CHAPTER 65

Dallas, Texas

Hardy and Sara managed the last leg of the trip without any recurrence of symptoms from her disease. She met every attempt to draw her into conversation with a stoic silence, only making hourly calls to Presley. Each call ended the same, with her hanging up without a word.

They made it to the safe house arranged by Presley, located in the middle of a quiet Plano neighborhood, on schedule. Presley waited for them as they pulled into the driveway that led up the side and around the back of the house, out of sight from the street.

She exited silently as Presley opened the door for her.

"Let's get you inside," he said, as he escorted her through the back entrance. She didn't make much eye contact with him, but allowed him to lead her into the safe house.

So far nowhere has been safe, Hardy reminded myself.

Hardy shook that thought from his mind, grabbed their bags, and went inside. Once inside, one of the inspectors bolted the back door and led him upstairs to one of four bedrooms. He set the bags down on a king bed with a flowery comforter and checked out the other rooms. Unger sat in the corner of one of them in a white doctor's coat, reading a magazine, surrounded by medical equipment. In the last bedroom he found Sara, Presley, and an enormous man in a dark suit. He had greased-back black hair, and one eye seemed larger than the other. His arms were crossed, and his expression was all business.

The stranger glared at Hardy. "Who the fuck is this?"

"I'm Nick Hardy. Who are you?"

"I'm Big Bill Billingsley, the fucking DA around these parts."

"Nick is helping me with Sara's security," Presley said. "He's cleared to know everything."

Billingsley gave Hardy a dismissive glance and returned his attention to Sara. "I'll ask you to describe what happened, just as we've rehearsed. The defense attorney will try to find a hole in your testimony. He'll try to attack you personally to damage your credibility in front of the jury. Once he's done we'll get you out of there."

Sara didn't respond. The attorney glared at Presley. Presley motioned for him to leave her alone for now, but he pressed on. "Sara, are you with me?"

Presley took Billingsley's arm and forced him out of the room. Hardy went in and sat on the bed next to her.

"We've overcome tough spots before," Hardy said. "We'll get through this one, too. We'll get them back safely."

"Do you think Manuel will trade for refusing to testify? Without my testimony the case is all circumstantial. Maybe getting Victor off is enough."

"Maybe," Hardy said.

"We need to find out what he wants," she continued. "We need to talk to his lawyer. The one trying the case. He'll be able to get us in a dialogue with Manuel."

"I think we should get Presley back in here. He'll have some ideas on how best to continue."

"Yes," she said. "By himself, please. That district attorney's a prick. He just cares about his case. Presley will want Esteban and Juan back as his first priority."

Presley walked in before Hardy could get up.

"Good," Hardy said, "Sara and I want to strategize on how to get Juan, Esteban, and Walker back."

Presley came in and sat down. He took his US marshal jacket off, and Hardy could see he'd lost too much weight in the past week. He struggled to meet Sara's hopeful gaze. "I wish I knew what to say."

"Sara thinks we should call Ortega's attorney," Hardy said. "He must be able to communicate with Rivera."

"Probably," Presley said.

Sara leaned forward. "I'm wondering if I don't testify, if that will be enough."

"Honestly," Presley countered, "I don't know if he'd go for that. It isn't just the trial for him. He feels you betrayed the family."

"He offered a trade," she said. "He must be expecting us to use the lawyer as a conduit for communications."

"We keep expecting a call," Presley said. "He has to feel some urgency here. The trial starts tomorrow, and you're testifying on day two. I'm surprised he's waiting for us to call him."

"I don't see how it can hurt," Sara said. She lowered her voice. "I'll do anything to get them home safely."

Presley stood. "I'll have the district attorney make the call. He needs to be part of any conversation with the other side."

"Will he do it?" Hardy asked.

"I won't give him a choice," Presley said as he went back toward the stairs.

CHAPTER 66

An hour later Presley rejoined them. Sara sat up. "Did you reach him?"

"Yes." Presley said. "Rivera's message was clear. If you don't testify *for* Ortega, your son and brother will be killed."

"I see," Sara said. "What he wants is for me to testify on Victor's behalf. To commit perjury."

"Yes," Presley said. "Anything to get Ortega off. There's one more thing. They want to meet tonight at midnight. In a park off the toll road in the Turtle Creek district."

"What for?" Hardy asked.

"They say they'll release Walker as a show of good faith," Presley continued. "They'll give you proof your son and brother are alive and well. They insist you're there, so they know that you get the message."

"What do you think?" she asked Hardy.

Hardy exhaled. "Can we really protect her if she goes? Rivera could have an army out there."

"It's a risk," Presley said. "We can send in the bomb squad ahead of time. We can have helicopter coverage. We can put Sara in a vest and surround her with marshals, but there's no guarantee. They might try to tail us back here, where they could launch another assault. They could try any number of things. But, if they're true to their word about Walker, I have to consider it."

"Trusting Manuel is a mistake," Sara commented.

"No argument there," Presley said. "The logic seems to hold together, though. If he can turn you to testify for Ortega, he'll want you alive for the trial."

"Can I even do that? They have all my testimony from the pretrial interviews. Won't it jeopardize my status in WITSEC?"

"If you change your testimony in real time," Presley said, "I'm sure the DA will treat you as a hostile witness. He'll probably charge you with perjury. The attorney general will insist we drop you from our protection if you violate the terms of your agreement."

"The DA must be freaking out," she said.

Presley smiled. "I assured him that you're just playing along to buy us more time."

"He has to know I'll do anything to save my son."

Presley shook his head. "I think his ego won't let him acknowledge that possibility. He did tell me to do my job and get your family back before the trial starts. He's irritated that he has to deal with the distraction."

"He's irritated?" Hardy said. "What a nimrod."

Presley laughed. "I believe he is. Anyway, he doesn't have a clue that you're thinking about it."

Sara shifted to get more comfortable. "What happens if I testify for Victor, he gets off, and I get jailed for perjury? Will Manuel release them? Leave me alone?"

Presley shook his head. "That would be out of character." Presley leaned down so he could speak in a lower voice. "Sara, we both know you have to do whatever it takes to keep your son and brother alive. If you're going to change your testimony, please don't tell me. I would be obligated to tell the DA and attorney general."

"What do you think I should do, Nicholas?"

"I think we get Walker back. She was there. She might be able to help us."

Sara let out a deep breath. "Agreed."

"I'll set it up," Presley said.

CHAPTER 67

The partly obscured quarter moon hid behind a moist haze that wasn't quite fog, nor anything else recognizable to a Southern Californian, which Hardy found oddly humorous, given the reputation of his home air. His clothes clung to him in the warm humidity. He didn't know whether to attribute that to the weather or the tension.

He and Sara sat in the second row bench seat of one of six black vans. Four marshals sat inside each van. Everyone wore protective gear. Presley rode with Hardy and Sara, in headgear that allowed him to communicate with two helicopters scanning the area around the park.

Sara held Hardy's hand as they pulled out. "Any word on how Flint's end is going?"

"He'll be ready on time," Presley said from the front passenger seat. "They're getting the offices set up. Alice and Raquel are there and excited to go. I think Flint's kinda fallen for Raquel. She's an impressive woman. Once you testify we'll be ready to make our move on Rivera."

"*If* I testify," Sara corrected him.

Presley started to reply and stopped himself. He sat back in his seat and listened to the helicopter and their lead car's communications.

They came to a stop on a residential street as the other cars dispersed throughout the neighborhood. One of the other cars would enter the park first, and wait for the car containing Walker. Only when Presley saw that Walker was alive would they move in.

Hardy reached forward and tapped Presley on the shoulder. "Any way we can listen in?"

Presley thought for a moment, finally shrugging. "Sure."

He flipped a switch on a control panel installed between the driver's seat and his, and they heard a deep, male voice. "This is chopper one. I have a visual on our van entering the park from the north. No sign of the bad guys."

"This is van one," another voice said. "Confirming entrance."

"Roger that, van one," Presley said.

"This is chopper two," a new voice bellowed. "We have company. Another chopper has joined from the south. I see a black sedan entering the park from that entrance. They're here."

"This is base one," Presley said. "Any sign of a sniper on that chopper?"

"Looking with infrared goggles now. Negative, base one. Just a pilot in there."

"Roger that," Presley said. "Everybody stay alert."

"Roger that, base one."

"So far, so good," Presley said as he covered the microphone with his hand. "Once we confirm Walker is there we'll go in."

"Base one, this is van one. The target has parked ten feet in front of us. The front passenger door is opening. A man in a mask with an automatic weapon is getting out. Jeez, he's huge. Must be six-seven, three hundred. Favoring his right leg. He's signaling for us to approach. Sending our point man over now. Showing he's unarmed. Walking halfway to the car. They're talking. The rear passenger door is opening. I have a visual on Walker. Gagged and bound. They want to see Sara."

"Roger that, van one," Presley said. "Tell them we're on our way in. ETA is two minutes."

"Roger that, base one."

"All vans move in," Presley announced. "Surrounding formation. Let's get Walker back."

The van moved forward toward the park. Presley turned back to Sara. "Sara, you ready?"

"I'm ready."

"I'll escort you out of the van when I'm sure it's safe," Presley said. "We'll get you back to the safe house when we have Walker."

They passed through the park entrance and the other vans joined them. They pulled up to the meeting site and the vans formed a circle. Both of the marshal's helicopters flew low right above them. Rivera's helicopter stayed off to the side.

"Okay, I'm stepping out now," Presley said to Sara. "When I'm convinced it's safe I'll signal you to join me. You'll be surrounded by marshals, and you're to stay at my side, which will remain inside the perimeter. Understood?"

"Yes."

Presley opened his door and stepped out. Three marshals from each van simultaneously jumped out and formed a circle inside the perimeter set up by the vans.

Presley stepped to the edge of the perimeter and called to the giant at the sedan. "I'm US Marshal Presley. Who am I meeting with?"

The giant grinned. "You can call me Tiny."

Hardy fought off a grin.

"Okay, Tiny," Presley said. "We have Sara here. You see her once you put that gun down and release my inspector."

Tiny shook his head. "Let's get one thing straight. You're in no position to demand anything. If anything doesn't go exactly the way we expect it to her son gets offed right now. I'm sure you've seen our helicopter. They're in constant communication with the men who have her family. If they fail to report in every twenty seconds that everything is going to our specifications Rivera will send her son and brother back in bite-size pieces. Do we understand each other?"

"We do," Presley answered. "We just want to complete the deal you offered. You give Sara your message in person in exchange for your prisoner."

"So let's see her," Tiny said. "I've shown you your marshal. She's all yours once I talk to Sara."

Presley turned and signaled for Sara to join him. She gave Hardy a hopeful glance and they both joined Presley within the circle, surrounded in close quarters by the other marshals.

"I'm right here," she announced. "Now prove to me my family is okay."

Tiny held up his free hand and showed it to the marshals before slowly reaching into his pocket and pulling out a cell phone.

"I will let you speak to your son," Tiny announced. "We won't risk a message being transmitted by your brother. I will toss the phone to you. It will ring, and Rivera will be on the other end. He has the boy with him, and you can speak to him. The boy thinks he's on a family vacation with his cousins, so no need to worry him. After that, you'll toss the phone back. Then I'll get back in the car, and we'll leave. The marshal stays standing right here until we're gone. If anyone tries to get her or stop us, the men in the helicopter will give Rivera the word to kill your family right now. Are we clear?"

"We are," Presley answered. "Toss me the phone."

Tiny tossed the phone and Presley caught it. Seconds later it rang, piercing the night with its shrill tone, and Presley handed it to Sara. She opened it up and placed it on speaker so they could all hear.

"Yes," she answered.

"Hello, Sara," came Rivera's voice, which even Hardy recognized. "You have been quite difficult to locate. I'm glad we're finally able to reunite."

"Fuck you," she said. "Let me talk to Esteban."

Rivera paused. "I see the years haven't changed you one bit. I've always admired your feistiness. But you should be careful. You don't want me to change my mind about my generous offer."

"Just let me talk to him."

"*Sobrino. Ven aquí! Su madre está en el teléfono!*"

The sound of excited squealing came from the background. Moments later Esteban was on the line. Sara's knees buckled slightly at the sound of his voice, and Hardy held her steady while she talked. "Esteban. Oh, I've missed you so much."

"I miss you too, Mama. Uncle Manuel says you'll be coming to visit soon."

"Yes, I'll be there soon. Are you okay?"

"I'm fine. Mama, Uncle Manuel says I need to go now. We're going swimming in the pool, and having a sleepover outside under the stars."

Sara started to protest, but before she could say anything Rivera's voice came back on the line. "There, you have your proof. You know what you need to do."

"Let me speak with Juan," she said.

"No. You have my word he is here and doing well."

"He needs medical attention."

"I know all about the family curse. I will take good care of him. If you do your part."

"How do I know you'll let them go?"

"What choice do you have?"

"I can't guarantee the outcome of the trial, no matter what I say," Sara pointed out. "If I change my testimony they'll probably throw me in jail for perjury. I need to know that you'll let them go if I do my part and testify Victor didn't do it."

"If you testify for Ortega, *and* he gets off, you have my word your family won't be harmed. Ortega must be acquitted of all charges. You must be compelling to the jury. I think after further reflection you'll finally admit that your husband killed your neighbor. That's why you've been lying to the police about Ortega."

"You want me to implicate Sam?"

"It's a win-win. He's already dead, so what more can they do to him? Who knows? Maybe admitting the truth will be the start of a reconciliation between you and Ortega. The way it was meant to be."

"You're a monster," Sara said.

"Don't you dare lecture me," Rivera screamed back at her, his rage finally emerging. "You sold out your own family. You're lucky I'm giving you this chance, you ungrateful bitch. You don't want it, fine. I'll dice up your precious family into little pieces and FedEx them to you."

Presley reached over and took the phone. The marshals ushered Hardy and Sara back into the van, leaving Presley to stand alone facing Tiny.

"We're done here," Presley said into the phone as Hardy strained to hear. "We kept our end of the bargain. Tell them to release my inspector and we'll leave peacefully."

"The *great* Marshal Presley, isn't it?" Rivera said. "Garcia told me you were a tough SOB. Very impressive that you escaped my trap down here. If you ever want to make some real money you should come work for me. I could use a man with your skills."

"I'm going to toss the phone back to your man now," Presley said. He motioned to Tiny and slung the phone back to him with the line still open. Tiny caught it, mumbled something to Rivera Presley couldn't make out, listened for a moment, and hung up the phone. After hanging it up he removed the SIM card, dropped the card and phone on the ground, and crushed them under the heel of his cowboy boot.

"I'm getting back in my car now," Tiny announced. "Remember, we are watching. Once we are gone and it's clear I wasn't followed you can come get her. Your cue will be a flash of light from my helicopter. If either of you moves before the signal we'll know it and her family is done. If you follow the helicopter, her family is done."

Tiny eased himself back into the sedan and the driver pulled away at high speed, filling the heavy air with dust.

After a few long minutes passed, a flash of light shot down from the sky and Presley rushed forward to Walker. He took the gag out of her mouth and undid her hands.

"Oh, Marshal, I'm so sorry," Walker blurted out. "I should have seen them coming."

Presley pulled her toward him and held her. "Shhh. Don't worry about that now. Let's get you back to safety and have the doctor take a look at you. Did they hurt you?"

"Nothing to worry about."

"Good," Presley said. "Let's get you back and you can debrief us on what happened."

He led her back to their van, where Sara waited.

"Sara, I'm so sorry," she said. "You must hate me."

Sara took a deep breath and gave Walker a genuine smile. "I know you did your best. There's no time for regrets. Let's just focus on getting Esteban and Juan back."

"I think I can help with that."

CHAPTER 68

They drove back to the safe house without incident. The helicopters split up and half the vans went one way, half the other. Rivera's helicopter didn't try to follow them.

Unger gave Walker a once-over, tended to some cuts, and proclaimed her fit for duty before turning his attention to Sara, who wanted nothing to do with any medical attention. Hardy could see the bronze hue returning to her face. They relocated to the bedroom with the medical equipment, and she participated in the debriefing while getting her transfusion going.

Presley, Walker, and Hardy took a seat around the bed as Unger hooked her up.

"Comfortable?" he asked her before he inserted the final needle.

"I'm fine," she said.

"That's odd," he said. "This treatment is supposed to be uncomfortable." He gave her a wink. "I must be doing it all wrong."

She returned his wink. "Thanks, Doc. Sorry to drag you all the way to Dallas for me."

"I needed a vacation anyway," he said.

Sara cocked her head. "Doc, if babysitting me is your idea of a vacation we're going to need to send you to remedial vacation training."

He patted her on the arm. "I'll be back to check on you in a few." He slowly ambled out. They could hear the stairs creak as he walked downstairs.

"Okay," Sara said, "let's get to it. What happened in Malibu?"

"Your brother arrived and we didn't see anything suspicious," Walker said. "Then, that night, when I was on the phone with you, there was a loud crash in the direction of the bedrooms. Before I could react a half-dozen men crashed into the room and subdued me. I saw a big military style 'copter hovering low over the yard before they put a dark hood over my head. They knew exactly where we were. It was a professional job."

"How is that possible?" Hardy asked. "Did he turn another marshal? Your chief of police friend?"

"No," Walker said. "I overheard them talk about how another man tailed you in Malibu when they attacked our house, and later at the beach. In a second car. I think he saw what went down on the beach, and knew to track us through the chief of police. Maybe even planted a tracking device on her car while we were on the beach. It was just a matter of surveillance from a safe distance and doing their homework on the layout. Once they had a second team ready, they struck."

"If they were watching, they knew I wasn't there," Sara said.

"Yes," Walker said. "I'm guessing they couldn't round up another team in time to move in on you in Eureka. They'd already lost one, and even Rivera has to have some limitations on his available resources. They figured they'd catch up with you through your boy. Then your brother showed up, and they had them both to use as leverage."

"Did they say anything else?" Presley asked.

"No," Walker said. "They all wore masks and long-sleeved gear. I didn't see any identifying marks or features before they put the hood on me."

"Any idea where they took you?" Presley said.

Walker shook her head. "I couldn't tell which direction we went, but it wasn't too long a flight. Probably out over the ocean to avoid anyone paying much attention to us. After we landed they loaded me into a small plane. Once here in Dallas I was kept in an abandoned building."

"What about Esteban and Juan?" Sara asked.

"The chopper left shortly after they dropped me off. My guess is they were still on it."

"We know they're with Rivera now," Presley said. "The chopper took them to him in Mexico."

Hardy licked his parched lips. "Can't we just storm in there and take them back?"

"We'll need an extraction team. It's a fortress."

"So go get a team."

*****

Unger completed Sara's treatment as Hardy sat on the side of the bed, watching her sleep. He could see her normal coloring returning.

Unger took her pulse. "No organ damage. She'll be back to her normal self in the morning. She'll need multiple treatments per week going forward. The rate of iron buildup in her intestines is overwhelming her ability to process it."

She stirred and slowly opened her eyes.

"Hey," Hardy said as he took her hand. "The treatment worked fine and you should feel better soon."

"Thanks. I do feel better," she whispered. "Can you get me some water, please?"

He fetched her water bottle and helped her take a few small swallows.

"Time for sleep," Hardy suggested, kissing her on her forehead. "Unger gave you something to help with that. You should sleep through the night just fine."

"How come you're so good to me?"

He smiled at her. "Just rest."

She made the effort to put her hand on his cheek. "God only knows what I'd do without you in my life," she whispered as she started to doze off.

"No worries about that." Hardy kissed her on her forehead again. "Now go back to sleep. We'll talk tomorrow."

She smiled and fell asleep.

Hardy watched her for another hour, knowing that she'd have a hole inside her until they found the most important people in her life and they were safe.

CHAPTER 69

Hardy woke up in a contortionist's posture in the chair next to Sara's bed. The morning sunshine cast a bright hue across the room, and several birds with yellow breasts and black heads and wings chirped outside the open window on a branch at eye level. A surprisingly cool breeze flowed in through the window, promising a cooler day.

Sara sat up in bed, the tubes removed from her arms. She stared at the birds and hummed something Hardy couldn't quite make out.

"Morning," he said.

"Morning. Did you get much sleep in that awful chair?"

He stretched his back out and tried to loosen up a crick in his neck. "I'm good. Just a little stiff."

"You men and your morning stiffness," she said.

Hardy laughed. "Clever. But I think I must be doing it all wrong. How did you sleep?"

"Fabulously. I'm so excited. Hear those birds singing? They're a sign."

"A sign?"

"Yes. Something *very* good is going to happen today."

"How do you do that?"

"Do what?"

"Stay so up all the time. After all you've been through."

"I have my moments, as you well know. Life is short. Worrying is just a big waste of time. Besides, most of my life is dominated by happiness and joy."

They heard someone rumbling coming up the stairs. Hardy half expected Rivera's men to be storming the place. Thankfully, it was Presley and Billingsley who rushed in.

"We have eyes on Rivera's compound. If Juan and Esteban are there, we should know soon."

"I came by to see how you're feeling," Billingsley said.

"I'm fine."

"Are you ready for tomorrow?" Billingsley asked.

"Sure," she said softly.

"You better be," Billingsley said. "Or your deal is off, and you'll have to face Rivera on your own."

"That's enough," Presley said. "Let her rest."

Billingsley poked Presley in the chest. "You be sure she shows and is ready to nail that bastard to the wall. I'm holding you responsible for that. So far, you and your team have been all hat and no cattle."

Presley didn't react right away. After Billingsley removed his hand Presley walked him to the door. "You ever put your hand on me again you won't get it back in one piece. Understand?"

Billingsley laughed and walked out. Presley slammed the door behind him.

"That guy really is a prick, isn't he?" Hardy observed.

"You have no idea."

Presley's phone rang. He answered, then put it on speaker. "Okay, go ahead and repeat that."

"I repeat, we have a visual on the boy," they heard over the phone's speaker.

Sara threw off the blanket and scooted down to be next to Presley and the phone.

"He's in the compound," the voice continued. "Well guarded, as you'd expect. We haven't seen Juan or Rivera yet, but we think they must be here if the boy is."

"Roger that," Presley said. "Do you have schematics for the compound?"

"Nothing," the voice reported. "We'll be flying blind."

"How many men do you have?" Presley asked.

"Just two of us right now," the voice said. "You wanted to keep our search quiet so word didn't leak to Rivera, so it's just us. How should we proceed?"

Presley thought about that for a few moments. "Well, two of you can't go barging in there, that's for sure. Whatever we do, it will have to be swift enough to catch them by surprise so they can't hurt Sara's family."

"Roger that," the voice said. "I wish I could tell you I could get a few dozen guys to go in there that can keep a secret, but the truth is Rivera has his fingers in everything and almost everyone down here. I can't go recruiting without attracting the wrong sort of attention."

"Agreed," Presley said. "Let me think about that and get back to you in thirty minutes. For now, stay out of sight."

"Roger that. Out."

Sara shook Presley by the shoulders.

"I knew you'd find them," she told him. She turned to Hardy. "Didn't I say we'd find them?"

"You did," Hardy confirmed.

"What are we going to do to get them back?" Sara asked Presley.

Presley sat and pondered. "Hardy?"

"Yeah?"

"Would you and Flint be willing to go in there after Esteban and Juan as part of the extraction team? With Sara's coverage at the courthouse, we're a little shorthanded right now."

Hardy didn't hesitate. "Of course."

Sara reached out and took Hardy's hand. "Oh, no, Nicholas, it's too dangerous. These are professionals. Your martial arts training won't be much good against their guns."

Hardy smiled. "My place is with that extraction team. The most important thing in my world right now is getting Esteban and Juan back to you. I *have* to go."

She gave him an uncertain smile. "Oh, Nicholas, what am I going to do with you?"

"You're going to let me help you." Hardy gave her a huge grin. "Besides, if Bret goes down there and plays the hero without me he'll hold that over my head forever." Hardy turned to Presley and raised his eyebrows a notch. "Okay, boss, what's the plan?"

"Call Flint in Costa Rica. He needs to get to Ensenada right away."

"Okay. When do I leave?"

Presley glanced at his watch. "In two hours. I'll have a private jet drop you and a few others there. Off the books. We'll find a stretch of desert to land in that won't get Rivera's attention."

"When and where should Bret meet me."

"It's a three hour flight from here, so in five hours. He has his plane with him. You can coordinate the meet location from the air. Then he can fly you all out of there."

Presley headed back out to put a plan together, closing the door behind him.

Hardy picked up the phone and dialed Flint's cell number. Flint answered on the first ring. "Flint."

"Hey," Hardy said.

"Nick. I heard about Esteban and Juan. How's Sara holding up?"

"Better than I would be. Listen, we found them at Rivera's compound just south of Ensenada. I'm on my way down there in a few hours to help with the extraction. Can you get there?"

"Shit, yeah. I can be there in four hours."

"Perfect," Hardy said. "We'll be landing in the desert somewhere around there. Presley says to call you with the exact location from the air."

"That'll work, pard. Is Presley coming?"

"No, he won't leave Sara's side until the trial is over."

"All right. How many of us are there going to be?"

Hardy wasn't sure. "I suspect we will be badly outnumbered."

"Just the way I like it," Flint said. "That will give the bastards a fair chance."

Hardy laughed. "Yes. I'll call you from the air. How's everything there?"

"Awesome. This CEO from Spain is unreal. Smart and sexy."

"Down, boy."

"Hey, you know me. It's all business."

"I do know you, so cut the crap and behave."

"Well, I am behaving," he said. "At least until after the sting."

"I'm proud of you," Hardy joked. "Talk with you later."

Hardy hung up and Sara took the phone and tossed it aside. "Nicholas?"

"Yeah?"

"I don't know what to do about tomorrow."

"I know. Hopefully, we can get Esteban and Juan out of there before you take the stand. I want to be there for you at the trial."

"That would be perfect. To have all three of you back."

Hardy stroked her hair. "Whatever you decide, I know it'll be the right answer. I have complete faith in you, you know."

She shook her head. "I'm not that good."

Hardy heard a knock at the door and opened it for Presley, who handed Hardy a black ski mask and introduced him to three marshals, two men with a woman in between, that would accompany Hardy on the flight.

Hardy considered their black combat gear. *Jesus, it's like a Ninja convention.*

"Nick," Presley began, "this is your team. It's best if we avoid their true identities. We'll use the seven dwarfs as call signals."

"Who am I?" Hardy asked.

"We voted you Sleepy."

"Man, Sleepy sucks. What did you name Flint?"

"Dopey."

Hardy laughed. "Okay. I can live with that."

Presley pointed at his team, from left to right. "Meet Grumpy, Doc, and Sneezy. Happy and Bashful will meet you in Mexico."

As if on cue Sneezy cut loose with a violent sneeze. Grumpy punched him in the arm. "You better get those allergies contained."

Sneezy wiped his nose. "It's the fucking pollen in Dallas. Drives me crazy. Mexico will be fine."

"One more thing," Presley said for Hardy's benefit. "The US Government can't send mercenaries into a foreign country. Getting caught by the police down there isn't any better than getting caught by Rivera's men. We won't have any clout with the authorities. You're on your own."

"Well," Hardy said, "we better avoid the authorities then. Right, guys?"

Grumpy, Doc, and Sneezy just stared back at him.

"Right," Hardy answered himself.

"There'll be bulletproof vests on the plane," Presley said. "Along with a complete weapons arsenal. Grumpy's the team leader. He calls all the shots. Understood?"

"Yes, sir. No ad-libbing."

"Let's get going," Presley said. "The plan is you'll be back here in the morning with both of them, and Sara will have a worry-free time at the trial."

Sara came up to Hardy and moved her lips toward his.

Hardy leaned in. *Finally. I knew she'd come around.*

She hesitated, then altered course and kissed him on the cheek.

Hardy sagged.

Sara whispered, "Sorry," then faced everyone else. "Thank you for trying to save my family. I'll be praying for you all."

The team trudged downstairs. Hardy held back, but Sara wouldn't turn to face him. After a few moments, he slipped past her. "Be safe."

"You, too," Sara said. "I need you to come back to me."

Hardy turned at the bedroom door. He saw tears streaming down Sara's face.

"You better go," she said.

She turned and fled into the bathroom.

Hardy shook his head, then went to join the rest of the team. Presley stopped Hardy at the front door and pulled him aside. He handed Hardy a wad of cash. "In case you need to bribe your way out."

"Let's hope it doesn't come to that."

"One more thing. If you or Flint get a shot at Rivera, I want you to take it," he whispered so that only Hardy could hear. "I can't order a marshal to do it. I'll have your back. Off the record, of course."

"I'll tell him," Hardy said. "When this is over you're going to owe me a favor."

"What kind of favor?"

"You'll see."

CHAPTER 70

The turbulence knocked Hardy around some—an E-ticket ride as he would call it at Disneyland. He passed the time listening to his "No Worries" playlist, which he normally reserved for walks on the beach.

They made decent time and landed on schedule. Flint was waiting for them in pitch-black clothes from head to toe. His plane sat to the side of the landing strip in the desert. There was no sign of civilization anywhere. A Rembrandt sky, ablaze with stars, washed over them.

"Good to see you," Flint said as he shook Hardy's hand. "Anyone else coming?"

"Two more. They've been watching the compound and have the operational plan."

"Excellent. Rivera and his men won't stand a chance," Flint said, a big grin on his face.

Hardy smiled. "We all have code names. Yours is Dopey."

Flint grimaced. "Seriously. Your idea, no doubt."

"Actually, it was Presley. But I approved."

*****

Happy and Bashful pulled up in an SUV caked in mud and they all loaded the gear and themselves. The plane that had brought Hardy took off, and they were on their own.

On the way to the compound Grumpy went over the logistics and the details of the retrieval operation. They had little to go on. Sara's family could be almost anywhere within the compound. Halfway through Flint glanced up and gave Hardy a concerned expression.

"No worries, Dopey," Hardy assured him. "Piece of cake."

"Oh, I'm not worried about me," he said. "I'm worried about you."

"Just worry about getting Esteban and Juan back to Sara," Hardy said. "That's all that matters."

"I'm sure Sara has other concerns," Flint countered. "If I don't bring *you* back in one piece she's going to beat the shit out of me."

They both laughed at the image.

The SUV came to a stop. They'd been driving the last few miles without any lights, and now they'd arrived at a bluff over the ocean. Hardy could see the main road into the compound a hundred yards to their left, where a brightly lit guard shack stood out in the night. A fence with barbed wire surrounded the perimeter of the property.

"We're here," Grumpy said, then pointed toward the beach. "You can see the house down by the water. We'll dig under the fence in case they have sensors, then head to the beach so we can go in from the surf. Sleepy, as we briefed you, you'll stay here and provide recon for us until we're inside. Then you'll come extract us."

"I still think I should go in with you," Hardy said.

"Someone has to be our eyes from up here," Grumpy said. "You have the least weapons training, so this is best operationally. Trust your team. We'll get them out. You have the handgun should you need it."

He handed Hardy a set of night goggles that must have weighed fifty pounds. "These have infrared night vision, so you'll see anyone with a pulse. Just flip the switch on the side." He next hooked Hardy up with a communications system. "These will allow us all to stay in constant communication. Remember, code names only."

Flint patted Hardy on the back as he exited the SUV after the other five. Hardy grabbed Flint's sleeve before he could get away. "Presley said to take Rivera out if we get a chance."

"You can count on that," Flint said. "See you down there. With Juan and Esteban." He started to move away, turning back with a huge grin. "You're so getting laid for this."

Hardy shoved him and watched them approach the fence below. A few minutes of digging in the soft sand and they were under it and safely on the other side, jogging toward the beach in single file.

Hardy focused on the compound in the distance. A dozen armed men were milling around a huge fountain in a high-walled patio area. A two-story mansion sat on the far end of the square. Men with automatic rifles were stationed in turrets on all four corners of the compound.

The waves crashed below him, providing good cover for the team as they approached the compound. The moonless sky made it impossible to see them without the goggles.

The sound of a foot stepping on a branch behind Hardy startled him. He spun around, and a man stood in the dark, a pistol aimed at Hardy's heart.

"Easy now," the man said in broken English. "Put both your hands behind your head."

Hardy did as he was asked, while measuring the distance between them.

"What are you doing out here?"

Hardy knew an obvious lie or denial would likely arouse his suspicion even more, and he might call down to the guards below. "I came looking for Rivera."

The man gave Hardy a curious expression. "So you know who you're spying on. You're either stupid or insane."

"I lost my brother to one of the drug lords trying to horn in on Rivera's business. I figure Rivera and I have a common interest. He'll want to eliminate any new upstarts. So I came to offer my help."

"By staking out the compound in the middle of the night?"

"I just arrived. It's too late to go knocking tonight, so I thought I'd check out the layout so I know how to approach him tomorrow."

The man stared at Hardy. "You alone?"

"Yeah."

The man motioned for Hardy to step aside and took a quick peek inside the SUV. "Señor, just what do you think you could offer a man of Rivera's resources?"

The team could call on Hardy's headset at any moment and all of their covers would be blown. He needed to hurry.

"I've been investigating the operation of this upstart since my brother died," Hardy said. "I know everything about them."

"Tell me what you know."

Hardy knew that the drug business was competitive and violent in these parts. Other than that he had nothing credible to offer. "I want to see Rivera. My information is for him."

"I think you're lying. I should shoot you right now. Rivera will probably give me his best whore just for doing it."

"Then shoot me," Hardy said, figuring a control freak such as Rivera didn't grant the authority to minions to take matters into their own hands. "I have nothing left to lose."

The man pondered Hardy's statement for a few moments. He waved him to step ahead of him, toward the compound. "We're going to walk down the hill. You will stay ten feet in front of me and walk very slowly. If you deviate I shall shoot you in the back, and you'll be just another victim found shot in the desert by the *Federales* when they do their next patrol. Do you understand?"

A shout from the compound startled both of them. They turned toward it and saw all the lights in the compound go out.

"What the fuck?" the man said, reaching for his walkie-talkie, his gun drooping slightly.

Hardy took advantage of the momentary confusion to lunge at him and knock him to the ground with a powerful kick to his chest. The man tried to swing his handgun back up but Hardy pinned his arm. Hardy slammed his head, complete with the heavy goggles, down onto the man's forehead, and he released the gun. Hardy slammed his head one more time, and the man went limp beneath him.

Hardy rose to his feet, taking the man's gun and walkie-talkie and throwing them into the SUV. The man surprised Hardy by stirring.

Hardy didn't want to hurt him—he was just a dumb soldier and killing him wouldn't do anybody any good, but he didn't need him getting in the way. He took his pistol out and pointed it at him.

"I don't want to kill you," Hardy said, "but I will. Don't underestimate what I'm willing to do."

"Do you know who you are messing with? Rivera is the most powerful man in the country. You're going to die. There's an army down there, and another on the way now that the alarm has been triggered."

"I'll take my chances. Tell me, how can you work for a monster like that?"

The man laughed. "Señor, you have no idea what life was like here before he came along. There was despair and hopelessness throughout the region. Now we have money, plus we have all the women, liquor, and drugs we could ever want. He's bringing in American porn stars for us. The police leave us alone. It's as if I've died and gone to heaven. You know what else? He's not even down there. He has a movie studio. They're filming tonight. You're wasting your time."

Hardy changed his mind about hurting him. He kicked him in the face to shut him up, and drove his pistol butt into the back of his skull to knock him out so he could tie him up.

CHAPTER 71

After tying the sentry's wrists behind his back, Hardy returned his attention to the compound. He saw men scrambling around in the dark, several with high-powered flashlights. He knew power outages in Baja were commonplace, and the team counted on that fact to buy them some time to maneuver without Rivera's guards being alerted to their presence.

"Sleepy, you there?" Flint's voice whispered over the comm system.

"I'm here," Hardy whispered back.

"We've cut the power and we've scaled the south wall without being seen. We're perched right below the top. What's the story outside?"

Hardy scanned the courtyard. "Two men right below you, just smoking cigarettes. Three more about ten feet to their left. One of them has a flashlight and is scanning the opposite wall. Five more across the courtyard. Plus the armed lookouts perched on the wall in each corner."

"Roger that. I need you to count to ten, then take the light built into your goggles and turn it on, aiming it at the men on the far side of the courtyard. That should get everyone to turn your way. We'll be over the wall and have them all disarmed before they realize what hit them. Once we have the courtyard in our control we'll move inside the mansion. That's your cue to drive down here and bust through the wooden gate into the courtyard."

"I'll be there," Hardy assured him.

He counted down and flipped on the light, pointing it toward the guards at the far wall, which set off a chain reaction, and all flashlights swung in his direction. He stood still, hoping a sober sniper wasn't setting his crosshairs on him.

Within seconds he heard the spitting of silencer-equipped pistol fire, followed by some frantic movement of lights and silence. No yelling. No alarms. Just bodies lying in the dirt amidst the flashlights.

Hardy switched off his light and climbed into the SUV. Just as he started it an alarm went off down below, followed by shouting in Spanish. The element of surprise was gone.

He shifted the SUV into gear and started the descent toward the compound. The SUV turned the wire fencing into a tangled piece of modern art.

A spattering of automatic weapon fire barged in on the night. Hardy's imagination pictured every possible battle going on down there.

"I've been hit," Bashful yelled over the communication system. "I'm cornered in the back stairwell."

Hardy heard several more rapid-fire shots from down below. A few shouts. A flash of light.

An explosive device went off in the courtyard at the base of the mansion's entrance, shaking the ground and lighting up the night.

Hardy could see fire ignite the curtains in the room facing the courtyard and explode up the wall, followed by more shouting and some screams.

Oh, Jesus, he thought, *where are Juan and Esteban?*

"Sleepy, we need the SUV down here now," Flint's voice pleaded over the comm system.

"On my way!" Hardy screamed into the microphone. The SUV careened down in uneven jumps and starts, and his head slammed against the roof. He managed to strap himself in and braced himself for more. Halfway down the hill another, larger, explosion rocked the SUV and sent a plume of smoke up into the sky.

Hardy reached the bottom of the hill as flames engulfed the mansion, flooring the SUV and aiming for the wooden gate that led into the courtyard, covering his eyes just before smashing into it. The gate splintered into dozens of jagged pieces. Hardy was inside the courtyard.

A man stood in his path, just ten feet ahead. He aimed his automatic weapon at Hardy.

CHAPTER 72

Hardy floored the SUV toward the shooter, taking out his own pistol. They simultaneously fired at each other, and Hardy jerked his head down. He felt bullets whiz past his temple, miraculously missing him. At the same instant he saw a red hole in the assailant's forehead, and he crumpled to the ground. Hardy slammed on the breaks, skidding to a stop just yards away from the burning mansion.

"Sleepy." It was Flint's voice. "We have Juan and Esteban, but we're trapped in here. We're holding the guards off, but the smoke will get us soon."

"Where are you?"

"Second floor," Flint's voice gasped. "Far side of house. Guards downstairs have us pinned. Windows are barred. Stairs burning. Can't see. Hard to breathe."

"Hang on," Hardy said, looking at the blaze engulfing the only entry from the patio. "Give me a sec."

"Hurry," came Flint's choked reply.

Hardy checked the rest of the building for a way in. Directly above the entry was a balcony. He could see smoke pouring out of an open door up there.

"There's an open door to a balcony right above the entry from the patio," Hardy said. "Can you get to it?"

"Can't move," Flint said. "We're pinned in one of the bedrooms. They can't come get us because of the fire on the stairs, but we're trapped."

"Okay. I'll get them off your ass. When I give the word run across to this balcony. The SUV is right below it."

Hardy looked down at his pistol, then at the burning mansion. Knowing there were men with automatic weapons inside, he didn't have much going for him as a distraction for the team. He covered his nose and mouth with a handkerchief and charged inside, feeling the heat explode around him.

He stepped into a large entertainment area. The walls on all sides were ablaze, the smoke was thick, and breathing immediately became a chore. His eyes watered and stung, and the room became a blur in the dim light and haze.

He dropped to the floor and crawled toward the center of the house, where automatic gunfire blasted. He came around a corner and found four armed assailants firing rounds up into the second floor, which hovered above in a sea of flames and jet-black smoke. Red-hot embers lay where the stairway used to be.

He lay prone on the wood floor and fired at the four snipers. "Go now!" Hardy yelled into the comm system.

Two snipers were hit by his first volley, and fell to the ground. The other two spun around and fired in Hardy's direction, but in their haste they didn't recognize Hardy was lying on the floor. Their bullets flew over his head, and he had time to squeeze off two more shots which found their marks. Both assailants crumpled to the floor.

Above, Hardy saw shadows flash across the hallway toward the balcony.

He took one last look at the snipers, who seemed to be out of commission, and spun around to head back out the way he'd come.

An explosion from the kitchen rocked the house and knocked him down, flames multiplying until every wall was engulfed. His skin started to blister. The wood floor was now letting off steam and appeared on the verge of going up in flames as well. He had only a moment to get out of there.

He scrambled to his knees and thrust himself around the corner and back into the entertainment room. He couldn't see the entrance through the smoke but pressed ahead on faith. The heat and smoke were debilitating and he could feel his body starting to shut down.

Just as he thought he had no chance to get out, another explosion ripped through the house and lifted his body clear off the floor and propelled him through the exit, slamming him against the SUV. He fell in a heap at the side of the car, stunned but conscious enough to recognize the worst of the heat was gone. There were voices around him.

He saw Esteban being placed in the SUV by Juan, with Flint closing the door behind them.

A strong arm picked Hardy up and helped him into the front passenger seat.

"Let's go!" came Grumpy's command from behind. Bashful was at the wheel and floored the SUV toward the broken patio gate.

"Did everyone get back?" Hardy asked.

"All accounted for," Grumpy said, nodding toward Happy, Doc, and Sneezy squeezed in the back, with Esteban across their laps.

Hardy smiled. "Any sign of Rivera?"

"Nope," Grumpy said. "You did a helluva job back there. You saved us all."

Shouting came from ahead and three figures appeared in their path, each with automatic weapons.

"Duck!" yelled Bashful.

Several rapid-fire shots exploded next to Hardy's ear, causing a loud ringing throughout his head. "Clear," came Grumpy's voice from behind. Hardy raised his head and saw the three assailants prone in the sand.

They passed through the patio and drove up the driveway that led to the main gate.

"There'll be guards at the main gate," Grumpy said. "They'll be frantic from watching the scene at the compound. Once they see us coming up the hill they'll let us have it with everything they have. Which may include small rocket arms."

"Like a bazooka?" Hardy asked.

"Something like that," Grumpy said. "Only more advanced. Probably heat-seeking missiles like those favored by terrorists. American Red-eyes or Stingers, or perhaps Soviet Grail SA-7s or Chinese HN-5s."

"What do we do?" Hardy asked.

"Fight fire with fire," Grumpy said.

The side window behind Hardy opened and a huge handheld missile barrel appeared to his right. "This is going to be loud," Grumpy's voice warned as he leaned out as far as he could.

Hardy braced himself for the shock wave, or so he thought. The actual sound far exceeded anything he could have imagined or expected. Fire and burning heat spewed from the barrel just feet from his shoulder.

Fifty yards ahead of them the gate exploded. The pathway out glowed.

"Again," Grumpy warned.

A violent explosion rocked Hardy's head, with singeing pain along his right arm.

The missile obliterated the guard shack, leaving only burning scattered pieces of wood. No one could have survived the blast. Bashful floored the SUV and charged up the hill.

They drove past the main gate and escaped the compound. Now they needed to get past the town and to Flint's plane at the airstrip without being stopped.

CHAPTER 73

In the distance Hardy saw red, blue, and white, in quick flashes.

The *Federales. Heading toward us.*

"See that?" Hardy asked Grumpy.

"Yeah," Grumpy said. "There isn't an alternate route that gets us where we're trying to go. We'll have to pull off into the desert and wait for them to pass."

"If we can see their lights, can't they see ours?" Hardy asked.

Bashful shook his head. "Our headlights are off."

"I see a second set," Hardy added as the SUV came to a stop. "Looks as if we need to deal with two cars."

"Hang on." Grumpy stepped out of the SUV and walked twenty feet out into the desert, then returned in a jog. He climbed back in and shook his head. "The sand out here is too soft and deep to drive on. If we get off road here we're screwed."

"What else can we do?" Hardy asked.

"We fight," Grumpy said. "I need everyone out now. We'll hide in the desert and ambush them when they arrive." Grumpy pointed to each side of the SUV. "Two attack teams, one on each side. Sleepy, you'll take the packages to a spot to the side and way behind us so they're clear of the firing lines. I figure we have about two minutes before they get here. Let's move."

Hardy climbed out and opened the door behind the driver's seat. Grumpy handed him a blanket as he carried a wide-eyed Esteban onto the sand. Hardy and Juan followed Grumpy into the night, barely able to see him a few feet ahead. They moved down the road about fifty feet before angling into the desert at a ninety-degree angle. After running twenty feet into the desert Hardy set the blanket down and Grumpy set Esteban on top of it.

"You stay here," Grumpy instructed. "Don't move or speak no matter what you hear or see. Once we've neutralized them I'll come back for you."

"Okay. Good luck."

Grumpy patted Hardy on the back. "Luck has nothing to do with it." He ran back up the desert to join his half of the team.

"You came for us," Juan said, his voice weak. "You saved us."

Hardy smiled at him and whispered, "We still have work to do. Let's stay quiet for now and wait for the team to chase them off."

They waited in silence as two police cars came over the hill and stopped when they saw the deserted SUV two-dozen yards ahead. Policemen with automatic weapons took defensive positions around their cars.

"This is the Ensenada police," a voice boomed over a loudspeaker. "You're surrounded. Show yourselves, hands behind your heads."

The good guys opened fire from both sides, first taking out their lights, then shooting at their feet. Most of the police officers panicked and fled into the desert. A few chose to stay and fight, which cost them their lives.

The gunfire stopped, leaving a void of eerie silence. Hardy started to relax, then heard a humming sound approaching, getting gradually louder. At first he couldn't quite place it, but after a few seconds a sobering recognition struck him.

A helicopter was coming from the direction of the compound.

It came up over the hill with a bright light scanning the ground. Hardy froze, praying that it wouldn't flash on the three of them. As it flew over, the light temporarily blinded Hardy.

The helicopter moved past them before banking into a turn that would take it right back to where they were.

CHAPTER 74

Hardy knew he couldn't outrun the helicopter. He did the only thing he could think of—he moved over Esteban to shield him from the expected gunfire.

The helicopter came about and bored in on them. Hardy expected to hear gunfire at any moment.

The gunfire didn't bring the expected pain, only a scream from above. Hardy saw a man's body falling toward him. It landed with a thud a few feet away, a bullet hole in the forehead.

More shots rang through the night and someone on the team knocked the helicopter's light out. Hardy heard bullets piercing metal and glass, followed by the whining sound of a helicopter spiraling out of control.

Directly above him.

He didn't know where it might come down, but he knew that even if the helicopter missed them the explosion and shrapnel would be deadly.

He lifted Esteban up off the blanket, signaled for Juan to follow, and carried him farther into the desert as fast as he could run in the soft sand.

The whining increased in intensity and tempo, and the helicopter crashed into the desert about thirty feet away. A deafening explosion followed and the force from the impact blew sand, glass, and metal in all directions. Something sharp lodged itself in Hardy's shoulder.

A second explosion erupted as the helicopter's fuel went up like a torch on steroids. The heat from the burning fuel surrounded Hardy and he could sense his skin starting to burn again and knew that Esteban and Juan couldn't be any better off.

He forced his legs to keep pounding through the sand. Gradually the heat dissipated. Once he couldn't feel it any longer he lay Esteban down as gently as he could, sat Juan down next to him, and collapsed at their side.

*****

Hardy woke up to a gentle rocking motion, as if in a soothing dream. His mind pictured being in an oversized hammock on the beach in Hawaii, rocking to the steady beat of a low surf, with a mai tai in his hand and Sara curled up next to him.

He opened his eyes a sliver and saw Flint staring down at him instead. Hardy chuckled, which turned out to be a bad idea, irritating the pain in his shoulder.

"What's so funny, pard?"

Hardy managed a smile through the pain. "I don't want you to take this the wrong way, but you're so not who I was dreaming of."

Flint laughed. "Maybe you'd prefer the *Federales*?"

"I'll settle for you." Hardy poked his head up a touch, which also lit a fire in his shoulder, and saw that they were airborne on Flint's plane. "Juan and Esteban?"

"They're great. Just a few scrapes. You saved them. The heat from the helicopter fuel would have ignited all of your clothes if you hadn't moved them."

"Well, maybe."

"No maybe about it. The guy that fell from the helicopter went up in flames. Nothing left to even identify him. We thought it was you at first. After a short search we found the three of you. You have some first-degree stuff on the back of your neck and arms, but the gear protected most of your body. Juan and the boy appear to have a slight sunburn, but that's it."

"Who's flying the plane?"

Flint grinned. "They told me you were waking up, and I wanted to be here for that. Bashful is holding it steady while the autopilot does the work. I'll go back in a sec."

Grumpy joined Flint at Hardy's side. "How do you feel?"

"I'm good."

"Your shoulder will need patching up," he informed Hardy. "A piece of metal got in there, but the vest took most of the blow and it didn't sever anything. The cuts on your face may need a plastic surgeon, but you'll live."

"Have you called Sara yet?" Hardy asked.

"Still in radio silence until we get across the border," Flint said. "Which should be in a few minutes. I better get back in there. I think it only fair that you be the one to tell her."

Flint moved back into the cockpit, leaving Hardy with Grumpy.

"They're really okay?" Hardy asked.

"Yep. Playing cards a few rows back."

"You guys are unbelievable."

Grumpy shook his head and smiled. "Without you we'd all be fried to a crisp or gunned down. You did good."

Flint's voice rang out from the cockpit. "We're in US airspace. Two more hours and y'all be on the ground at Love Field in Dallas. That should be about eight a.m.—plenty of time to get you to the courthouse on time. What say you give Sara a call?"

Grumpy passed Hardy a satellite phone. Hardy dialed the safe house twice, fumbling the first attempt owing to nerves.

Sara answered on the first ring. "Hello?" She sounded awake but tired.

"Sara, it's Nicholas. We have Juan and Esteban. We're back in US airspace and we'll have them in Dallas in two hours." He received nothing but silence from the other end. "Sara? You there?"

"I'm here. I guess I'm kinda speechless."

"It's almost over."

"Did everyone make it out okay?"

"Yeah. We didn't see Rivera. But we destroyed his Baja compound. He's going to be pissed."

"Can I talk to them?"

"Of course. I'll pass the phone back. See you soon."

Grumpy passed the phone back, and Esteban squealed in excitement at the sound of his mother's voice.

Hardy spent the rest of the flight with his eyes closed, hoping to feed his exhausted body some sleep, but instead thinking about Sara. He imagined a future together, and he couldn't put that idea aside.

What's the matter with you, dude? She's resolved to stay in WITSEC.

His eyes blasted open.

So this is what love feels like.

CHAPTER 75

Dallas

They landed just after 8:00 a.m. at Love Field. Presley, Sara, and a dozen marshals met them on the runway. They escorted Juan and Esteban off first and hustled them to the van carrying Sara. Hardy watched them drive away, longing to speak with her.

Presley waited at the bottom of the steps for Hardy and Flint.

"Congratulations," Presley began. "I understand you overcame incredible odds down there."

Hardy let Flint respond. "Thanks, Marshal. Everyone came through."

Presley eyed them both. "Well done. Are you both still game for the next phase?"

"Absolutely," Hardy assured him. "I want to bury Rivera."

"Once Sara testifies the three of us will head to Nosara," Presley affirmed.

"What about Sara?" Hardy asked.

"Once she testifies," Presley said, "she'll be relocated to her new location with her family. They'll have a new US marshal. My time with her will be over. I won't even know where she is."

"That must be hard," Hardy said. "You've put so much into her protection."

"It's how it works."

"Still, it has to suck."

Presley showed a hint of emotion for the first time since they landed. "Yeah, it sucks." He gave Hardy a knowing look. "For both of us."

*****

Hardy rehearsed his pitch for Sara all the way to the safe house. He was pumped up, certain that his revelation of loving her, no, of being *in love* with her, would change everything. He knew she felt the same way about him. He *knew* it.

They parked in the back and Hardy ran inside. He scrambled up the stairs, ready to barge into her room, when he saw Grumpy at her closed door.

"Hold on, Sleepy," Grumpy said. "She asked for some privacy with her family while she gets ready for her testimony today."

She can't mean me, Hardy thought.

"Sara," Hardy called out. "It's Nicholas."

After an awkward silence, she answered. "Not now, Nicholas. I have to get ready."

All of the air in his lungs vanished, and he gasped. "Sara? I have to tell you something. It can't wait."

Presley came up behind him. "What's up?"

Hardy turned to him. "I need to see Sara before you leave for the trial."

Grumpy said to Presley, "She says she wants to be left alone."

Presley stepped to the door and spoke softly. "Sara? How you doing in there?"

"I'm okay. I'll be ready."

"Did you get a chance to thank Nick personally for what he did in Mexico? It might be your last chance."

Hardy watched the door open a crack and saw just enough of Sara's face to see she was crying.

"Thank you, Nicholas," she stuttered. "I'll never be able to re-pay you."

"Can I come in?"

She shook her head. "I can't do this right now. I need to focus on my testimony. So I can move on with my life."

"Your life should be with me," Hardy blurted out. "You know I love you. And I know you love me, too."

Sara stared at the floor. "Nicholas, I told you that's never happening. Please leave me alone now."

"How can you say that?"

She closed the door. "Good-bye, Nicholas. Thank you for everything. Marshal Presley?"

"Yes."

"I'd like to go to the courthouse, just you, me, and Juan. Can we do that?"

Presley lowered his head and didn't make eye contact with Hardy. "Of course."

Hardy took one step toward the door, which caused Grumpy to straighten up. "Don't do it, Sleepy."

"My name is Nick. Nick Hardy." Hardy glared at Presley. "And you both suck."

Hardy careened down the stairs and stormed out the front door.

CHAPTER 76

Hardy ignored the yelling behind him and ran. A zig here and a zag there, through yards and open fields, and he was convinced he'd lost them.

He still had Presley's wad of cash in his front pocket, and a parched throat. Everything he needed.

Poker and tequila. That will cure what ails you.

He found a main drag and hailed a cab. He climbed in and threw a C-note in the front seat.

"I need a private poker game. One where the cards are hot, the women are hotter, and the drinks are cold."

The Hispanic driver smiled a yellow, rotting mess in Hardy's direction. "There is a club downtown. You a cop?"

"No. And if you see any US marshals, don't tell them where I went. Deal?"

"Sí, señor."

*****

A tiny Asian man glared at Hardy at the club's entrance. Hardy flashed a grand at him, and he let Hardy by. Ahead, a lone nine-seat poker table. A dealer in a green vest, matching the table's felt, hand shuffled a single deck and dealt two hole cards to six players. Hardy grabbed an empty seat and a blonde right out of the adult film industry brought him chips. After ordering a tequila straight up, he turned his attention to the room.

The dark room reeked of tobacco and nicotine. Surrounded by wood paneling from the seventies, and no windows, he couldn't help feeling claustrophobic.

Tequila. That's what will fix that.

As if on cue, his drink arrived. He downed it in one swallow and signaled for blondie to bring him another one.

They finished the hand and he got dealt his two cards, facedown. He peeked and saw two queens.

He had few superstitions, but one he held dear was to not win the first hand. History had taught him those nights were some of his worst.

But he had two queens. He bet. Some skinny lady in sunglasses and a cigarette burned to the nub raised him.

Superstition aside, he went all in for his grand. Right after draining a second tequila and ordering a third. This place had found a way to make tequila taste mediocre, but he didn't care.

All aboard for a tequila sunrise.

The skinny smoker grunted and folded.

Hardy didn't know whether to be happy or sad. He collected his money and tipped the dealer generously.

What the hell. I'm playing with free money.

He drank and bet and bet and drank. Somehow he stayed erect, and his chip stack stayed close to even.

Blondie came by again and he signaled for more, but she ignored him and walked past.

"Hey," he yelled, watching her wiggle by. "Blondie. Busty. Whatever your name is. I asked for another shot."

She ignored him, which is more than he could say for the beefy Asian who came out of the shadows. He grabbed Hardy by the front of his shirt and ripped him off of his chair.

"Excuse me, sir, but you're no longer welcome in this establishment," he said in a thick accent, twisting Hardy away from the table.

Hardy tensed to apply some of his martial arts training, but stumbled over his chair and crashed to the floor. He heard laughter.

He popped back up, but found his arms held against his back by two more bouncers. They dragged him to the door, and threw him into the street, where he crashed onto a layer of trash.

"Hey, my money's in there," Hardy yelled.

The door slammed and the man guarding it stepped in front of it. He eased his jacket off his hip just enough to show Hardy his pistol.

"My money," Hardy repeated. "I'll go. But give me back my money."

The guard smirked and slammed the door.

Hardy laughed. He wasn't sure why.

Yeah, buddy. The joke's on you. You may have taken all my money, but I got free drinks. On top of that, I got dissed by my girl. Yay, me.

A black SUV with no plates came screeching around the corner and skidded to a stop in front of Hardy. He stared at the darkened windows, wondering who might be inside. The front passenger window cruised down and Hardy was face-to-face with Flint in the driver's seat.

"Nick, get in," Flint said. "Presley's having a conniption."

"But not Sara."

Flint shut off the engine and got out, standing on the far side. "Dammit, Nick, get in the car. This isn't the time or place."

Hardy chuckled. *Like there's a time and place for any of this.*

"You can go back. I'm not coming."

Flint charged to Hardy and shook him. "Sara's getting ready to testify, and you're going to be there. Do I have to whip you, or are you coming voluntarily?"

"How'd you find me, anyway?"

"There aren't that many poker clubs still going at this hour. Now, do I have to kick your ass?"

Hardy got in the passenger seat. "Whatever."

"How smashed are you?"

"You know I can handle my liquor. I'm fine."

"You better be when you see Sara. Or I'll be the least of your troubles."

CHAPTER 77

Sara opened her bedroom door and stepped back at the sight of Hardy. She wore a dark-blue skirt and jacket with a white blouse. The skirt was short enough to expose her upper thighs as well as her curvaceous legs. She wore a bulletproof vest under her blouse. "I'm glad you came back. I need you at the trial. I'm sorry if I hurt your feelings."

Hardy glowered at her. "And I'm sorry you didn't care enough to feel any remorse discarding me like that. I wasn't even worth saying good-bye to."

Her face flushed and she charged him, stopping right in his face. "You idiot. Don't you know how hard this is for me? Don't you know how much I love you?"

Hardy raised his voice to match hers. "You sure have a funny way of showing it."

She slapped him. Hard. Tears were running down her cheek. "I couldn't see you because it hurts too much. My life isn't mine. I don't get to choose to do any of the things I want to do. I thought you, of all people, knew me well enough to know how badly I ache at being forced into seclusion again."

"Then don't do it."

She clenched her teeth and screamed at him. "I don't have a choice." After a short pause, she continued at a new, improved decibel level. "And why would I want to be with you, anyway. Look at you. The first sign of trouble you run to your poker and your booze. You're no better than the addicts Manuel lives off of."

Her words stunned him. He tried to reply, but had nothing.

Sara took a deep breath and leaned into Hardy. "I'm sorry, Nicholas. I didn't mean that. I'm just so upset."

"You have every right to be. I'm the one who should be sorry. You made it clear from the beginning that this wouldn't last."

"I'm too dangerous to be with. Certainly you can see that."

Hardy kissed the top of her head. "You know I want to be with you, no matter what. But you're right about one thing. I have an addiction, and I need to get it under control."

Presley stepped up and cleared his throat. "Sara, are you ready to testify?"

She smiled at Hardy. "Are we ready?"

Hardy winked. "Absolutely."

"Let's end this once and for all."

Presley eyed them both. "Once you testify, you'll be taken from the courthouse to your new life. With a new marshal."

Sara felt Hardy sag and looked up at him. "This is the hardest thing I've ever had to do. But it's the right thing. For you, me, and Esteban."

He hugged her, knowing none of this was right for him, but not wanting to burden her any more.

They drove to the courthouse in silence.

CHAPTER 78

They rolled down the private driveway of the courthouse toward the underground entrance. Getting underground calmed Hardy. He'd seen too much in the last week to feel comfortable out in the open, in spite of Presley's assurances and the convoy of vans.

"Rivera has to be going crazy," Sara said. "He could try anything today."

"Yes," Presley said. "His hope of you testifying for Ortega is gone. Now he needs to stop you from testifying at all. We'll be ready for anything he tries to throw at us."

The inspectors in five other vans emptied and surrounded Sara's van before Presley opened the doors. Juan joined her and they exited single file, with a dozen armed inspectors surrounding them.

Keep sharp, Hardy thought. *Don't underestimate Rivera's influence.*

Presley explained the precautions being taken. "The garage has been cleared and swept for bombs. We'll be taking a dedicated stairwell from the garage. The courtroom is on the fifth floor, and the exits in our stairway are barricaded at each floor other than the fifth, with marshals at each door inside the building. The fifth floor has three marshals standing watch within the stairwell. Once at the fifth floor we will be escorted into a windowless side room. The room has reinforced steel walls and doors, and a combination keypad that only I and the local US marshal know the combination to.

"The marshals scan everyone who enters the building, and perform random searches. They repeat the scans and searches for anyone entering the fifth floor, which can only be done by way of the interior stairwell, and then again at our courtroom. Two dogs at the entrance and the fifth-floor stairwell check for explosives. The courtroom windows are all sealed and fitted with bulletproof glass, and an electronic scrambler in the courtroom makes it impossible to listen to the proceedings from outside the room.

"We'll be escorted up our dedicated stairwell by three marshals in the lead, followed by our party, followed by three more marshals. Sara is scheduled to be the first witness after court reconvenes, so we'll only be in the side room for a few minutes. Another team of inspectors is inside the courtroom."

Still, Hardy couldn't help feeling anxious. Presley looked like a man feeling the same thing.

When they reached the stairwell Presley motioned for Flint to get in behind the three marshals on escort duty, followed by Hardy, Juan, and Sara. He brought up the rear of the fivesome, followed by three more marshals. They started walking up to the fifth-floor courtroom in single file.

They made it as far as the third-floor landing when Flint flinched.

"What?" Hardy whispered to him, looking up the stairwell to see what Flint saw.

Three men in US marshal jackets stood on the fifth-floor landing. They all showed emotionless faces.

"The guy on the right," Flint whispered back without turning his head or taking his full attention off the fifth-floor landing above. "He hasn't taken his eyes off of her. The others are all taking in everything. And he's leaking oil."

"Is that surprising?" Hardy asked. "She *is* the alleged target."

Hardy knew Flint's instincts to be impeccable, and he stood a little taller to try to make it harder to see Sara from up there.

His movement triggered an immediate reaction from the marshal Flint had pointed out. In one smooth and quick motion he pulled his handgun and aimed down the stairwell at Sara.

CHAPTER 79

The marshal's move caused a chain reaction in the stairwell. The other marshal's all assumed he had seen a threat to Sara, and pulled their weapons while shouting, "Gun!" Flint and Hardy tried to move toward Sara to protect her, but were tackled by the marshals in front of them as they sorted out the threat. Sara and Juan were dropped to their knees to shield them.

Hardy was slammed to the concrete steps. He saw Presley frantically spinning around to locate the threat. Presley screamed at the marshal who had started it all. "What do you have?"

The marshal who had ridden Hardy to the ground had left himself vulnerable to a few simple countermeasures, and Hardy was back on his feet in a second, staring up at the marshal who'd drawn first. Hardy's escape brought more attention as a threat, and now all the guns were pointed at him. "Freeze!" came a command from half a dozen marshals all at once.

Presley grabbed Hardy's arms and pinned them behind him. "Stand down!" he commanded. "I have him."

He leaned into Hardy and whispered, "Are you out of your mind?"

"Flint didn't like the look of the marshal that drew the gun," Hardy whispered back. "I tried to get between Sara and him. That's when he drew the gun."

The marshal in question sweated profusely, his hand shaking.

"Okay, everybody relax!" Presley commanded. "Shoulder your weapons."

The marshals all looked at each other, then start to comply. Even the suspect on the fifth floor.

Presley addressed the marshal who'd drawn first. "You, on the stairs. What did you see?"

"The man you're holding started acting suspicious," the marshal called down.

All the weapons were squared away. Presley signaled to let Sara, Juan, and Flint allowed back on their feet. "Okay, listen up. This guy is with me. I vouch for him completely."

Hardy kept his eye on the marshal who'd drawn the gun. Presley whispered something to Flint, who leaned into Presley and then stepped back toward Sara.

"I'm going to release him now," Presley said, "and we'll start back up the stairs. Are we clear?"

He was met with concurrence.

Presley started to release Hardy when the marshal at the fifth floor again drew his gun with lighting speed and aimed it at Sara. In that split second Hardy knew none of the other marshals had time to draw in time.

A shot rang out from behind him, echoing violently throughout the stairwell.

The marshal collapsed, a bullet hole square in his forehead, just as the two men with him grabbed him, again shouting, "Gun!" and pulled him down to the ground.

Hardy turned and saw Flint holding a smoking gun.

The gunshot brought an immediate reaction from the marshals on the stairs. The marshals again shoved Juan and Sara to their knees, a sea of bulletproof vests around them. Flint was grabbed, disarmed, and brought to his knees with guns pointed at him.

Presley let go of Hardy and shouted to the marshals, "It's over! The marshal up there was the threat."

Presley's declaration was met with confused looks, but gradually everyone seemed to recognize the fact that the marshal had pulled his gun twice, even after being told to stand down. The marshals released Flint and he dusted himself off.

Presley reached down and picked up the gun that Flint had used. He raised it in the air and slowly moved in a circle so that he could see every marshal and address them face-to-face.

"This is my weapon," he announced. "I asked this man, a former police officer and highly trained in small-weapons fire, to take it out of my holster while I was occupied with Mr. Hardy in case that marshal drew his weapon again. I asked him to use lethal force if necessary to protect our witness. So he was acting on my orders."

Presley holstered his weapon. "Now, for the record, I fired that shot. Flint was unarmed, and I fired it. Does everyone understand?"

The marshals all nodded.

"Good," Presley said. Then, pointing up the stairs, "Now get that piece of shit out of my sight."

The marshals at the fifth floor removed the rogue inspector before Sara arrived on the fifth-floor landing, a pool of blood the only remnant of his existence.

Big Bill Billingsley met Sara at the entrance of the reinforced side room, and Hardy, Presley, Flint, and Juan went inside with them. The rest of the marshals stood guard around the perimeter of the room.

Juan and Sara took seats while Hardy fetched them each a bottle of water from an ice bucket on the credenza. "You okay?" Hardy asked in a soft voice when he returned to them, belying the fact that his heart raced out of control.

Sara held onto Juan. "What would the day be without a little excitement."

Hardy cracked up. *In spite of being the subject of numerous murder attempts, she makes us laugh.*

"We can postpone your testimony if you'd like," Presley said, which drew a frown from Billingsley, who Hardy disliked more by the minute. "The judge knows what's going on, and he will give us plenty of leeway."

She shook her head vehemently. "No. I want to get it over with. The sooner we testify the sooner I can reunite my family and get on to our new life."

Presley looked up at Billingsley. "Okay. Let's do it."

Hardy went to the corner with Flint, and Presley joined them. Presley held his hand out and Flint shook it.

"How did you know he was dirty?" Presley asked.

"Just a feeling," Flint said. "I didn't like his stance and demeanor. He looked too focused. Like a polecat eyeing its prey."

Presley took a deep breath. "Exceptional work."

"Do we know who he is?" Flint asked.

Presley shook his head. "One of the local inspectors. I interviewed him myself, and he passed all the checks. He's probably been under Rivera's influence since they set the trial here in Dallas."

Hardy lowered his voice so Sara, who was going over her testimony with Billingsley, couldn't hear easily. "Is it safe for her to go in there?"

"I'll be with her the entire time."

Billingsley rose and joined them. "It's time. She's ready. I'll go in first. Wait five minutes, then bring them in. Don't screw it up for me now."

Presley lost his professional demeanor with that last crack and shoved Billingsley up against the wall. Nobody made a move to restrain him. It took all of Hardy's self-control to keep from piling on.

"You prick," Presley said. "You think I care about your reputation? I care about her. She has put her life, her brother's life, her child's life, on the line every day while you sit back and work your career. She lost her husband. You're nothing compared to her."

He shoved the startled Billingsley aside and glared at him, daring him to say another word. Billingsley might have been an egomaniac, but he was smart enough to know to get out of there without saying anything else.

He slunk out and Sara came up to Presley and hugged him. "I'm going to miss you."

"Me, too," he said as he allowed himself to be hugged.

She let go and came over to Hardy and Flint. "I guess this is it. Later today Juan and I will be on our way to a new home, and you'll be on your way to Costa Rica. Thank you both for everything. Obviously, without you I wouldn't have made it."

Before Hardy could respond she leaned up and kissed him on the lips. "I don't know how to say good-bye to you."

"I don't either."

Presley opened the door, Sara took Hardy's hand, and the five of them marched to the courtroom.

CHAPTER 80

Once in the courtroom Sara went directly to the stand and was sworn in. Hardy and Flint took reserved back-row seats. Juan sat surrounded by marshals near the front of the courtroom. Men and women in US marshal jackets sat at the end of each row. Presley sat at the table with Billingsley, and two marshals stood on each side of the witness stand where Sara sat.

Victor Ortega sat in the defendant's chair next to the defense attorney. He, small in stature, gasped when Sara walked in.

Billingsley asked Sara about the events of the night of the murder, and she gave an accurate recount without flinching. She described the history of Ortega and Rivera's pattern of violent behavior, often over the objections of the defense attorney, who repeatedly was overruled. Sara effectively solidified the case against Ortega, and the twelve jurists appeared mesmerized by her and her story. Ortega was in big trouble, and he knew it. He became more agitated and vocal with his attorney as the testimony progressed, powerless to stop the guilty verdict that seemed inevitable.

Finally the pressure grew to be too much for Ortega, who stood unexpectedly.

"You traitor," he screamed at Sara, who kept her composure. "You're lying to protect your dead husband."

The judge pounded his gavel as the entire courtroom broke out in murmurs and uncomfortable shifting around. "Order!" he commanded. "Counsel, get your client under control or I'll have him removed."

The defense attorney tried to assist Ortega in being seated, and Ortega threw his arm off to the side and glared at him with an angry, warning look. "Don't you touch me, you incompetent fool. This is all your fault. You're letting that piece of trash tell lies about me."

The judge pounded his gavel again and signaled to the marshal standing watch by the defendant's table to take control of the situation. The marshal came up behind Ortega and shoved him into his seat. He clearly relished doing it.

"One more outburst, Mr. Ortega, and you'll be removed," the judge warned.

Ortega seethed in his seat as Sara completed her testimony. Once Billingsley finished he turned it over to the defense attorney, who did his best to attack her character and her story. He tried to paint Sara as a bitter woman who had been dumped by Ortega and was trying to extract a measure of revenge.

Ortega watched Sara deflect the defense attorney's desperate salvos easily, until Ortega stood again and screamed at her. "You will pay for this. You will be struck down for your filthy lies."

The marshal grabbed Ortega from behind to escort him out. Sara responded before he could leave the courtroom.

"Victor, you made your own bed, and now you have to lie in it. One day we will all be judged. I've made mistakes in my life also, and maybe God will judge me harshly. But I've told nothing but the truth here, and I'll take full responsibility for everything I've done in my life. You might want to do the same. God will listen."

The marshals ushered a thrashing Ortega out. Meanwhile, the defense attorney returned slowly to his table, defeated in his attempt to discredit Sara. His face showed the hopelessness of a man with little time left to live.

Presley whisked Sara off the stand and escorted her back to the reinforced side room, Hardy and Flint following. Once inside she fell into Hardy's arms and they held each other for several minutes.

"It's all over," Hardy said. "You did great. I'm so proud of you."

"I'm so glad that's behind me."

Presley came up and cleared his throat. "Sara, sorry to break in, but you and I need to go now. A team of US marshals is waiting to take you and your family away to your new location. Meanwhile, the three of us have some unfinished business to take care of in Costa Rica."

"Don't take any chances down there," Sara said. "If he won't go for it, or if he suspects anything, get out of there. I need to know you're all coming back in one piece."

She turned back to Hardy and held him again. "I wish everything was different." She kissed Hardy one last time and then stepped over to Presley. "I'm ready."

Presley escorted her back outside. A sea of marshals surrounded her and she left in an instant.

"She's going to be fine now," Flint said.

"I suppose," Hardy said. "Do you really think we can put Rivera in a position where he can't hurt her?"

"Pard, I doubt we'd get good odds in Vegas. Then again, I didn't think we'd get this far."

CHAPTER 81

Nosara, Costa Rica

Hardy, Flint, and Presley landed in Flint's plane on a single runway in the jungle.

"Any other marshals coming?" Hardy asked Presley.

He shook his head. "I'm on vacation. We're on our own."

The thick air smelled of burning animal fat and salty ocean breezes. Howler monkeys wailed from high in the trees. A National rental car rep met them and turned over the keys to a minivan.

They took the unpaved main drag through town and into the beach community. The only ones moving with any urgency were surfers scurrying to the sand.

"Where is everybody?" Hardy asked. "It seems deserted."

"Just surfers and folks hiking the jungle," Presley said. "The road in isn't paved. Keeps most of the tourists away."

Hardy admired the palm trees and thick green vegetation. "It reminds me of Kauai. I bet it rains every day."

"Mostly inland." Presley said. "When a storm hits, it hits hard."

They pulled up in front of a quiet office building two short blocks from the beach. They climbed the stairs to the top floor, which consisted of one large office suite. They had rented the entire floor for the month, and Hardy could smell fresh paint. They stepped off the stairs and into a reception area decorated in an array of pastels, with two large vases and several paintings of local landmarks. A large sign announced the entire floor as the home of Salazar Enterprises.

There were two doors behind the reception desk, one on each side. The one on the left had a nameplate for the owner, Raquel Salazar. The one on the right was unlabeled.

Alice and Raquel waited in the reception area. Raquel's long black hair shimmered in the fluorescent light. She wore a tan skirt that showed off firm legs, a matching blouse that showed off her full figure, and black boots. She could just as easily have been a magazine cover model as a successful businesswoman.

Flint took Hardy directly to her. "Nick, this is Raquel Salazar. Raquel, Nick Hardy."

"It's a pleasure to meet you," she said with a smile that lit up the room with straight, white teeth.

Hardy shook her hand. "Good to meet you. I can't tell you how much we appreciate you doing this. I assure you we'll have your back."

"Thanks. It'll be fun."

Hardy gave Flint a "just what did you tell her?" expression, but Flint just smiled.

Alice opened the door to Raquel's private office. "This is where we'll meet with Rivera. The room has a video camera and microphone installed in the smoke detector. The feed goes into the room next door, which is set up to monitor everything in here. The suite also has five beds and two bathrooms so we don't have to leave the building tonight."

"Nice," Hardy said. "What about wireless?"

Raquel moved to the laptop on her desk. "We installed a private network and you can get access anywhere on the floor."

Hardy pulled out his cell phone to test it. "Password?"

Raquel smiled. "KickRiverainthenuts."

"Oh, I like the sound of that," Flint said, raising his eyebrows at Raquel.

"I thought you might," Raquel continued. She walked past Flint and gave him a sexy smile.

Alice glared at them both. "Can we get back on task here?"

Hardy pulled up a news website on his cell phone to test the router access. He stared at the screen in shock.

"Guys, we have a problem."

CHAPTER 82

"What's wrong?" Presley asked.

Hardy showed him the screen. A picture of Hardy and Flint in the Dallas courtroom sat under the caption "US Marshal Gunned Down in Dallas Courthouse." Under that was the subcaption "Two Men Wanted for Questioning."

Presley glared at the screen, his face turning a darker shade of red. "What site is this?"

"CNN. How'd they get this? How'd they get our picture from inside the courthouse?"

Presley shook his head. "Let me see that."

Hardy handed him the phone so he could read the story. Flint came over and read it over his shoulder.

Presley handed the phone back. "That prick."

"Who?" Hardy asked.

Presley put his hands on his hips. "Billingsley. He put this out. That attention-mongering moron. Must have snuck someone inside the courtroom with a camera."

"What do we do?" Hardy asked.

Presley thought for a moment, then said, "Nothing. I'll take care of it. You guys aren't going to get questioned about what happened in there. The Dallas US Marshals will get the investigation closed."

Presley stepped to the side and made a call on his cell phone.

Flint took advantage of the lull to scramble into the bathroom, emerging moments later in shorts, sandals, and a green island shirt with a golf course etched on the back. "That's better. Now I can work."

"Okay," Presley said as he returned. "That's handled. The picture and story will be pulled and Billingsley will be ordered to stand down. Now, let's see where we are." He motioned for each of them to take a seat around the desk.

Alice sat at the laptop. She took a remote and turned on the flat screen mounted on the wall, which displayed her computer screen. Pictures of Rivera and Delgado came up, which turned Hardy's stomach. "Here's the target on the left. We should know in twenty-four hours if he's going to take the bait. He's vulnerable right now. Not only has he failed in eliminating Sara before the trial, but his thirst for power has him expanding his business in many directions, which has him taking money from underworld figures and promising outrageous rates of return."

"I've been able to confirm with knowledgeable sources he's extended himself quite a bit," Raquel added. "It's a classic case of ego and greed driving business decisions. Happens all the time. Especially with people who have been protected like he has. He feels invincible."

"The man on the right is Delgado," Presley said. "He never leaves Rivera's side, and he'll be armed."

Next Alice displayed a newspaper article and a website page side by side.

"Here's the bait," she continued. "Two articles, one in the local paper we know he reads every morning, and one on the Internet. The article talks about how Raquel is expanding her financial empire and looking for partners in the region. It references her investment performance over ten years."

She moved the cursor over to the website. "The website has more details, and has enough true background that will give the story credibility. All the financial declarations are public and verifiable when he checks into her."

Hardy squirmed. "He can't use the information we're handing over to him against her in the future, right?"

"Oh," Raquel said, "don't worry about that. I'm impossible to find if I don't want to be found. I have no corporate address. No one knows what country I live in. I work at my estate, and it's well protected. He won't get near me without a hundred people knowing it."

"We found you," Hardy said.

"I saw Flint coming long before I let him find me. I'm not worried about it. You shouldn't be either."

Alice continued. "The article states Raquel is in Nosara for just two days and will choose her partner before she leaves. We've included two of her pictures to show off her beauty. Rivera will see her as both a person that can make him more powerful, but also as a personal conquest. He'll see Raquel as the holy grail for his affirmation as a romantic figure in the region."

Alice flipped to the next screen, which showed financial summaries. "Here are Raquel's official financial ledgers. The track record speaks for itself. He'll want in on the ground floor."

She flipped to the next screen. "Here's the fund we've set up. We put the Marshals Service five hundred million in here. Once Rivera wires his money in here, we'll have crippled him. We close it down, take his money without a trace, and he's left without the cash to pay back his investors. Even if he can keep his operation afloat for a while, his investors will want his neck."

"What if he shows but doesn't go for it?" Hardy asked. "Do we let him walk out of here? We were prepared to kill him in Baja. We can just take him out."

Presley fidgeted. "The situation in Baja was different. We were on a rescue mission, and we knew there'd be resistance and shooting. So if he'd been killed as part of meeting our objective of getting Juan and Esteban back, so be it. If we kill him, someone will take over his empire and will just continue operations. Our best play is to get rid of him as a threat and cripple his operation."

"What if he won't come?" Flint asked. "Don't we have extradition treaties with Costa Rica?"

Alice answered. "We knew we needed to get him out of Mexico so we could set up shop without him knowing about it. We picked Costa Rica because we think he'll feel safe here. He gets some of his drugs via the main highway through the country. He can get here discretely. We weren't going to get him to a country that didn't have extradition. We thought Costa Rica was our best shot."

"If he doesn't show," Presley said, "we go home. We're not going to chase him on his turf. The Marshals Service is prepared to protect Sara. But I think he'll come. The hard part is getting him to transfer enough money to damage his chance to operate and survive." He turned to Hardy. "That's where you come in. You'll be his competition. For the right to be Raquel's business partner and get in on the ground floor on her stock choice."

Flint shook his head. "Why Nick? He's heard Nick's voice. He hasn't heard mine. We'll all be in the room in disguises, but Nick has a big speaking part."

"I insist, my friend," Hardy said. "I know you could pull it off, but this is my chance to assure Sara a safe future. I need to do it. My makeup specialist from Hollywood will be here later. She'll take good care of us."

Flint fidgeted in his seat. "I still don't like it."

Hardy waved away his concern. "Don't worry, you'll be watching the whole time. In the unlikely event he recognizes me, I know you'll have my back."

"If that happens I *will* take him out," Flint said.

Hardy shook his head. "Remember, our most effective play is to get his money. Then his creditors will take care of him for us, and his drug operation will be in chaos."

Presley turned to Raquel. "Do you have any questions or concerns? We can stop if you're uncomfortable."

Raquel shook her head. "Alice tells me Sara is a special woman, and we can end her nightmare right here. I'm in."

Hardy still felt uncomfortable. "Do we really need to use Raquel's real name and business info? Can't we make something up so he can't trace it back to anyone?"

"He'd see through it," Alice said. "His people are paid handsomely to be thorough. It has to be a legitimate business to pass his smell test."

"Okay," Hardy said. "I guess you know best. How is Rivera supposed to reach us?"

"Answering service in Spain," Alice said. "We didn't want them coming unannounced. The service will set up an appointment with him, then they'll call."

"He has to be out of his mind with rage," Hardy said.

Presley grinned. "We're counting on it. Sara says that when he's angry he gets impulsive, needing to feel better right away. Just another consideration on our side of the ledger."

"What else is there to do?" Hardy asked.

"Now we wait," Presley said. "See if he takes the bait."

Presley's cell phone rang. Hardy sat up straight, hoping the call was the answering service. After a short conversation Presley put the phone to his chest. "Ortega's jury came back with a guilty verdict of murder in the first degree. Sentencing to come."

Flint stood. "This calls for a celebration. There's a liquor store around the corner. What's your pleasure?"

"Don Julio," Raquel said. "Several bottles."

Presley continued on the line. "What do you mean? When? How?"

Hardy felt his heart race. *Now what?*

"Okay," Presley said before hanging up. He bowed his head.

"What?" Hardy asked, terrified to hear the answer.

"Sara's disappeared," Presley said.

CHAPTER 83

Hardy stiffened. "What do you mean, disappeared?"

"She evaded her protection detail and vanished. Before she was reunited with Juan and Esteban."

"Could Rivera have gotten to her?" Hardy asked. *Of course it's Rivera. Who else can it be?*

Presley shook his head. "No sign of a struggle. No demands about her family. The marshal thinks she just left."

"Without Esteban?" Hardy said. "No way."

"Pard's right. Something's wrong."

Hardy gulped. "Rivera's the only explanation."

"I don't know what to think," Presley said. "We have everybody looking for her."

Alice's text message tone caused them all to jump. She glanced at her screen. "Excuse me. Urgent business back home." She stepped away into the hallway.

"Does this change anything?" Raquel asked.

"No," Hardy said. "We go through with it. We end him, no matter what."

CHAPTER 84

Arena Jones, a makeup magician and legend, and onetime former lover of Hardy's, showed up in a tight-fitting tube top, short shorts that showed off thin, firm legs, and two large cases that were rolled in by a male assistant with massive arms. She was the most sought-after makeup artist in Hollywood, and not because of her looks. She was peerless in the talent department.

Everyone was introduced and she got down to business. She had the three men who needed disguises sit next to each other on a couch and studied them.

"We need to assume he knows what we all look and sound like," Hardy said.

She reached into one of her cases. "Okay. I'll fit you with a mouthpiece that will cause a natural adjustment to your voice. It's my own design."

She turned her attention to Presley. "You'll be the attorney, right?" Then to Flint. "And you don't have a speaking part."

Flint laughed. "Yeah. What a waste, eh? If I do need to say something, he's never heard my voice."

She pulled out several tanned masks and hairpieces. Hardy felt like he was on the set of a *Mission Impossible* movie.

"Let's try these on and see how you look."

She began with Hardy. Once she was satisfied she handed Hardy a mirror.

Jeez, Hardy thought. *No way he'll know it's me.*

Hardy sold the investment banker look in his zillion-dollar suit. His hair color was now pitch black, with a local tan and a mustache that hinted of graceful aging. She gave him his mouthpiece and he croaked, "Nice, Arena. He'll never know." The voice was deeper and grating.

"I've known you for years and I wouldn't recognize you on the street." Arena said.

Raquel circled him, looking for any sign of a flaw in his disguise. "It's amazing. I had no idea this could be done. I always assumed the camera hid some flaw in the costumes."

"There's no hiding anything these days. High def shows it all."

Once Flint and Presley were in costume, Arena approached Hardy, took his hand, and whispered in his ear, her tongue making light contact and sending a chill down his spine. "Maybe you and I should go have our own private party. Like that time in the dressing room?"

Hardy lay his forehead gently on hers. "That was a long time ago."

"All the more reason to get together soon."

He smiled and kissed her on the cheek. "It's complicated."

"Hmm." She leaned into him, her breasts rubbing up against his chest. "Well, if you ever want uncomplicated, you know where to reach me. I'll hang around to help you all get in costume tomorrow."

*****

"Anybody seen Alice?" Presley asked an hour later.

"She stepped out," Raquel said.

Flint cocked his head. "Alone? Is that a good idea?"

Raquel shrugged. "She's a big girl. 'Why' is none of my business."

*****

Raquel's cell phone rang an hour later. Alice was still missing.

"He went for it," a German voice told her. "Six tomorrow morning. You'll have ninety minutes before the stock market opens, and two hours before the local banks open."

She hung up and grinned at Hardy. "Rivera took the bait. You're up first thing tomorrow."

Just then Alice walked in, meeting their stares with disdain. "What? Can't a lady go for a walk?"

"Rivera will be here in the morning," Raquel said. "Before the open."

Alice didn't look up. "Then we know what we have to do." She walked away, texting.

CHAPTER 85

Flint woke up to whispers. He checked the time—four hours to showtime—and sat up. Hardy and Presley were sleeping near him on cots in the video surveillance room. The voices were coming from the next room, where Raquel and Alice had bunked.

He leaned forward, as if the extra few inches would help him hear. When that failed, he grumbled and crawled out of bed. After a stretch and back crack, he opened the door and entered the women's inner sanctum.

Alice stood at a sink with a glass of water. Raquel sat on a sofa. Tension was selling for two cents a ton.

"Hey," Flint said. "Can't sleep?"

Alice glared at him. "This doesn't concern you, Mr. Flint."

"Whoa. I'm a white hat. Remember?"

Raquel motioned for Flint to join her, which intensified Alice's glare. "She's just a little on edge. Maybe you can calm her down."

Alice slammed the glass down, shattering it in her hand. Blood splattered the counter. "You condescending bitch."

Flint wanted to get the hell out of there, but couldn't ignore the blood. He ran to Alice and wrapped her hand in some paper towels. He tried to get her to focus on him, but Alice's attention was firmly placed on Raquel. "Raquel, get me the first aid kit under the sink."

Raquel rushed to comply, which seemed to irritate Alice even more. She handed the kit to Flint, who pulled out some tweezers and anti-septic. "Hold still. I need to clean the wound."

He dabbed at Alice's hand. Satisfied the wound didn't contain any glass, he poured a generous dose of antibiotic on it. She clenched her teeth, and her eyes watered, but she didn't scream.

"What the hell was that all about?" he asked.

Alice straightened her posture. "It seems I've been deceived."

Flint looked to Raquel for clarification, but got no reaction.

"About tomorrow?" Flint asked. "Because if there's a problem, I need to wake the others up and we need to figure it out."

"No," Alice said. "Nothing about that. No need to involve the others. I'm sorry to have troubled you." She let Flint wrap it in a bandage and tape some gauze to it.

"You'll need to see your doctor when we get home," Flint said.

"Fine. Now, if you'll excuse me, I would like to get some rest." She gave Raquel and Flint one last glare for the night and trudged off to a cot in the corner.

"What was that all about?" Flint whispered to Raquel.

Raquel sighed, watching Alice crawl onto the cot. "I hurt her feelings."

Flint waited for clarification.

"Apparently she thought there was more going on between us than there is."

Flint almost choked. "You're . . . ?"

Raquel shook her head. "Not really, no. I've played both sides, including some wonderful time with her, but my preference is to be with a man."

"And she wants more."

"I told her I was more interested in you than in forging a deeper relationship with her."

Flint's heart kicked it up a notch. "Um, that's great, but maybe this isn't the time to get her all riled up."

Raquel grinned. "You're cute when you don't know what to say. But, you're right. We have a job to do and we don't need any distractions." She leaned in and kissed Flint on the cheek. "But when this is over . . ."

CHAPTER 86

The team rose at five and readied themselves. Arena got the men in costume, then examined Raquel. She wore a white blouse under a yellow blazer that showed off her deeply tanned skin and tiny waist. "Lovely, dear. He won't be able to resist." She kissed Hardy on the lips and excused herself. "See you in Hollywood, Nick."

Hardy watched her go, wondering if he'd ever see anyone in Hollywood again. Or anywhere.

Raquel and her "attorney" Presley set up next door and waited while Flint rechecked the electronic surveillance equipment, which worked perfectly. Hardy, Flint, and Alice would be able to watch, hear, and record everything that happened between Raquel and Rivera.

Flint turned to Alice. "You okay?"

"Why wouldn't I be?" Alice said over a cold stare.

Hardy glanced at her. "It's natural to be nervous. He's a bad dude. No way to predict how this plays out."

"Raquel is going to invest in a stock before the market opens," Alice said, "and it will move the stock so much that we'll make a killing. And the competitor's stock will crash. Just like we planned."

Hardy admired her confidence. He wished he shared it.

"That part is easy," she continued. "The hard part is getting away without him knowing we conned him. He may have already been tipped off by his attorney."

"Presley says Rivera's attorney jumped at the chance to get out."

"We'll see. Rivera's a vengeful guy. Presley's offer of protection and a new identity might not be enough."

"Presley offered him some serious money. This is his chance to be free of Rivera."

"His money won't do us any good if we're all dead," Alice said.

"Hey," Flint said, "enough with what can go wrong. We have a good plan."

Hardy felt edgy about Alice's monotone. *There's something off about her. Nerves? She's certainly justified. But there's something more.*

At six sharp someone knocked on the outer door of Raquel's office, and Hardy watched Presley open it just a crack on the video screen. He heard a few muffled voices, followed by Presley swinging the door open.

Rivera had arrived.

Rivera's bodyguard Delgado came in first, wearing a gray business suit with a bulge on his hip. He signaled back to Rivera when the room checked out, and Rivera and a small man, both in black suits with white shirts and red ties, followed him in.

Raquel stood and extended her hand. "You must be Mr. Rivera. Welcome to Salazar International."

Rivera looked like he'd seen an angel. "Ms. Salazar." He kissed her hand. "It's a pleasure to meet you."

"The pleasure is *all* mine."

Hardy smiled at Flint. "She's playing Rivera perfectly."

"This is my attorney," she said, pointing at Presley. "Señor Martinez."

"And this is mine. His name is unimportant."

Hardy focused on Rivera's attorney. *He looks scared. Shitless.*

"Can I get you anything?" Raquel asked, obviously enjoying herself. "Anything at all?"

Hardy thought Rivera might start drooling. After a moment to reflect on his response, he sat down in the chair across from Raquel.

"Perhaps another time. After we agree to do some business together you should come visit me at my Hacienda."

Raquel sat down. Both attorneys and Delgado stayed standing.

"*After* we agree?" Raquel said. "You're confident we will be doing business, Mr. Rivera?"

"I am. I'm exactly what you need to establish yourself here."

"Oh, I don't know about that. I have many attractive options."

"You have only one *best* option," Rivera countered. "I can open doors that no one else can. I have an unrivaled power base. And I have the capital to match your investment and make for a true partnership."

Raquel cocked her head. "I was thinking more of a limited partnership."

"I know how much you're staking to get off the ground here. I'm prepared to match it. I'm prepared to be a full partner."

She tilted her head. "That information is closely held, Mr. Rivera."

He grinned, proud to have impressed her. "Please call me Manuel. Trust me, I don't take chances. I had you and your firm checked out from top to bottom in the last twenty-four hours. I know everything there is to know about it. I'm prepared to match your investment."

She paused. "I've done my homework as well, and your personal liquid assets don't match my investment."

Rivera appeared caught off balance by her knowledge of his business. "True, but I have my own set of investors. They're counting on a big return with my business expansion. I can cover your stake."

Raquel contemplated his offer and raised her eyebrows. Hardy could see the sexual tension building in Rivera. *She's driving him crazy.*

"Manuel," she said, "I like to be direct. I know about your businesses, your business partners, your investors, and about your influence. I find the influence impressive. I find other aspects of your business distasteful. I won't have drugs and pornography as part of any operation I'm involved with."

Hardy held his breath. *Rivera isn't used to being challenged, especially by women. But she had to say it to be convincing.*

"If you've studied my business interests," Rivera countered, "you know that I am expanding in diverse ways that are consistent with your own growth plans. Together, we can have it all."

Raquel smiled. "I like to have it all."

"I can see that in you. You know what you want, and you go get it. You're my kind of woman." He said that last sentence with obvious multiple messages.

Raquel leaned forward. "Let's say, for the sake of argument, that I'm interested. How quickly can you move?"

"I have the matching funds in an offshore account, liquid, and ready to wire."

Jackpot. Hardy felt so excited that he could hardly bear to sit still and watch.

"Just like that?" she asked, trying to appear marginally interested.

Rivera shook his head, still smiling. "Of course not. There are proper business procedures to follow. My attorney will need to review everything."

Rivera's attorney stared at his shoes. Rivers of his sweat dripped onto the carpet.

Don't lose it now, Hardy thought. *We've almost got him.*

Raquel gave Rivera a sexy smile. "Attorneys. A necessary evil. Personally, I use mine to follow orders, not give advice."

"As do I. Perhaps we can consummate our relationship?"

"Manuel, are we talking business or pleasure?"

"Perhaps both. I know *the* restaurant in Nosara. On the beach."

"Sounds wonderful," she said, "but I have a deadline. I must make my move before the US market opens. That's in about an hour. Then I need to leave the country this morning. I do have another potential partner coming in a few minutes."

"You don't want to work with anyone else."

"I have two excellent options. I'll choose the one willing to meet my terms, including my deadline."

"I can't have my investors approve any deals that fast," Rivera said.

Raquel stood and gave him her hand, which he kissed again.

"That's too bad," she answered. "We could have been *very* good together. If you change your mind, the paperwork and transfer must be complete by seven fifteen."

That was Hardy's cue to move. Hardy and his "bodyguard" Flint, in their disguises, walked around a back exit and back into the reception area.

Raquel's office door opened and Hardy was face-to-face with Rivera. Rivera glared at Hardy, but didn't show any sign of recognition. Hardy walked past him, showing him no respect and bumping him on the way by. Flint followed Hardy into the office.

Rivera spun and Delgado reached for his gun. Rivera's attorney closed his eyes.

"Don, how good of you to come." Raquel kissed Hardy on the cheek as if they'd known each other for years. "Tell me, how is the family? I bet the boys have grown so much since our visit last summer."

"They are well," Hardy answered. "Huge. They eat so much."

Hardy pretended to check out the office just so he could see what affect his appearance was having on Rivera. He was seething. Rivera gave an irritated nod to Delgado, and they bolted, along with the attorney.

Hardy waited until he heard them leave the floor via the stairwell before relaxing and getting out of character.

"Did you see the look on Rivera's face?" Flint asked. "He was going nuts."

Presley exhaled. "That only matters if he comes back. And if that attorney keeps it together."

Hardy gave him a reassuring smile. "Don't worry. We have him."

"Are you sure?"

Hardy patted him on the back. "We had him when he decided he needed to be who he thinks he is. Now, we finish him off."

CHAPTER 87

The minute hand slogged ahead. Hardy thought it might actually be moving backward.

"He's not coming back," Flint said. "Should we go after him?"

"He'll be back," Hardy said. *I think.*

Footsteps in the hallway. A knock on the door.

Hardy made a fist pump and the team moved into position.

"Come in," Raquel called out.

Rivera, Delgado, and his attorney entered single file. Rivera looked determined. Delgado looked cautious. The attorney looked green.

"Manuel," Raquel said. "Don and I were just completing our paperwork."

Rivera fumed. "You are making a mistake."

Hardy took a menacing step forward. "Hey, buddy, you heard the lady. I'm ready to transfer five hundred mil in right now, to get in on the ground floor. Based on her track record, I'll double that today."

Rivera's face flashed bright red. Raquel pointed to the computer screen. "Manual, look at this."

Rivera stepped behind her. "What am I looking at?"

"My portfolio." She switched screens and displayed a specialized stock chart. "See the movement when the last five stocks went public?"

"Sí."

"I drove those increases. It will be the same with this one." She showed him another stock chart, then flipped back to her portfolio screen. "See the cash withdrawals and deposits, and the big jump in value for each stock. It maps directly to the stock price moves." She flipped back and forth between the pages to demonstrate the link between her investments and the stock. "The reason I'm so excited is that I've found the Latin American equivalent of those two. They both have initial public offerings in thirty minutes, and the one I choose to invest in will have a monster day."

Rivera narrowed his eyes toward her. "They are priced to rise fifteen percent on the first day."

Raquel laughed. "That's nothing. Once the other big boys see what I'm doing, they'll all want in."

Rivera leaned over the couch, hovering above her. "How sure are you about this?"

She winked. "Positive. Once institutional investors see me make a move, they'll follow in bunches. I just have to pick one of the stocks."

Rivera turned to her. "I need to get in on this."

"Well, that only happens if you agree to my terms. You want to be partners with me, you have to show me you're serious. Or, I suppose you could wait to see what happens. But you'll get in late, and your profits will lag."

Raquel let him stew for a good minute. Finally, she leaned forward. "We *would* make an amazing team. Professionally, and *personally*."

"Can you open your account for me? I'd like to see the money in there."

"You don't trust me, Manuel?"

"I don't trust anybody with five hundred million dollars."

"Of course. I wouldn't either. Here."

She opened a new computer screen that displayed the brokerage account they'd set up for her with the Marshals Service money. "Here's the account."

Hardy stepped closer to Raquel. "We don't need this bum. I'll get rid of him."

Rivera grabbed Hardy by the lapel. "Do you know who you are talking to?"

Raquel stepped between them and forced Rivera to let go. "Gentle-men, I will have none of this cock fighting. If you want to go outside to measure yourselves, that's your business, but in here you will behave."

"My apologies, Raquel," Hardy said. He pulled wire instructions out of his pocket and handed it to her.

"Five hundred million dollars. For our partnership. You can wire it while I'm signing the paperwork."

Rivera edged over to look at the wiring instructions. Panic set in on his face.

"Don," Raquel said, "you won't regret it." She motioned to Presley, who provided legal documents to Hardy.

"Where do I sign?" Hardy asked.

"Here, here, and here," Presley said. "This gives you access to the account. It takes both of you to withdraw any money."

Hardy signed. "I love it when I'm about to make a fortune."

"Call in the wiring instructions," Raquel said. "We've only got fif-teen minutes." She turned to Presley. "Notarize this, fax it in, and make a copy for him. The bank will give you the confirmation code for him."

"Yes, ma'am."

While Presley handled the paperwork, Hardy called Alice and put the call on speaker.

"Cayman Islands National Bank," Alice answered.

Hardy gave a series of instructions and authorization codes, while Rivera bit his lower lip. Alice said with a confirmation code. Moments later Alice's computer dinged, and her portfolio grew to a hundred million.

"There," she said. "It's been transferred. Welcome to Salazar En-terprises, Don."

Presley handed him his completed paperwork. "Here you are, sir."

Rivera's face flushed bright red, and he stepped around the couch toward Raquel. "Raquel, I am still the man you need."

"I'm sorry," she said, "you came all the way down here for nothing." She smiled at him. "Too bad we won't be consummating our relation-ship after all."

Rivera glared at Hardy, his face getting a darker shade every moment. Hardy cleared his throat. "I'll let myself out."

"Wait!" Rivera yelled. He pointed to his attorney. "You. Check those papers. Tell me if they're sufficient."

Presley handed the attorney a fresh set. The attorney studied them, then turned to Rivera. "They provide the proper protection. You'd have equal rights to the account."

Rivera checked the time. Five minutes left. "What about a three-way partnership? We can all go in for five hundred million and have even more clout."

"I don't really need more," Raquel said. "There are only so many shares to get at the IPO price."

Rivera sat down next to her and put his hand on her knee. "Three equal shares, three board members. You can have the controlling vote on the board."

Hardy waited a good ten seconds before responding. "Raquel, what do you know about this man?"

"He is, perhaps, the most influential man in the region."

Hardy rubbed his chin and addressed Rivera. "Do you have the money ready to transfer before the market opens?"

Rivera clenched his teeth.

Raquel's cell phone rang, which signaled Alice was calling in, on cue. She flashed sad eyes at Rivera. "I know you need approval from your investors. Perhaps it's best this way."

Rivera gritted his teeth.

Raquel answered the phone. "Hello? Yes, I want a hundred million dollars worth at the opening bell. That will give my partner and I the largest voting bloc." She laughed. "Yes, I said one hundred million. I know the risk, but I like my chances. It's not like I'm new to this." She hung up.

"Which stock is it?" Rivera asked.

Raquel giggled. "Now, Manual, do I look like the kind of person who gives away my advantage?" She glanced at her phone. "You'll see in a few minutes, like everybody else. Maybe you can get in before it goes up thirty percent."

Rivera stood. "I have investors who just invested five hundred million with me. I'll give you a finder's fee if you tell me which stock."

Raquel shook her head. "And create competition for those shares? Not a chance. I'm the only one making this play. The only question is, do I invest one or one and a half billion? Up to you."

Rivera's face turned radish-purple. Hardy held his breath. *He can't resist. We've got him.*

"Give me the papers," Rivera said. "And the computer." Raquel moved aside so he could sit down next to her. Rivera typed frantically as Hardy stepped behind the couch to see the screen.

An investment account flashed onto the display. Hardy could see the five hundred million dollar balance. Rivera typed in the wire transfer instructions Raquel had provided, and stared at the screen.

Hardy swallowed nothing but dry air. *One more click and we've got you.*

Raquel leaned into Rivera and stroked his leg. "You know we will make an amazing team."

Rivera ground his teeth, streams of sweat dribbling down his cheek. He stared at the screen as the clock on the display counted down. One minute remained.

Hardy did his own teeth grinding. *C'mon, you son of a bitch. You know you want to.*

Fifty seconds.

Rivera tapped the side of the keyboard with trembling fingers. "If this doesn't work, they'll kill all of us."

"It's going to work," Raquel said.

Hardy was sure she believed it, and the Marshals Service was about to score big. *Another side benefit.*

Thirty seconds.

"I need time to modify the order," she said. "Are you in or out?"

Rivera's finger hovered over the enter key. He started to move it down when the door to the room burst open and Alice barged in, ahead of schedule.

"Stop!" Alice yelled.

CHAPTER 88

Hardy stared at Alice in horror. He wanted to scream, but could only glare at her. *What are you doing?*

Rivera lifted his finger from the keyboard and jerked to his feet. "What is this?" He shifted away and stood behind Delgado. "Who are you?"

"My name is Alice Polk. I'm with the SEC. Ms. Salazar is the subject of an ongoing investigation."

What the fuck? Hardy felt dizzy and nauseated. *She'll get us all killed.*

Delgado pulled out a pistol and pointed it at Flint, keeping an eye on all of them. "Everybody stand still."

Alice stepped toward Rivera. "I know who you are, Mr. Rivera. You and your party are free to go. Dozens of US federal agents are surrounding the area. If you want to avoid being detained as part of this, you need to leave right now."

Federal agents? Are you kidding me? This can't be happening.

The computer dinged again. "You need to leave now," Alice said.

Hardy debated whether to snag Rivera himself. *We didn't get his money. Alice didn't hide all of it in another account. What do I do?* He glanced at Presley, who appeared as stunned as he felt.

Delgado grabbed Rivera's arm. "Come on, boss. You can't be here."

Rivera's attorney stared at Presley. Hardy could see the pleading in his expression. *He's going to lose it. If Alice hasn't gotten us all killed, he will.*

Another ding.

"What is that?" Rivera asked.

"The market opened," Raquel said. "Must be my stock purchases."

Rivera narrowed his eyes. "That's still my account on your computer." He bolted to the couch and lifted the laptop to eye level. His face blanched. "My money." He turned to Raquel. "Who authorized these stock buys and sells?"

"You didn't wire any money to my account," Raquel said. "How would I know?"

"Let's go, boss," Delgado said. "The fed's will be here any minute."

Rivera stared at the computer. "No one is going anywhere."

CHAPTER 89

Hardy slid over to see the laptop screen. A series of stock buys and sells streamed down the screen. He saw the account balance in free fall.

How did we do that?

He shook his head. *Who cares? He lost his investor's money. We got what we came for.*

Rivera shook the laptop, as if that would stop the sells and the drainage of funds. His wide eyes shifted to Raquel. "You did this." He dropped the computer and pulled out a knife. Before Hardy could react, he had Raquel in his arms, his knife ready to gut her. "Undo it."

Alice gasped. "No. She didn't do anything."

Delgado waved his pistol at Hardy, Presley, and Flint. "You three. On the couch. Sitting on your hands."

Hardy calculated his chances of reaching Delgado before he found a hole in his chest. *Not good. And even worse to get to Raquel in time.* He acquiesced and the three of them complied.

Once they were seated, Delgado put his gun to Alice's head. "What do you know about this?"

Alice curled her lip. "You're making a mistake. I'm just here to arrest them."

Rivera put a little pressure on Raquel's throat, and a sliver of blood trickled down to her dress. Yellow turned to orange. "If you think I won't kill all of you, you're mistaken."

Rivera's attorney broke cover and got on his knees. "Boss. I know who this attorney really is. It's US Marshal Presley."

Hardy felt Presley stiffen next to him.

This is all going to shit. Better do something, or it'll be too late.

Rivera stared at Presley, then at his attorney. "How would you know that?"

"I, I pretended to make a deal with him. So I could get him here. So you could capture him. Use him to find Sara."

Hardy could see Rivera ease up on the knife. "Really? And you just decided to tell me this now?"

The attorney's face showed his uncertainty. "I was trying to protect you." His voice and expression gave away that even he knew how lame that excuse was.

Rivera laughed. "I see. How long have you worked for me?"

"Ten years."

Rivera motioned to Delgado, who put a bullet into the attorney's forehead. The attorney dropped face first as blood spilled onto the carpet.

Rivera put more pressure on the knife. "Marshal Presley. Interesting. Tell me. Where's my money?"

"I took it," came a voice from behind them.

Sara stood at the door, Flint's tranquilizer rifle in her hand.

CHAPTER 90

Sara?

Delgado wheeled toward her, his gun aimed at her head. Unlike Sara's, his gun was filled with bullets. One shot and Sara would have her head blown off. Hardy lunged forward, but could only watch as Sara fired a shot, knocking Delgado back into the three on the couch. Hardy could see the tranquilizer dart sticking out of Delgado's chest.

Rivera held the knife tight against Raquel's throat. As much as he wanted to kill Sara, right there, he wanted to live more. He clung to Raquel, using her as a shield. "Hello, cuz."

"Let her go, Manuel. It's over."

"Oh, it hasn't even started yet." He dragged Raquel to the exit leading to the reception area, keeping her body between he and Sara. "Are you willing to kill her, just to get to me?"

Sara pulled another dart out, but fumbled it onto the floor. *No, no, no.*

Hardy shoved Delgado's unconscious body onto the floor. He measured the distance between himself and Rivera. He knew the slightest miscalculation would cost Raquel her life.

"Keep Sara and Alice safe," Hardy whispered to Presley and Flint. "I'll save Raquel and get Rivera." He stood. "Sara, stand down."

"We can end him right here. End all of it."

"We've won." *I don't know how, but we got him. Now, we just have to get everyone out of here alive.* "His investors will take care of him for us. You don't want his blood on your hands. It's not who you are."

Hardy faced Rivera, who had reached the exit. He pulled his mask off, exposing himself. "Leave her. Take me instead."

Rivera's eyes almost popped out of his head. "Hardy."

"That's right. Remember when you said it wasn't over between us?" He showed his empty hands. "Here's your chance."

Rivera's face turned red. "You are a dead man."

Hardy eased toward Rivera. "Let her go. You know you want me. I can even tell you where your money is."

Rivera jerked up out of his crouch.

"That's right. I know how they did it. I know how to fix it."

Rivera shook with rage. "Tell your girlfriend to drop the rifle."

"Do what he says, Sara. Please."

Sara's trigger finger flinched, but she acquiesced and set the rifle on the floor.

"There," Hardy said. "No threat. Just you and me. Let everyone else go, and I'll give you back everything that belongs to you."

Sirens approached from the distance. *Police sirens.*

"I want you *and* Sara," Rivera said.

"That's not happening," Hardy said.

Rivera smiled. "Just who do you think the local police will side with? Me, or a gringo from the US? If I stay, I'll get Sara anyway."

Hardy tensed. *Jeez. He probably owns those guys. No way to predict how they'll treat a US marshal.* "But your money will be long gone. I'm your only chance to get it back."

Rivera dropped his smile. He fidgeted with the knife at Raquel's throat.

Sara shocked Hardy by bolting toward Rivera. "Stop," he yelled, but Rivera already had tossed Raquel aside and grabbed Sara. He had her at knifepoint.

Raquel scrambled back to Hardy, who handed her off to Presley.

Tires screeched to a skid on the dirt road below.

CHAPTER 91

"You'll never get out of here," Presley said. "My badge carries more clout than you think."

Rivera laughed. "Your badge means nothing compared to my influence."

Hardy took a step toward him. "Once those police arrive you'll never see your money. Last chance. Let Sara go and I'll come with you."

Rivera sliced into Sara's throat, just enough to start a trickle of blood. "Come with us now, or I kill her where we stand. Then I tell the police you killed her. You'll never get out of this country alive."

Hardy considered his options.

"Don't do it, Nicholas. I'm already dead."

No you're not.

A noise behind Rivera caused him to glance back. Hardy expected a police officer, but a black dog edged in, eyeing everyone suspiciously.

Hardy grabbed his chance. He planted his left foot and shot his right leg out into Rivera's side, catching him by surprise.

Rivera doubled over, releasing Sara, who ran behind Hardy. Hardy's next blow was to Rivera's throat. Rivera fell to his knees, the knife falling to the floor.

"Go!" Hardy said to Presley as he kicked the knife out of reach. "Get everyone to the van before the police get up here. I'll catch up."

"Is he dead?" Sara asked.

"No."

Footsteps scrambled up the stairwell at the far end of the hall.

"Hurry!"

Sara moved toward Rivera, but Presley snatched her and forced her into the hallway. Flint, Raquel, and Alice followed. They disappeared into the opposite stairwell.

Rivera gasped for breath. Hardy picked him up off the floor, swung him around easily, and threw him into the doorway of Raquel's room.

The footsteps sounded like they were almost to his floor.

"Remember when you declared you were my enemy?" Hardy said. "How's that working for you? How does it feel to go up against me one-on-one, without your hired muscle?"

Rivera lunged at him. Hardy recognized the flash of a knife blade. He tried to block Rivera's thrust with his arm, but the knife grazed him, and Hardy could feel blood rushing from above his elbow.

Rivera's thrust sent him past Hardy. Rivera turned quickly and charged Hardy again, his red-tipped knife pointed at Hardy's heart.

This time Hardy was ready. He kicked the knife out of Rivera's hand, which stopped Rivera for only a moment. Rivera continued his charge, his bare hands now targeting Hardy's throat.

Hardy grabbed both of his arms and held him there, face-to-face. Rivera's knee shot up and Hardy instinctively twisted just enough so that his blow caught him in the upper leg. But the twist gave Rivera enough leverage to force Hardy backward, into the wall. Hardy's head slammed against it, and he lost his grip on Rivera's arms.

Rivera pulled free and grabbed a table lamp. Hardy ducked just in time. The base of the lamp missed his head by inches before puncturing the wall. Hardy drove forward and hit Rivera with his full force in Rivera's waist and piled him backward into the far wall.

Rivera's face lit up, a raging inferno. Before Rivera could get another knee raised Hardy pulled Rivera's head forward and rammed his fore-head into Rivera's. The blow stunned Rivera, and his legs wobbled.

"One last thing," Hardy said as he maneuvered Rivera over to the open doorway. "I don't know what happened to your money."

Hardy gave him a crushing blow to the abdomen with his right foot, sending Rivera flying across the room and landing in a heap in the hallway. Out cold.

Hardy could hear footsteps approaching. Part of him wanted to stay and finish Rivera off. But he controlled his innermost desires and ran out the window and down the fire escape into the alley just as yelling began upstairs.

Hardy melded into a crowd that had formed and walked briskly to the parked van on the next block. He climbed in, and they began the short and bumpy drive to the airport.

"Did you kill him?" Sara asked.

"I don't think so."

Sara sagged. "You couldn't, or didn't want to?"

Hardy gazed at the jungle on the way to the airport. "A little of both."

CHAPTER 92

"So," Hardy said to Sara, "what are you doing here?" He turned to Alice. "And what was that all about? You could have gotten us all killed."

"I called Alice," Sara said. "I wasn't convinced Manuel would go for it. So I asked her to help me put a backup plan in place."

Hardy glared at her. "You should have told us. You should have told *me*."

"I couldn't take the chance it would alter your behavior on the Lust Gambit. You had to be convincing."

"Where did his money go?" Flint asked.

Sara grinned. "I hacked into his brokerage account and invested it in the company competing with the one Alice bought the stock in."

"So he lost a fortune," Raquel said. "All from his own brokerage account. No wire transfers to trace. No money to hide. Clever girl."

"How did you hack in?" Presley asked.

"Remember, I used to do computer hacking for Manuel before I realized what business he was in? I used the same skills he taught me."

"How'd you get in? Hardy asked.

"He put his investment account on the computer. He entered his password. It was child's play to get in after that."

Hardy turned back to Alice. "How did you know to call off the Lust Gambit and switch over to Sara's backup plan?"

Alice's face turned red. "Instinct, young fellow. Instinct." She cleared her throat, a deep and gravelly affront to Hardy's hearing. "Also, I was pissed at Raquel, and didn't want to see her make any more money off him. So, this way, I win both ways, and Sara gets off."

Raquel leaned over and hugged Alice. "I'm sorry if I misled you." She reached over and took Flint's hand. "I think I've found what makes me happy."

Flint beamed. Hardy put a virtual finger down his throat.

CHAPTER 93

Thanks to Alice and her influence in the financial world, the front page of every major financial paper and website disclosed a financial scam perpetrated by Manuel Rivera, the notorious Mexican drug lord. Anonymous sources reported he'd invested much of his business fortune, including money from influential underworld investors, in highly speculative investments, and had lost it all.

Rumors were rampant that Rivera's lifeless body had been found in Mexico, mutilated in horrendous ways. The Mexican authorities denied finding his body, and officially listed him as missing.

Alice went home and back to being the "Stockbroker to the Stars." She hired a fresh, young female assistant with much to learn about investing. And about Alice.

Inspector Tricia Walker was promoted to Deputy US Marshal in the Santa Ana office.

Raquel went back to her business empire and reclusive life. At the time Hardy didn't expect to ever see her again, but life has a funny way of surprising.

Flint came back with Hardy, but soon received a call from Raquel, and chose to join her as her new personal bodyguard. Hardy was devastated. First Sara, and now Flint. But that feeling of loss was temporary, as it turned out.

US Marshal Presley received a special thank you from the President of the United States in a private ceremony at the White House. It had something to do with using his vacation wisely. It didn't hurt that he returned a 90% profit on the money he'd borrowed from the Marshals

Service Asset Forfeiture Program. The other 10% was reported as fees for services rendered by civilians.

And he still owed Hardy a favor. A big one.

CHAPTER 94

El Paso, Texas

A week later, Hardy and Presley sat in an empty diner on a deserted road off of Route 10. It wasn't the end of the world, but they could see it from there.

Vultures sat on a fence post that separated the diner from the parking lot, really just hard-packed dirt in a sea of sand.

Other than a middle-aged cook with a gut several sizes too large, they were the only two patrons in there. They had both tried the cherry pie based on his recommendation, and Hardy had managed to get most of it down out of courtesy.

A swirl of dust kicked up down the highway. Hardy sat up straighter and strained to see. A nondescript sedan came barreling down the highway toward the diner.

Presley stood. "Stay here."

He went over to the owner, who cooperated by going into the back to give them some privacy.

The sedan parked and two men in plain suits stepped out, Sara following. She was wearing the same dress Hardy had first seen her in. *Amazing.*

Presley opened the door to let them know it was all clear, and in she came. When she saw Hardy she ran up and they held each other for the first time in two long weeks. "Oh, Nicholas, I've missed you," she said as she took a half step back to look at him. "Are you okay? Everything healed?"

"I'm great. What about you?"

"I'm good."

Hardy motioned for her to have a seat and sat down next to her in the booth. The three escorts moved to the far corner of the diner and Presley put some money in the jukebox, selecting a Beatles tune.

Once seated, she took a deep breath. "That's something about Manuel. Do you really think he's dead?"

"I think so. His investors aren't the type to forgive."

"I can't believe I'm really free from him. What's next for you?"

Hardy held her hand. "That depends on you. I want to be with you."

She smiled and touched his cheek. "Oh, Nicholas, I'm still a horrible person to have a life with. Just because Manuel is dead doesn't mean someone won't come after me to avenge him or Ortega. You made it much less likely, but it's still a risk."

"I don't care. Any life with you is better than any other I can imagine. You made me realize that without some risk anything truly great is impossible."

She shook her head. "Oh, Nicholas. Without being immediate family they won't allow me to be with you. I'm amazed they let me see you today."

"Let's forget about them for a sec," Hardy said. "What do you want? What will make you happiest?"

She looked at him with all the love a human being can show. "I wish you could be in my life."

"Vices and all?" Hardy asked, grinning.

"Vices and all."

"If you want me around, I have a way."

She sighed. "I'm not ready to marry you."

Hardy pulled an envelope out of his pocket and set the contents on the table for her to see. "No need. This is better."

"What's in the envelope?" she asked.

"A gift from Presley. He owed me a favor."

Sara sorted through the contents, a puzzled look on her face. "These are a new set of identification papers. For you, me, Juan, and Esteban."

Hardy took her hand. "Yes. Presley arranged for them. They're off the record and untraceable. We can go anywhere we want and start over. No WITSEC, no constraints."

"Presley provided these? He always said I'd be in WITSEC for life."

"Well, that's how it's set up to work. The danger is assumed to always be there, so they make a commitment to protect you forever. But they can't make you stay if you refuse to."

She shook her head. "We'd be in WITSEC?"

Hardy shook his head. "No. Presley did this on his own. This is the favor I asked him for. No one else knows. He'd probably get canned if anyone found out."

"Why would he do that?"

"I think you're his favorite witness ever. He knows you hate being in WITSEC. He knows that if you just walk away, you're still in danger. This is his opportunity to set you up with the life you really want."

She wrapped her arms around Hardy and held him tight. "I can't believe this. It's what I've wanted since the day I met you. I just didn't know how to get it."

Hardy eased her face back so they could face each other. "If being together is what you want, there is a car waiting out back through the kitchen. We'll excuse ourselves to use the restroom and Presley will keep your detail occupied as we go. Bret has his plane waiting for us on a private airstrip in Juarez, across the border in Mexico."

She turned toward Presley. "I don't want him to get in trouble."

"He won't unless we get caught and confess. Your detail will be none the wiser that Presley was involved."

"How do we get Juan and Esteban away?"

"Your security detail is here, so they're not being watched. Bret is standing by to pick your family up and meet us at his plane."

"But they'll think I was kidnapped. They'll keep looking for me. And you."

Hardy smiled. "Presley gave me detailed instructions on how to get away and where to go. We'll be out of the country before they even know we're gone. Bret and Raquel have set us up with them, where we'll be safe. Raquel goes years without being seen. She has the infra-structure to keep us hidden."

"I don't know, Nicholas. I want to be with you, but you're taking an awful chance."

Hardy took her hands. "It's all that I want. Life without you is never going to make me happy. Will you come with me? Start a new life together? Maybe even have our own child."

Her eyes gave away her astonishment. "A child? You want children?"

"People change. I've changed. I've stopped gambling."

She kissed Hardy on the lips and grinned. "Okay. Let's do it. Let's bust out and start our own life."

"We need to make our move while the music is still going. That way they won't hear the car start out back."

Hardy called to Presley. "Marshal, we're going to use the head. Be right back."

Sara's detail started to follow when Presley motioned for them to stop. "Give them a little privacy, guys." He gave one of them a nudge. "You might walk in on something you'll regret later."

They acquiesced.

Hardy and Sara went down the hallway and left through the back of the diner. Their getaway car sat in the blistering sun.

Minutes later they were on the highway, starting their new, free life. They smiled as the vultures flew past and disappeared into the desert.

CHAPTER 95

Point Verde, France

Beep.

Hardy glanced away from the stock tables in his morning paper and toward his laptop. His seat on the veranda at Raquel's estate overlooked the Mediterranean, and birds chirped in the background. His month there with Sara had been perfect.

His mind had been momentarily puzzled by the noise, before realizing he had an email message, his first in the new account he'd set up under his new identity. He figured it could only be some sort of innocuous welcome from the email service.

Not recognizing the sender's name, he read the message's subject line.

We know about the stock scam.

He leaned forward and read the message inside.

You have twenty-four hours to pay it all back.

ABOUT THE AUTHOR

STEVEN G. JACKSON is a professional storyteller who writes thrillers, horror, and comedy, and has a long list off published and produced novels, short stories, and stage plays. He often combines these genres in his stories. His workshops on the craft of writing are always popular. An avid horror fan, he has a world-class collection of vampire first editions. His Yellow Lab, Bear, is a mainstay in his novels, and acts as both muse and inspiration.

To the best of anyone's knowledge, Steven has never been a part of the Witness Protection Program. That's his story, and he's sticking to it.

To see Steven's list of novels, short stories, and stage plays, visit his website at www.StevenGJackson.com.

ACKNOWLEDGMENTS

As always, I am grateful for my wife, Yann, who makes my dreams come true every day.

NOVELS BY STEVEN G. JACKSON

The Zeus Payload

Nick King is a computer programmer and the lead technologist at his grandfather's company, Gordon Defense Technology. When he's not developing sophisticated security software for private and government clients, Nick and his friend and roommate, Dean Wright, travel to the Middle East in search of the terrorist responsible for the 1983 Beirut embassy bombing that killed Nick's parents. Nick has promised his grandfather, Anthony Gordon, a former CIA operative, that he will find and kill the terrorist, Saleh, before his grandfather dies from heart failure and dementia.

When Nick is approached by CIA agents to complete his work on a cyberweapon that can infiltrate any computer system without being detected, he does so with the understanding that the technology will be used to protect the United States from future cyber-attacks. While completing the computer worm, King uncovers evidence of espionage and conspiracy within the CIA, with a trail that leads back to the Nazi Party. King, not knowing who to trust, and realizing the unstoppable power his product would bring to whoever controls it, commits treason, and removes the worm from the classified facility.

As the consequences of his creation are revealed to Nick, he goes on the run with Dean and a NSA agent, Tanya Rose, who originally accused Nick of being involved with the terrorist organization that killed her brother in Benghazi.

Saleh has been orchestrating the cyber weapon's development for his own purposes, and plans to use it to attack the United States. Saleh lures King to Beirut, where their drama began thirty years earlier, and King must fight off Saleh, al-Qaeda, the CIA, the NSA, a white supremacist group, rogue agents, and assassins, to keep the ultimate cyber weapon out of the wrong hands, and keep the promise he made to his grandfather.

As if there are any right hands.

The Lamia

Evil is preying. With the highest possible stakes, amidst a horrific and suspenseful race against time, a reluctant psychiatrist fights a demon, a global pandemic risk, and his own troubled past in a fight for his daughter's soul.

On a remote boulder on a beach in Costa Rica, an unorthodox family vacation turns into a fight to stop a global pandemic. Emerging from the jungle treetops during a thunderstorm, a vampire bat attacks teenager Taylor. When her mother drowns in the turbulent ocean during the storm, Taylor blames her father, Richard Morgan, when his medical training can't save his ex-wife.

The leader of a Costa Rican task force, a transplant from the nearby indigenous Bribri tribe in the Talamancan mountains, is determined to stop the spread of a deadly global pandemic originating from a Bribri demon. She tries to kill Taylor on the spot, but Morgan overcomes the task force and the family escapes home to Salem, Oregon.

But Taylor starts to change, and Morgan is conflicted between the science he relies on as a psychiatrist (and his atheist girlfriend) and the religion he abandoned. Linda, who lost her daughter to the pandemic, arrives to convince Morgan the unexplainable is real, and he eventually has no choice but to accept his daughter is possessed by an evil that is transforming her into a vampire. Morgan and Linda take Taylor to the Bribri village in a desperate attempt to get help from the Bribri shaman to perform an exorcism to rid Taylor of the demon. If this last-ditch attempt fails, he knows he'll have to destroy his own daughter to save her soul, and the world.

The Lamia is the ultimate battle between good and evil, offered from a master storyteller.

The Night Hag

Evil is back. With a vengeance.

In the sequel to *The Lamia*, the demon Lilith is freed from her Vatican prison by a Cardinal determined to trigger the birth of the AntiChrist, and start the world on a path to Christ's return. But partnering with a demon is fraught with deceit and danger, and Lilith has her own plans.

Lilith is focused on vengeance by repossessing the girl that got away - Taylor Morgan - and using her as a vessel for birthing the AntiChrist, while also destroying humanity with her legion of lamias, leaving her and the AntiChrist to rule a population of vampires.

Dr. Richard Morgan and his misfit team of cohorts must once again save his daughter from this unspeakable evil. He not only has to go up against the demon Lilith, but also the Pontifical Swiss Guard, a sect within the Catholic Church, international law enforcement, and his own personal demons, if he's to overcome the insurmountable and save his daughter, and humanity.

Once again, Morgan is sent on an international quest, with stops in Vatican City, Rome, the Cave of the Apocalypse on the Island of Patmos, Monaco, Nazareth, Pisa, and culminating with a chilling climax in the Sistine Chapel.

The Night Hag is a masterful sequel to *The Lamia*, and will leave you on the edge of your seat as you race to turn each chilling page.

www.ingramcontent.com/pod-product-compliance
Lightning Source LLC
Chambersburg PA
CBHW051124190726
48290CB00006B/1677